DEATH VALLEY

A JACK PRESTER MYSTERY

DEATH VALLEY

A JACK PRESTER MYSTERY

SANDY DENGLER

MOODY PRESS

CHICAGO

MYS
F
DEN

ISBN: 0-8024-2176-8

1 3 5 7 9 10 8 6 4 2

Printed in the United States of America

Contents

1

Jack Be Nimble

A hundred feet off the deck and eighty feet below sea level! He glanced again at his altimeter to make sure. Flatline. He did it! Now to get out of here before someone read his numbers.

Beneath his plane sped the broiling white salt pan of Death Valley. He could see his aircraft's shadow skate across the hellish salt. He could just make out detail as the hard, flat land whipped by below him. He paused. He saw—and it was gone. Perplexed, he jacked his bird out of the hole and howled back into the clear blue sky, his natural habitat.

Should someone lodge a complaint about his low-flying aircraft, his buddies would cover. Seven planes aloft, and if confronted they would all seven admit, "It was me," or, "Not me," depending how authoritative the complaint was. No way to tell who did what, if at all.

But now here he sat, faced with an ugly little dilemma. Keep his mouth shut and avoid sure retribution? Or speak and bring the wrath of God, not to mention the base commander, down around his ears? He could get grounded for this. And yet, he was a human being too, with a moral code. He was supposed to place honor above all. They could bust him for this. Besides, he couldn't be certain. It almost surely was not what he thought it was, out on that wicked salt flat miles from anywhere.

It couldn't possibly be a human body down there.

Jack Prester, when you came right down to it, disliked a lot of things in life, and airports were one of them. This airport in particular irked him. Las Vegas's airport is a microcosm of the glitzy, bawdy, twenty-four-hour-a-day city itself. Here it was 5:10 A.M., an hour when you ought to be milking cows if you're out of bed at all, but the airport bustled like downtown Albuquerque at midday. People swarmed everywhere. Banks of chrome-trimmed slot machines, a hundred of them, stuttered and clanged shoulder to shoulder in an island of chance at the center of the concourse. Booths and food wagons around the sides, garish lights, and vivid colors all invited you to buy, to gamble, to eat and drink. Anything but rest.

A female voice announced the arrival of 583 out of Dulles at Gate 57. They opened the doors at this end of the jetway. Moments later passengers came streaming out. Some gaped at this brilliant Vanity Fair, and others ignored the glitz, intently seeking friends and relatives. About halfway back in the parade, she emerged.

Jack assumed it was she. She obviously was traveling alone, and she resembled the description in his shirt pocket. "Dark h dark e 5'6 120 lb 24 yr old," promised the handwritten note Hal had given him. This lady fit.

"Dresses snazzy. Nice bod. Cold as Glacier Bay, but she looks good" was Hal's personal, private observation. He did not mention her short, Amelia Earhart hairstyle which, with her huge eyes, gave her a charming waif quality out of keeping with her all-business clothes and attitude.

Jack lurched erect from leaning against the support column and moved forward. "Miss Evelyn Brant?"

She looked at him, stepped aside out of the stream, and looked at him some more. "Brown hair, dark eyes, five eleven, hundred and sixty-five, thirty-four years old. John Prester."

"Good morning." He extended his hand.

She set down her suit bag and shook tentatively with a flimsy grip, staring at his elbow as if she thought a snake would stick its nose out of his sleeve. He reached for the suit bag and her laptop. "May I?"

She let him take them. Did this mean she was not a women's libber? Or did it simply mean she knew how blasted heavy both pieces were and was too smart to haul them if she didn't have to?

He watched her a few moments and decided on the smarts. "What's coming through baggage claim?"

"Two suitcases. Mr. Edmond told me to travel light."

Jack nodded. He didn't carry this much duffle when he went to Australia. They walked without speaking down the bright concourse and silently took the escalator downstairs. Jack sensed he was being studied, but if so she was discreet about it; every time he looked at her she was looking somewhere else.

Then all the glamorous and brilliant somewhere-elses seized her full attention, and she gawked, still discreetly, like any tourist from back East.

He dipped his head randomly at the scene about them. "A little gaudy for my taste, but the food isn't bad. Do you want something to eat before we take off?"

"I had something on the plane, thank you. If you want to, that's fine." She frowned. "Take off. We're flying?"

"Figure of speech. We're driving."

"Mm." She wore a feminine sort of gray suit, tailored, businessy, and she did not in the least look like she had just spent most of her night flying from Washington, D.C., to the corner of Nevada.

With his jeans, cowboy hat, running shoes, and chambray shirt, the sleeves rolled up to his elbows, Jack felt a wee bit underdressed to be walking beside this city lady.

9

Walk? March. And briskly. She did very well at maintaining the pace in those high-heeled shoes. He had to really keep it nimble to stay with her. Jack never did see the point of women's high-heeled shoes, except that they made the leg line more attractive. And that was probably the point right there.

Everything she did suggested vaguely that she was in a hurry to finish it and do something else. She walked fast; she gestured swiftly, the few times she made any motion at all; she spoke rapidly. Brusque. No nonsense. Tense.

She did not speak again until her suitcases came around the carousel, when she said, "That," jabbing a finger at her matched luggage. When you talk in monosyllables you need a few gestures now and then.

He gave her back her laptop and suit bag and carried the suitcases out to parking. They were heavier by far than her carry-ons.

Even before they approached the truck, Maxx expressed delight. His baritone bark echoed around the garage. The huge black lab was perched on top of the cage, his usual throne when Jack wasn't around. The steel-bar cage in the pick-up bed was three feet deep by three feet high by the truck width, and when big old Maxx climbed up there he could see for miles.

She stopped cold with her mouth open. "This is it?"

"Four-by Dodge Ram long-bed pick-up, gray with gray interior, drum box, and steel wire dog cage in the bed. One Labrador retriever comma, black comma, five years old comma, Maxx. Didn't Hal give you a description?" He pulled the cage door open and put the suitcases inside.

Maxx came bounding down off the roof to lick Miss Brant's hand. She shrank back in horror and disgust. Undeterred, Maxx belched and turned to lick Jack's pants leg.

"Maxx, cut it out!" He reached for the suit bag.

"Wait! That dog isn't riding back here with my things, is he?"

"Why shouldn't he?" Jack stuffed the bags in the cage and clapped his hands. Maxx jumped in, and Jack closed the door.

"That dog is not going to ride with my things! The laptop alone is worth over three thousand. I don't—"

"And it couldn't be safer, Miss Brant. Nobody but nobody reaches in that cage when Maxx is in there. Look at him. A head like a basketball and teeth that could dent an anvil. Besides, you don't want him up in the cab with us. Trust me." Jack paused for effect. "He licks. Constantly."

Her face tightened, and Jack couldn't tell whether she was going to start crying or explode in anger. She did neither. She marched around to the passenger door. "Let's get out of here."

On the outskirts of town Jack spotted a Gearjammer Truck Stop and pulled in. "Gas tank's full, but we're not. Breakfast for Maxx and me, and anything you'd like. You're still on eastern daylight time; you might be ready for lunch by now."

She climbed out her side without waiting for him to open her door. She was liberated after all.

He popped the ammo case, filled Maxx's dish from it, and stuffed the dish inside the cage door.

He followed her into the dining area of this vast truck stop, out of the brisk, cool dawn air into dank, languid, air-conditioned air. They slid into a Naugahyde booth, he ordered two eggs over easy without looking at the menu, she decided on a cup of tea, the waitress left, and social discourse took a nosedive. From nothing all the way through town to less than nothing now.

Oh, well. You can always fall back on business when all else fails. "Tell me what you know about this case," Jack ventured.

She shrugged. "I'm to walk into the superintendent's office with an open mind and start looking through his books. Mr. Edmond didn't brief me to look for anything in particular, but they think something is amiss."

11

"You're aware that George Gibbs, the dead man they pulled out of the creek, was from the Government Accounting Office."

She nodded.

"Murdered."

"Mr. Edmond intimated there might be foul play, but he assured me I wouldn't be in any danger."

"Then you're not. Hal knows the situation."

As a conversationalist she was a complete poop. She dropped the ball instantly and spent her time watching truckers come and go. Sleepy, unwashed men lolled in the booths, talking on the pay phones installed at each table along the wall. They brought in thermos bottles the size of oil storage tanks and left with them full of coffee blacker than Maxx. Through the tabletop-to-ceiling windows you could watch monster eighteen-wheelers come and go. And come, and come, pouring past the huge windows. Their drivers stood on stepladders doing the windshields as they filled up.

Jack had seen all this a million times. He was often a part of it. Now he watched Miss Brant's face awhile. "Your first meal in a real truck stop, right?"

The food arrived. She looked at his plate a moment and requested a side of white toast. When the waitress left, Miss Brant glared at him. "You sound bemused. And condescending. I can live with the bemusement. You'll get off the condescension right now."

"My apology. I didn't mean to sound condescending. There's a lot of places I've never been, either."

Her mouth dropped open. She was staring past his shoulder toward the door. Jack twisted around to look.

Bikers. Hell's Angels. Hippy Dippy Two-Wheelers. Whatever you want to call them, here they came, at least a dozen, straight out of the sixties. Their black vests, nickel-studded leathers, blue jeans, boots big enough to dip sheep in, all seemed to match their artful tattoos and sun-browned, unshaven phizzes. They swaggered, they laughed too loudly,

12

they took over. They filled up the huge dining area just by standing there.

Miss Brant looked stricken. "Do you realize what's wrong with those people?"

"I know a hundred things wrong with them. What's your analysis?"

Fervently she murmured, "They're between us and the only way out."

2
Jack Be Quick

The only difference between these bikers invading the Gearjammer and the bikers of thirty years before was that these guys were thirty years older than bikers back then. Jack watched the aging Angels scoot chairs, rearrange tables, and make remarks to the waitress, which they considered very funny. In a noisy gaggle they settled into a cluster of tables in the middle, disenfranchising a couple of diners already seated there. The diners moved without a murmur.

Miss Brant mumbled, "I didn't think such people really existed."

"Only in your nightmares. Actually, once you get past appearances, they aren't too bad. I broke down about a year ago north of Carlsbad. My old CJ-5. Half a dozen of 'em came ripping down the road, pulled in beside me, and rebuilt my water pump. It lasted long enough to get me into Roswell."

The waitress arrived with the toast.

Jack nodded toward the noisy bikers. "Regulars or in from outside?"

The waitress shook her head. "First time I've seen 'em, and that's already once too often."

One of them, a grizzly giant with a potbelly, stood up

and looked around the room. "Who owns that big black dog out there?"

Think! But you better be quick! The last thing you need is to tangle with this bunch of loonies. Jack stuffed his mouth full of sausage before he answered, the better to sound uncouth. He regretted shaving this morning. "The Lab in the steel cage? Me."

"That mutt showed his teeth and growled at me. He messes with me, and he's dead."

"Lemme know. He's not supposed to draw blood unless I tell him to. Where you guys headed? Anywhere in particular?"

"Death Valley. Our spiritual home."

They all guffawed loud and long.

"I hear Edwards is doing some joint ground maneuvers with Fort Irwin this week. If you go in the south end at night, don't run into any tanks. They're convoying up the Amargosa."

The grizzly grinned. "Wouldn't wanna hurt the taxpayers' tanks, would we!" and to Jack's blessed relief he sat down again amid the raucous guffaws of an appreciative audience.

Miss Brant was staring at him again. "Was any of that true?"

"Any of what?" He worked hard to put the sausage down without requiring a Heimlich maneuver.

"The tanks, and are they really going to Death Valley?"

"I have no idea if they're really going to the monument, and it's true about the joint maneuvers."

"How would you know about that?"

"Base commander told me." These hash browns were pretty good. But then, truck stop food is usually pretty good.

She nibbled her toast, looking either dubious or worried. Presently she asked, "What else did the base commander tell you?"

"I talked to him on the phone yesterday. Interesting. One of their fighter pilots walked into his CO's office and

15

gave himself up. Said he joined the Below Sea-level Club and in the process saw a body. Turned out to be George Gibbs, the GAO guy, of course. No way anyone would have spotted it from land level. The corpse was face down in a small salt pool in the creek bed, partially covered with sand, invisible except from overhead. Good thing the flyer decided to report the find and take the consequences."

"What consequences?"

"I have no idea. The Air Force does not smile on stunts, at least not officially."

"Stunts?"

"To get into the Below Sea-level Club, you have to fly a plane at high speed below sea level. Death Valley's the only place you can do it in the U.S. The record goes to a guy who refueled below sea level. The whole ball of wax, too—a tank transport connected to the fighter by the fuel line. *Rowrrr*, up the valley they went, fifty feet above the ground."

She hardened. "You think because I'm new out here you can tell me anything you want and I'll believe it. Well, Mr. Prester, you can just get off that right now too!"

He felt his own anger building, and that wasn't the way this was all supposed to go. The edge on his voice came without trying. "I have neither the desire nor the motive to lead you on with a merry tale, Miss Brant. So until you can be a little friendlier, it's *Dr.* Prester."

Her dark eyes narrowed. He didn't realize how gigantic they were until she closed them down. "Oh. Is it M.D., Ph.D., or snake oil?"

"My dissertation was on the use of play in communicating with murderers aged ten and under. You figure it out."

Her face softened. "What ten-year-old is a murderer?"

"You'd be surprised. Actually, I agree with you. Killer, yes. Manslaughterer, maybe. But not murderer."

She finished her toast in silence and made herself a second cup of tea. He polished off his breakfast and grabbed

16

the check in case she decided to get women's lib notions about paying, in front of that bunch of biker yay-hoos.

When they hit the road, cruising Route 95 north out of town, the sun was just coming up over Miss Brant's right shoulder.

The freeway leveled out into long, long straight stretches across featureless desert basins. A few low bushes grew here and there amid bare, gravelly dirt. No trees. No grass. Wide open spaces. Wide, *wide* open spaces. The sky glowed blue, the broad land glowed beige, the road before them glowed a sort of interesting gray.

Jack was born for this kind of country. He settled back contentedly and cocked his left foot up, hooking the heel of his running shoe into the seat.

Rinky-dink two-lane replaced the four-lane, and you never noticed the difference. Out here traffic was nearly as sparse as the vegetation. They drove for miles before another car passed southbound. Miss Brant grew noticeably squirmier.

Up there—he saw something. What? About three miles ahead on one of these endless straightaways. Motorcycles. It wasn't the bikers from the Gearjammer. They were still behind him. This must be another bunch.

As he approached he could see they were parked all over the middle of the road. A couple of cars, their brake lights glowing in the morning gold, sat along the berm.

Bikes, blood, and bodies were scattered all over the asphalt.

This day had started out rotten, two hours before it should have. Now it had really gone somewhere in a hand-basket.

Jack pulled to the shoulder behind a red Nissan. He jumped out, popped the lid on his drum box, and grabbed a bunch of flares. He thrust them into the hands of a skinny, wide-eyed teenager. "Middle of the road, about a hundred yards beyond that curve up ahead. Warn drivers to slow down."

The kid stared.

"Here." Jack pulled the cap and mimed the action. "Strike it like a match. Got it?"

The kid nodded suddenly and ran off down the road.

Jack dug back into the drum box for his medical jumpbox. "Who's in charge here?" he yelled.

No one spoke up, no one stepped forward. He could see the answer in their confused, shocked faces. He stopped, inhaled, and took a moment to look around.

Three bikers, one of them a woman, lay motionless on the asphalt, nowhere near their two mangled bikes. Another bike—no, two bikes—had been knocked into the ditch. One of their riders sat with his knees up and his head in his folded arms. The other lay curled on his side. A woman in a Toyota's driver's seat cowered, sobbing, but the car looked undamaged. Her husband on the passenger side was firing up a camcorder, for crying out loud.

Jack pointed to a hulking, unkempt mountain of a man who seemed to be in one piece. "We'll take 'em in order, left to right. You help me and assign workers."

The guy shrugged, heaving shoulders as big as microwave ovens, but he fell in beside.

Jack pointed at a young woman in cut-offs. "You organize traffic control."

And now Jack played a role he had all his years fervently hoped never to see. He got to play God, making what could be life and death decisions. Triage. Deciding who gets help first and who is beyond making it. And he prayed to God every moment to give him the wisdom to help instead of kill.

The biker at his side, a mountainous three-hundred-pounder named Hippo, got with the program right away. He didn't initiate much, but he could give and take orders like a mid-East general. They moved from fallen body to fallen body, assessing damage. This one just might need help breathing soon, possibly a full-scale CPR effort. Find someone with CPR training to keep an eye on him. We'll splint this one's leg after we see to the others. Fractures are low priority, the last thing you attend to. Keep this one on his side; if he vomits he won't aspirate. That means inhale, Hippo.

Jack told the massive man what was needed, and Hippo assigned people to the tasks. Three or four people tried to explain patches of what happened. He felt like a glob of kelp in an undertow, tugged in all directions.

A car pulled up right beside him. A neatly dressed young man in shorts and an alligator shirt swung his door open and handed Jack a car phone. "They want to know what you have."

Jack didn't ask who "they" was. He grabbed the receiver with a bloodied hand. "We have five fallen bikers, all struck by a hit-and-run semi. None of them had a helmet on. Four male victims alive and one woman dead. Two men in their late forties or early fifties with possible head and internal injuries. A possible leg fracture and one with bumps and scrapes. We need at least two units, three would be nice, an airlift would be even nicer for the internal injuries, and send out a pumper to hose the road down. Glass and fuel and metal shards all over." He handed the phone back. He had neglected to mention the pools of blood.

As he turned his back, the clean young fellow was studying his bloodied-up phone unit, gingerly holding it by two fingers.

The highway patrol came half an eternity later, followed after the other half of eternity by an aid van. No paramedic. Just EMTs. Emergency medical technicians, especially in volunteer outfits, are good, but you need someone who can administer drugs and perform invasive procedures.

Jack felt swamped. No matter how quickly he worked, he couldn't keep the lid on. It was like trying to hold two dozen corks underwater at once. He moved from victim to victim encouraging the drafted help and watching

19

for changes. One of the victims, Cat, with the broken leg, actually seemed to perk up a bit. The others were sliding.

That bunch from the Gearjammer came howling up. Instead of helping they gawked like everyone else. Rough tough tourists.

His heart did a little tickle. He could hear the *flub flub flub flub* of a chopper in the distance. Here it came. In moments the big "Medic 1" on its pontoons was legible. Amid a cloud of dust and sand that its blades spat thirty feet, it settled. Genuine paramedics came running. Another aid unit showed up. Talk about answers to prayer.

Jack was no longer in command, and he loved it. He held bags and otherwise helped with IVs. Hippo helped the EMTs package the leg fracture, strapping the guy splint-and-all to the backboard. The cops interviewed the cars that had arrived first. No one had seen the actual deed except the bikers themselves. Half a hundred people stood around watching now—now that there was nothing really useful to witness. Volunteers directed traffic along the far shoulder. Traffic still backed up, but the hustle was over. Jack didn't have to play God anymore.

He even got to step back and catch his breath. Hippo came waddling over lackadaisically and stood beside him. Apparently Hippo was out of things to do too.

"I don't get it." Jack glanced at Hippo's four-day growth of gray whiskers. "These people are saying a trucker ran over them?"

"We were cruising, y'know? Minding our business, enjoying the pretty. Bikers got a heart, too, y'know? He comes up behind us, hits his air horn and his jake brakes. We keep cruising."

"All over the road."

"Hey, man, it's our road, too, y'know? All of a sudden he shifts down, guns it, and starts plowing. I went in the ditch, but I managed to stay on my wheels. Cat and Arnie couldn't. They hadda lay their bikes down. But he—" Hippo stared a few minutes at the three on the highway, in particular at the blue tarp with the woman under it. He wagged his shaggy head. "You sure she's dead? Absolute total sure? Maybe CPR or something?"

"No pulse, no heartbeat, fixed pupils, and her brain is exposed, Hip. I'm sorry."

"Gonna get that—" His threat was drowned out as the bird took off for town, churning up another stinging cloud of dust.

"Get any ID at all?"

Hippo shook his head. "No writing on the trailer. Blue tractor, I think, but I didn't see any writing. Don't think anyone else did either. He was behind us, y'know? We'll find him."

"Just make sure you don't find the wrong one, OK? Some of my best friends are truckers, and I don't want you tearing them apart for no reason. They don't all mow bikes."

Hippo squinted at him. "Who are you, anyway?"

"Work for the Park Service. Got EMT certification as part of my ranger training."

"Cop."

"Tree fuzz, yeah."

"Going to Death Valley?"

"Yeah. I hear some of you guys are too."

"Yeah, we're all going to the Valley."

"Thought Sturgis was the rendezvous for you people."

"Sturgis ain't like the old days." Hippo bobbed his head. "We're bringing back the old times, y'know?" And his graying, hirsute face grew animated. "Man, this is like the old days already, y'know? With the cops and truckers down on us. Used to have a motorcycle rally in Death Valley every year."

"You mean like the moto-cross down in southern California."

"No, man, them idiots are creeps. Their little Suzuki dirt bikes whining around—" Hippo spat in the dust. "This was a legitimate rally, y'know? Motorcycle Association sponsored. Camp all over the valley, show off your hog.

21

Saw my first chopper in Death Valley. And this custom job they had there one year, man, it was a big bike with a Corvair engine rigged into it. A Corvair, y'know? A pancake six! Zero to sixty before you turn the key in the ignition. You had a couple jewels like that every year. It was happening. Then the authorities phased it out, y'know? Said it attracted too many undesirables."

"Which was you."

He grinned wickedly. "Which was me. All of us. One year, they checked all the bikes coming into the Valley. You hadda have a helmet, or you couldn't go through. They figured that'd sort out the scum, y'know? The AMA dweebs, they all wore helmets."

"Not you." And now one of them lay dead with her brains in the breeze, and two others were dying with head injuries.

Hippo waxed enthusiastic. "So a dozen of us, we mugged a party of them doofuses and took their helmets. Rode through the barricade pretty as you please with them stinking helmets on. Then we tossed the helmets away soon's we reached the other side, and off we went."

"Laughing like loons."

"You got it! The looks on the rangers' faces. They had their cruisers all tangled together to make the blockade and couldn't get after us. Not in time, y'know? Anyway, a couple months ago, Bo and Gizzard and some others were talking about the old times, and they said that's something oughta be done again, y'know? So they called around, a bunch of us, and we're doing it."

"How many you think are gonna show up for this thing?"

"Thousand. Twelve hundred. Like the old days, y'know?"

"One more big fling at life before life flings you."

Hippo stared at him a moment. "Yeah." That huge, pliant face spread into a bulbous grin. "Yeah! One last big fling! And hit's gonna be glorious! Y'know?"

3

Salt of the Earth

The sun burned hot now. The excitement had fizzled, leaving a lot of unused adrenaline behind. The carnage was cleared. The highway patrolman had amassed himself enough paperwork to build a tower of Babel. Which is what paperwork is anyway. Jack and Miss Brant rode as they had been riding for the last hour, in forced, tense silence.

The silence irritated him. More than irritated, it angered him. They would be working closely in this investigation, and they had to know each other comfortably. She was fighting it, fighting him, for no reason he could see, except maybe an urge to be difficult or something. And that irritated him even more.

"Miss Brant." He broke silence that begged to be broken.

Those huge dark eyes turned toward him.

"As I understand it, Hal borrowed you because you're a whiz at finding discrepancies on the books. The regional office suspects hanky-panky of some sort in the Death Valley accounts, but they can't find it."

"Region's not investigating. Mr. Edmond wants Washington to investigate. What I don't understand is where he borrowed you."

"He didn't. I work under him directly. It's a pilot program the National Park Service is trying. When you have an unusual case that takes a little extra work, you call in one of Hal's pals. That's me. It's new." Jack watched a hulking motor home go by and could not imagine driving one of those things all over the West.

"When did they cook this up?"

"After that incident at Yellowstone where the diplomat got assassinated."

Ev twisted in her seat to look behind them. The motor home—a tiny cubicle of civilization—grew smaller. Did that really bother her? "I see. And the Park Service took all that flak for botching the investigation."

"The Yellowstone crew is good. It wasn't really their fault. They didn't have the training or the manpower. They got crucified in the media. Hal's pals is an attempt to keep the media feeding-frenzy from happening again."

"Cosmetic." She snorted.

"No, ma'am."

Silence.

"So what then? You're the big hero who boils in, takes over, and saves the day."

"Hal sets me up as a coordinator, and I'm empowered to give orders, sort of, but I'm an adviser. The regular law enforcement specialists do the investigating, the FBI does its thing, and I fill in around the edges. I cover, or assign, those loose ends they either can't get to or don't know about."

She sounded weary. "I can't see you doing any good, then, unless you're stepping on their toes. I know how it works when we try to coordinate an audit investigation with other agencies."

"Lot of diplomacy involved. True."

More silence.

"When will we get there?" In the two hours they'd been on the road, not counting the incident with the downed bikers, she had constantly acted restless, angry, irritated for no reason, and otherwise obnoxious. If Jack had to work with this cookie for the next how-many weeks, he'd go nuts. Or strangle her.

"Hour or so."

She stared glumly, straight ahead.

He stared glumly, straight ahead. Finally he couldn't stand it anymore. "Where were you when I needed you back there?" And only when that exploded out of him did he realize that this was what really angered him so.

"I stayed in the truck and didn't get involved because I didn't know what to do."

"Neither did Hippo, and he came through like a champ. You didn't try." Without meaning to, he was snapping at her as Maxx would, if Maxx ever snapped. She turned on him, snapping more viciously than Maxx ever would. "When a person's life is at stake and you don't know what you're doing, the worst thing you can do is try to help. You do more damage than good. You know that." She took a deep breath and let it out slowly. "It was not a matter of not getting involved, in the usual sense. For the victims' sake I stayed out."

"Sure."

If glares were thermal, she would have fried him like a potato chip.

Her voice sped up even faster, spitting words out staccato. "I don't have ranger training, or training as a law enforcement specialist, or EMT training, or training on what to do at an accident scene, or anything like that. That doesn't mean I'm stupid or cowardly, Dr. Prester. I earned my bachelor of arts at twenty and my M.B.A. by twenty-one. I've been three years with the Washington office and accepted a GS-12 almost a year ago. I can't do what you do, but you can't do what I do, and what I do I do very well, thank you!"

"Training is for career purposes. When life throws you a loop, like it did this morning, you don't stop and think about what you're trained for. You dive in and do your best and let God fill in around the edges. None of the volunteers at that scene, except for the two who knew CPR, had training of any sort. But they served, and they did just fine."

He turned to look at her and almost got lost in those big dark eyes. He must drive his point home before he forgot what it was. "You and I are not going to work together closely because we love it and we hope someday to marry and have five kids, all future rangers. We don't have any choice. We're working together because our mutual boss feels the two cases, the Monument's finances and the Gibbs murder, might be related, and therefore we were both sent to handle it. If you need me beyond the scope of my training, you have every right to expect me to do my best for you. And I expect no less from you. Are we understood?"

Had her face been much closer to his radiator, the ice in her voice would have gelled his antifreeze. "Perhaps we'd better say in so many words now exactly who's the boss here."

"Neither of us. Together means two Indians, no chiefs. We ask of each other whatever's needed to get the job done, and if—"

Not again. Bikers up ahead. They were lolling, going maybe fifty, taking their time, contemplating their navels, whatever it is bikers in no hurry do. The road was straight enough that Jack could pull out wide and pass them, despite the fact that the inside three were left of the centerline.

He passed four more just this side of Death Valley Junction. And another dozen sat around under the shade frames at Zabriskie Point. He mused to himself that if these guys were typical of the breed, there was now enough methamphetamine in the national monument to sink a garbage scow.

As they came down out of the last of the low, naked hills, Death Valley splayed out before them in its shimmering heat and glory. White salt flats, ruler level, paved the floor as far as the eye could see up valley. Dark mountains ran north-south to either side, creasing and folding in muted earth colors. Where hill met plain, like verandas on old houses ran sloping skirts of smooth rubble, bajadas. Subtle earth tones and shades graced the bare hills. No vegetation to speak of. No trees or buildings to get in the way of the scenery.

Nothing significant had changed since Jack last saw this place ten years ago. And that, he reflected, is what the National Park Service is all about.

Miss Brant stared in shock. "There's nothing here. It's—nothing. No grass. Not a tree, not even a bush. It's empty."

"That's what the Forty-niners said too. You're both wrong; there goes a bush right there, for instance."

Her head swiveled as it whipped by. "It was ten inches high. And it was alone."

"It's a bush. I won't go into the sales pitch yet. Let you get used to it first."

"Don't hold your breath waiting."

Clumps of bikers by the dozen and the score wandered all over the road. Hippo and his buddies weren't the vanguard, they were the stragglers. Jack threaded among them, slowing when he had to, and all the while Maxx barked joyfully in back.

The road followed the bajada roughly north, the vivid, flat valley to their left, the sun-drenched dirt hills to their right.

"Look! Green!" Eagerly she jabbed a finger at the windshield.

And green it was, a minuscule oasis of human habitation in the midst of nowhere. Jack pulled into the visitor center parking lot and slid out of the cab. He stretched mightily, stiff from the long haul. The temperature was probably eighty-five or ninety—not at all bad for Death Valley on the first of October.

Miss Brant crawled out and stood by the tailgate in

27

the brilliant sun. "Furnace Creek. This is called Furnace Creek."

"Mm-hmm." Jack waved an arm, identifying the surrounding hills. "Panamints there, those are the Black Mountains, Funerals there. A kid hired by a gold mine up there once wrote home to his folks that he was working graveyard shift in the Funeral Mountains of Death Valley."

"How whimsical." Her voice dripped bitterness.

"Bet you don't like the Addams Family, either." Jack opened the cage door and motioned to Maxx. The dog bounded out and trotted off to oil a yucca.

From beyond the VC a voice called, "Prester?"

Jack wheeled. He vaguely recognized the face, but he never would have come up with the name without the guy's name badge.

Durwin Rice jogged up. He extended his hand. "Welcome to the precinct."

"Precinct." Jack grinned. "Sources inform me you'll have over a thousand bikers in here, twelve hundred, maybe."

"Where'd you learn that?" Rice's blue eyes flashed anger. If it weren't for his graying moustache he'd have looked like a five-foot-ten Arnold Schwarzenegger, a square-built, burly rock. But despite the bulk, if plain old fat were gold, he wouldn't have enough to buy a pencil.

"From a biker. And I understand it'll be glorious. Miss Evelyn Brant out of the Washington office. Durwin Rice is chief ranger here."

The way Durwin looked her over, you could tell he was between marriages. "Miss Brant. Welcome."

She shook hands with him as she had shaken hands with Jack, hesitantly. He was in the short-sleeved gray uniform shirt, so she couldn't possibly be suspecting snakes.

Durwin clapped his hands. "How about you two change your clothes or whatever inside, and we'll take a walk out to the scene. It's not too hot today—good for hiking."

Jack nodded. "I'd like to see the area. Which suitcase do you want, Miss Brant?"

"Mr. Edmond never suggested I was going to be out hiking."

Jack shrugged. "Flying all night and riding in the truck all morning—my suspension system's no picnic in the park. Good way to loosen up. Gives you an interesting perspective on the place."

"Wonderful." She didn't let it sound wonderful at all. She sighed. "And you're certainly right about the suspension."

The conversation held Rice's ear, but Miss Brant held his eye. His attention kept drifting toward her as he spoke. "We have absolutely zero leads. Walking out there isn't going to give you anything new, but it'll show you what we're up against. Brick walls from here to eternity."

It took Miss Brant almost half an hour of digging through everything she brought to come up with a cotton blouse and a pair of khaki shorts. The only shoes near suitable that she owned were mall walkers.

Jack put Maxx on a leash because dogs are supposed to be on leashes and he didn't want to tempt the tourists into turning their mutts free. He dug out his spare canteen to carry water for both Miss Brant and himself.

Rice rubbed Maxx's broad, silk-upholstered head, probably unaware that by so doing he was elevating himself in Maxx's eyes to the rank of Minor Deity. The dog slobbered all over him and otherwise expressed warm affection.

"Ever been here before?" Rice asked.

"Seasonal. Prowled every square mile of this place on my lieu days. Love it."

Rice snorted. "What else is there to do on your lieu days out here?"

The three of them plus Maxx started out across the flat, through blazing sun and sullen silence. The air didn't move, let alone whisper or anything. Jack compared the

29

sparkling natural brightness of this day and this place with the artificial lights of the Vegas airport. No contest. And he wished heartily that Rice had suggested eating before they started. Poor Miss Brant must be starved. An airline breakfast and a side of toast?

"Seasonal here." Rice's eyes seemed to focus on infinity, or maybe on nothing at all. "So was I, mid-sixties."

"Fifteen years before me."

The flat hat dipped slightly. "The way to get into the Park Service then was to build up a couple years' seasonal experience and get a high score on your FSEEs. Bingo. A season or two, and you were in. Not many transferred over from other agencies then—or left the service for other agencies."

"Lot of things have changed."

Jack glanced at Ev. She was already at least one pay grade level ahead of Rice, and in the Park Service one tenth the time. For that matter, Jack had fifteen years' less experience than Rice and he was a 12, too. Did Rice resent it? Some rangers did. Some didn't.

"Edmond sent a one-sheet dossier on you. Except for the last year or so, your positions were all out in the field."

"And this last year in the Washington office convinced me to grab the first thing that came along that would get me out of there. That's why I took this job. To get out of town."

Rice smiled and nodded. Kindred soul. There are those, like Ev, Jack speculated, who thrive on asphalt and bright lights, and those who breathe in rhythm with the land. Obviously Rice, too, was one of those who could live forever without traffic lights.

They stayed with the visitor trail, winding out across half a mile of ironing-board flatness. But instead of walking on west to the creek, they cut southwest and took off across the crisp, crunchy salt, picking their way carefully through the many boggy places. The albedo of this bare and sun-drenched whiteness made Jack's eyes hurt.

He knelt and scooped Maxx up onto his shoulders, the way Bible story books show shepherds carrying sheep. Maxx squirmed a bit—he hated being carried like this —but he gave up arguing pretty quickly and settled down.

Rice frowned. "I'm surprised a big dog like that would get tired so fast. Out of shape?"

"No. The travertine will cut his feet up." Jack shouldn't have had to spell it out for a chief ranger. For Miss Brant with her wide-eyed innocence, maybe, but not Rice.

Speaking of whom, she slogged along with a weary, humorless determination. Minute after silent minute she put one foot in front of another. She tended to drag her feet. She was no hiker.

"Just a couple hundred yards yet, Evelyn," Rice purred.

In that case . . . Jack let the dog down and took off the leash. "Find, Maxx. Find."

Maxx ran ahead, slowed almost immediately to a walk and began picking his way cautiously over the crunchy, jagged ground.

Salt Creek is salt, but it can hardly be called a creek. It runs, on the surface at least, only in wet weather, of which there is precious little. A few permanent pools here and there support inch-long, salt-tolerant desert pupfish, endangered not just by low numbers but by the vagaries of nature. The creek drains extensive, strongly saline desert marshes, a contradiction in terms if ever there was one, spreading out across the flat floor. Saltbush and pigweed grow in patches along it, as well as up nearer the foothills where drainage is a little more favorable.

At this particular place, the dry creek bed cut a meandering, flat-bottom groove a couple feet deep and eight or ten feet wide across the barren whiteness. Maxx caught on fast and hopped down into the creek, where footing was a wee bit smoother. His feet flying joyfully, he dropped to his back and rolled in the loose, salty sand.

31

Jack saw a lot of footprints now, all over the place. The area was trampled past any hope that either he or Maxx might read some sign of who had been here. Maxx loped north upcreek, came back this way, trotted off south downcreek.

Maxx stopped. Nose to the ground he started cutting tiny circles, snuffling and snorting with his cavernous nasal passages. If his bark was baritone, his sniffing was bass. He dug a few test strokes with one paw in loosened dirt. He gave up that site, circled cautiously an open pool of salt water, and moved farther down the creek to begin again that hollow snuffling.

Rice smirked. "Not bad for a dog. Where he was sniffling around there, that's where we brought the body up out of the water. You can see there where we dragged it a little."

Jack dropped down to look at the churned sand. "Tracks?"

"Nothing you could read. A tussle maybe, but not much of one. He was oriented head-toward-the-south, weighted down with sand. Floated anyway, kind of. Water's so salty, in another week he probably woulda been just one big pickle."

Jack glanced at Miss Brant. She didn't look at all well.

Rice rolled on. "I have the coroner's report for you in my office. Blows with a blunt instrument around the head and neck. Toxicology tests won't be available for another day or so."

"Who's doing them?"

"Inyo County."

"How'd you spot it?"

"Based on the flyboy's tip, we scouted the area in a chopper. That took a little over two hours. The kid wasn't sure exactly where. He was going too fast. Soon as they spotted it, they ferried us in, and we choppered the body out."

32

Fifty feet downstream of the salt pool, Maxx barked. He began digging in the dry creek bed there in earnest, shoveling out a couple scoops with his powerful front legs, pausing to snort, digging some more.

Rice growled, "Hal Edmond said your dog is special and I should be tolerant, but, hang it, Prester, this is a national park. Let's not tear it apart, huh?" Jack jogged down the creek bed to Maxx, but not to discourage the dog from digging. He squatted beside Maxx's rapidly growing hole. The pit was a foot deep now, and the salty dirt flew. Maxx snorted and snuffled and rooted with his nose.

Miss Brant moaned weakly and turned aside. You'd think someone who hasn't eaten for nine hours wouldn't have much down there, but she managed to toss her cookies anyway. Durwin Rice said some indelicate words Jack hadn't heard since he quit riding in schoolbuses.

Triumphantly, knowing he had just counted coup, Maxx dragged to light a big, hairy, decomposing arm and hand.

4
Jack of Spades

Jack liked the instant ramada that Cheryl Ashley had created. Supported by four aluminum-tubing triangles that made stakes unnecessary, a lightweight plastic tarp flapped.

She grinned when he complimented it. "Just don't try this thing in any little breeze—like for instance your dog breathing on it."

Partially translucent plastic, it cast an oceanic sort of blue tint across the scene, giving this hideous dig a surreal quality.

Miss Brant sat back onto the corrosive salt and wiped off her sweaty face. "I don't understand. Why are you doing it—digging up this person—this way?"

Jack kept working with his paint brush and tea-spoon. "It's amazing, when you disinter a body using ar-cheological methods like this, how often you come up with telling forensic evidence. Digging it up with a spade, sort of the heavy-handed approach, you might lose the clue that fingers your perp for you."

"A spade would get it over with. And I point out that my work here is not supposed to be fingering murderers. You seem to have lost sight of that."

This coming-out party, as parties go, was small but very smart—a dozen guests or so, counting the guest of honor, who still reclined in his grave: a medical examiner, Gunther Chu; the law enforcement specialist, Bob Hodges; a couple of rangers; Cheryl, the curator/anthropologist; Miss Brant; and Rice. Some reporters out of Vegas, not having the requisite party dress of tie and tails, were left waiting. Maxx, having both leash tie and a tail, snoozed under the ramada, bored senseless by the slow progress and not allowed to participate anyway. It was his find too.

Normally, work accomplished is inversely proportional to the number of people around to do it, but despite all the people standing around, the work was actually proceeding quite well.

They removed loose dirt bit by bit, examining and sifting it. Were the remains a millennium old, they would be sifting for artifacts—potsherds, a bit of linen or cordage, stone things, antler. The human remains would look more or less detached from humanity, being bones and teeth only. There was nothing detached about these, a millennium younger. The flesh still covered the bones. Only the search for artifacts remained the same.

And he stank. Bikers are not known for zephyr breezes from their armpits under the best of circumstances, but this bloated corpse really stank. And even before the disinterment had reached bare skin, the flies had arrived. Not a fly for miles. For counties. Suddenly here were buzzy little black ones and large blowflies, hundreds of them. Where had they all come from? Their constant *brrrrrrrr*, alternately rising and subsiding as progress disturbed them, sounded like a distant alarm clock.

"Now what's this?" Cheryl bent deep in the hole, her nose eighteen inches from her work, her blonde ponytail dangling within millimeters of the body.

Jack admired the way she ignored unpleasantness. The bloated corpse, dead possibly four days, didn't look good either. A male, probably early fifties, tattoos (one of which said "Cheryl"; Miss Ashley delighted in the irony of that), biking leathers, beard, shoulder-length hair. Not only

35

were these guys all over the landscape, they were inside it.

The undertaker had apparently stretched the body out straight, nose down, dug the grave beside it, and rolled it in. One arm was trapped beneath a hip. Sightless eyes, dulled by grit, stared wide open at the sky. The grave wasn't a millimeter bigger than it had to be.

With tweezers Cheryl picked up a cigarette butt an inch long. She sat back and studied it closely. "Unless this guy used lipstick, Jack, you had a woman on the scene."

"Do tell!" Jack held out an evidence bag.

She dropped it in with a flourish.

Jack glanced at the dispirited accountant. "Does that answer your question, Miss Brant?" He looked at Rice. "Where's the best place to get lipstick analyzed?"

"Vegas. It takes longer; they always complain about a backlog. But they can do all the fancy stuff. Neutron analysis, that kind of thing."

Back to work. Maxx lay in the shade pressed against Jack's leg, not in any expression of affection but because the shade frame wasn't big enough for him to stretch out farther away.

A news chopper out of Vegas whirred by, fluttering the blue plastic. The ramada shielded them from anything picturesque. With a swoop they rattled off to Furnace Creek, to sit in air-conditioning until some bit of photo-graphable news turned up.

With a paintbrush, Cheryl flicked the last of the dirt off the corpse's chest. She lifted two gold chains with her dental pick and let them fall. "The motive wasn't robbery."

"Apparently not." Jack's stomach growled. That breakfast and a skimpy box lunch didn't go far enough. One sandwich. An apple. A bag of tortilla chips. Period. When Rice called in the request for Cheryl Ashley, Jack had asked him to send out a couple of lunches with her. Cheryl had arrived promptly and apologetically with word from the concession kitchen: If you want box lunches, give twenty-four hours' notice. The sandwiches and apples

36

were from Cheryl's own scantily stocked refrigerator.

Miss Brant gave up her shallow semblance of helping. She looked like a terrier who had just gone through the rinse cycle in a washing machine. "Why do his fingers —uh—look like that?"

"Someone tried to take the fingerprints off with a cigarette lighter or something."

She studied Jack with abject woe. "None of this is real."

"All a figment of your imagination. You gotta quit eating that cheap salami. It upsets your system."

At the mention of salami Maxx stirred. He rolled up onto his belly and began idly licking and chewing on his feet, making mildly disgusting slurpy noises. If he wasn't going to be allowed to help, he would, by cracky, do his level best to annoy.

The diggers freed up the body and the last of the loose dirt. Whoever dug the grave did not worry about straight lines or flat walls.

Rice got on his handy-talkie and called the chopper in. Cheryl folded up her instant ramada ("Before the helicopter gets here and the backdraft blows it clear to Ubehebe Crater"). By the time the bird arrived forty minutes later, they had the body out of the hole and packaged.

Jack hated messes. Two bullet holes had entered the victim's back; none had emerged out front. No wallet, no watch. But a front pocket held several hundred dollars in bills. He videotaped the empty grave from all four sides, with its black caked blood in the bottom, as he had taped the initial scene. End of exhumation, end of documentation.

Here came the superintendent, Emery Leighton, strolling casually across the searing salt. Again, that name tag proved handy. Jack had memorized the names and positions of all the park employees before he arrived, as well as those of the concession supervisors. He could match names with jobs. Now he had to match names and jobs with faces.

The superintendent's face, fortunately, was memorable, so long and angular was it. Em Leighton had to be nearing retirement age. He stood taller than Jack by a couple inches and probably weighed twenty pounds less. His salt-and-pepper hair had turned misty white at the temples, and his eyebrows had long since grayed to near invisibility. He wore the flat Smokey Bear hat at a jaunty sort of angle, a regulatory no-no, but who's going to call the superintendent on a minor breach of regs?

The lady beside him had to be his wife. She stood nearly as tall as he, and weighed more. Her battered old Reeboks with their dusty tongues hanging out told Jack she was up to hiking from sea to shining sea if she felt like it. Her deep natural tan would have told him that, even if her walking shoes had kept their mouths shut. She wore her white hair short and wavy, like so many older women did, and Jack wondered where she found a hairdresser out here. She was introduced as Myrtle.

Jack now knew lots of Barbaras, several Brendas, and a score of Karens, but only one Myrtle in the whole world.

Myrtle bubbled, but Emery shook matter of factly when introduced and managed to remain aloof in the face of the second homicide in his park in four days. Standing about listlessly, he asked few questions as they finished up. Hal had said this Em Leighton was pretty laid back and easy going. But the man acted absolutely detached, as if it were someone else's park, some other supervisor's worry.

Myrtle asked a million questions, none of them her business. Rice answered most of them.

Maxx gave Emery one sniff and turned a cold shoulder. Snub the superintendent, the Park Mugwump? *Takes guts,* Jack thought. Maxx fawned all over the missus for some reason, rubbing his head against her designer sweatpants, ingratiating himself. She took it in good spirits. There are dog tolerators, and there are dog lovers. She was a dog lover. And Maxx, who could spot a potential treat-

38

deployer a mile away, returned in kind.

They sealed the open grave and its separate dirt pile, if you call throwing a plastic tarp and some sand over it "sealed." Rice offered cigars around, but only he ended up smoking one. Miss Brant watched him light up and looked physically ill.

Miss Brant just might be physically ill, Jack speculated. Half of her sandwich and her apple rode in Cheryl's daypack, untouched. Her face was a sort of cherry red. The unaccustomed heat, or fever? Jack wondered how he could tactfully find out which. Illness would explain her unrelenting grumpiness. But then, the heat and stench were bad enough that a college graduate from a sheltered childhood had every right to feel ill.

Maybe he'd better just scrub this notion of "We're together on this" and work by himself. Let her do, or fail to do, whatever she wished. On the other hand, their success with this case would make or break Hal Edmond's pilot program here. He hated to see the concept go up in smoke because some accountant didn't feel like cooperating. He'd call Hal tonight for advice.

The rangers wandered off. With a hearty wave, Gunther Chu, the medical examiner, flew out with the body. Rice led the way home. Miss Brant fell in behind him.

Jack walked behind her, more or less to crowd her and keep her moving. He was a little sorry electric cattle prods went out with the sixties. She was really starting to drag. Maxx rode on his shoulders again until they reached the tourist trail and he leashed up.

Behind him, Cheryl babbled enthusiastically. "The only bodies I usually get to dig up have been dead five hundred years. You sit there brushing the dirt off this ancient skeleton and wondering what it looked like when it died. This is the first I've ever been able to—uh—handle a dig from the other end of the time scale." Her voice paused. "That didn't come out right."

Jack grinned. "Hear what I mean, not what I say. Romans eight and the intercession of the Holy Spirit."

She laughed melodically. "Right on!"

Miss Brant twisted around and shot a scowl at him. Now what was bugging her? She said nothing and kept slogging.

It was nearly seven when they finally got back to what passes in Death Valley for civilization. Half a dozen rangers kept the small press corps at bay. Rice did an impromptu press conference. Death Valley uses seasonal help, primarily. When they signed on, did any of these seasonal rangers, three of them women, realize they'd be herding cattle at a genuine murder? Probably not. Our national parks are not normally considered murder venues on the same scale as, say, Miami or Chicago.

Cheryl still bounced, Myrtle Leighton gabbed and asked questions with the enthusiasm of a ten-year-old learning about reproduction in snakes, and Miss Brant moped. Jack let Maxx into the cage and coiled the leash. He made appointments with Hodges and Leighton for the next day sometime. Miss Brant crawled into the passenger side. She pressed her shoulders against the seatback and let out a shuddering sigh.

Jack climbed in. "I put our rooms on the card, just to make sure they're waiting for us. You'll be home soon." He torched it off and backed out of the parking slot.

"I won't be home for weeks."

He let it go by. As they passed the date grove below the Furnace Creek visitor center, he expected her to ask about it. She didn't even notice the tall date palms above their straight, shadowy avenues. How do you miss something that size?

The road skirted the east side of the flats. On the bajada, the gentle rise of land at the foot of these mountains, sat the inn, surrounded with enough vegetation to make it look livable.

In silence they turned off the main road and wound

up the lane, past silvery shrubs and creamy yuccas, to the inn. At the door he left her to her own devices while he set his duffle bag and her four pieces on the curb and put Maxx on his leash. She slid out of the truck by herself and stood forlornly beside her bags, an orphan in the storm of life.

From nowhere a college age kid appeared, pushing a rack cart. "Help with your luggage?"

"Sure. Kennel?"

"Yes, sir." The kid eyed Maxx with trepidation. He obviously was weighing the value of his hide against his job, and the job was coming in second.

"Kennel him for me, then, would you please? It's probably safe. He usually doesn't eat adult males."

The kid trundled their stuff into the lobby with Maxx's leash over his left wrist, the dog heeling patiently. The mutt's obedience pleased Jack. Maxx did not always bother to behave.

Miss Brant had lost the discreet way with which she had gawked in Vegas. Now she gawked openly, appreciative, even say awed, like some little farm kid on her first visit to Disney World. Jack signed them in as she scanned the lobby.

Her head whipped around, and she stared at the girl on the desk. "The what?"

The girl stared back. "The Jacuzzi. It's a hot tub with water jets. Very relaxing. It's past—"

"I know what a Jacuzzi is. I just didn't expect—" Miss Brant closed her mouth.

The girl pointed beyond the double doors of the dining hall. "It's past the outdoor pool, through the exercise room. You will enjoy our completely equipped exercise area." She handed them each a ticket. "This entitles you to a free drink. Happy hour is four to six-thirty. An in-house movie list is on your television set. The satellite channels are free." She assembled a smile and put it on automatic. "If you want anything, just call."

The bellhop disappeared with the bags and Maxx.

Jack nodded to the girl, wished her a good evening, and scooped up his key. He piloted Miss Brant through the swinging doors into the corridor. "I have no idea what your plans are for the evening. I have none. I'm not much for happy hours unless there's a clear business purpose. I'm very much for Jacuzzis and swimming pools. If you prefer to be alone, you'll not offend me a bit." He stopped beside door 18, her room. "If you wish to join me, we can dine together either before or after a dip. Your choice."

"You won't be offended if I want to eat by myself?"

"Not at all. The business day just ended. From here on out it's strictly social, if at all."

She stared through him a moment. "I have never felt so sticky and gritty in my whole life. I'm going to shower and spend some time in the Jacuzzi. Then the pool. Then dinner. You may join me if you wish."

He nodded. "Good enough!" He walked to his own room, 21.

For being more than a hundred miles from civilization, the Furnace Creek Inn manages to put on the dog, an oasis of cosmopolitan culture in a tree-clad oasis in the barren waste. The rooms are lavishly appointed, the amenities all right out there in the open.

Jack ignored the TV and the sealed bar cabinet and the fresh ice water in the ice bucket. He took his specialty, a thirty-seven-second shower. He loved wallowing in large bodies of water like, say, Lake Powell, but he hated showers, with all those little pieces of water jumping on him. He dug out his swimming trunks and headed for the Jacuzzi.

She had beaten him there. Clearly she must have perfected a twenty-five-second shower, and he envied that. She lolled in roiling water with her head back and her eyes closed. Her face had softened, the perpetual frown melted away to nothing. He dismissed his speculation that she might be ill. She appeared a totally different woman from

42

the hard, critical lady Jack had met at the airport over fourteen hours ago.

Fourteen hours. Two bodies and four severely injured people later. The crushed and bloody biker mama on the asphalt still haunted his thoughts. The stench from the latest corpse still clung in his nose.

He slid down into the water and let its swirling, bubbling warmth massage him. He closed his eyes. Bit by bit, the harrowing fourteen hours tiptoed away. Her voice asked, "Do you go out camping much?"

"A lot. Keep my gear stashed behind the seat. When I need to, I can set up in five minutes."

"I thought so. Mr. Edmond said the area was remote, so I steeled myself for the worst. It turned out to be worse than the worst I could imagine. The moment we left Las Vegas—not a decent tree, not a spark of life anywhere. So bare—the ground, I mean. And to drive so many miles without seeing a thing. In over an hour I counted seven buildings, and some of them were abandoned. Seven. And I'm thinking, what in hades—literally, hades—have I got myself into? Fire and brimstone. Desolate. This country is like the hell I learned about in Sunday school."

He smiled. "I think you'll be pleasantly surprised."

"I certainly haven't been so far. Except for this place, this hotel. I expected something a lot more—" she paused, sifting for words "—primitive. I was even afraid I might end up having to live in some primal cabin or tent, like camping. You can't imagine how glad I am that this place is the way it is. The rooms are really quite nice, for being in the middle of nowhere."

"Ever been anywhere besides Washington?"

"Not really, I guess. I was born and raised in Annapolis. My father's with the Naval Academy. School in Baltimore. I came into the Park Service in the Washington office and always worked there."

"Never been west of the Mississippi."

"Never been west of the Potomac."

The water splashed to Jack's left. A skinny, red-headed woman sloshed down onto a bench seat by his elbow. She was very skinny and very redheaded, in fact, with enough make-up to take ten years off her appearance or die trying. Jack glanced at the crowsfeet and bags that makeup can't hide and guessed her age at anywhere between forty-five and fifty.

She brandished her lighted cigarette. "Mind?"

Jack shrugged. "If you think you can keep it lit in this class three whitewater." He offered his hand. "Jack Prester."

"Gladys Gibbs." She accepted the handshake.

Gibbs. He frowned. "Related to George Gibbs?"

"Widow."

Now what do you say? A dozen thoughts spun around in his head, all clamoring for attention at once. "I'm very sorry."

"Thank you." She took a long, deep drag. "I'm not."

Jack shrugged again. "You knew him better than I did. Your first time out here?"

"To Death Valley? Yes."

"Current events implications aside, how do you like it?"

She burst into a harsh, raucous laugh. "Current events implications: lovely!" She chuckled a few moments, not at all raucous. "I like the area well enough, Jack, that I flew back home for the memorial service yesterday—they won't let me bury him yet, you know—and flew right back out here last evening. I have ten days left on the room, and I'm going to enjoy it."

"So you and George were supposed to be here ten days yet."

"The poor slob never could do anything right. Not even take a working vacation."

"If you went with him everywhere he went, you've been to some gorgeous places."

"And some real holes too. Glacier Bay, Alaska. Two

44

hundred and seventy days of rain a year. It rained every single day."

"How long were you there?"

"Me? A week. George stayed three weeks longer. Not one single day of sunshine that whole month. Same way with Mount Rainier. Overcast every blessed day. And North Cascades. Even longer there. I stayed in town the whole time he was out there, inside the hotel where it's warm and dry."

"And not one single day of rain here for months. I see the picture." Jack stood up. "Mrs. Gibbs, it was a pleasure to talk to you. And my condolences anyway."

"Thank you, Jack. And from now on it's Gladys, you hear? Good night."

"Good night." Jack climbed out and up. He heard Miss Brant speak to Mrs. Gibbs—Gladys, that is—and follow him to the pool.

His wet feet splacked on the tiles. He slipped over the side at the three-foot end, from hot churning water to cool languid water, and shoved off deeper, backstroking.

Miss Brant inserted herself into the pool gracefully and dog-paddled out.

"Maxx swims like that." Jack grinned.

"This is supposed to be the best kind of swimming exercise, dog-paddling." She stopped near him and stood up. The water came just to her armpits. She lowered her voice. "I can't believe that woman! A widow for four days and look at her."

"Interesting. But what I really want to look at is her lipstick and her brand of cigarettes."

5

Hogs and Bacon

Jack paused briefly on his way down the hall to peek in an office doorway. Most of Death Valley's administrative personnel worked in this airy, open office, with its many desks, dividers, printers, terminals, the obligatory shredder, and even more essential Xerox copier. It's tough to get enough paper to shred if you don't have a copier to manufacture shredding material.

Miss Brant's work station sat in the very middle, a three-by-eight-foot folding cafeteria table covered with spread sheets and printouts. Not one but four Magic Markers that spread a broad stroke of transparent color lay about, and Jack probably wasn't seeing all of them. Why ever could she need four colors?

She hovered above the table poring over printouts, occasionally Magic Marking an item, now and then punching something into a computer terminal at the end of the table. She was not a hiker. She was not a disinterrer. She was not worth mud in an emergency. But she looked perfectly content here, even say eager. Jack shuddered at the thought and continued on his way.

"Hey, Prester!"

Jack stopped in the chief ranger's doorway. "Good morning."

"Morning." Rice stood up and came around the end of his desk. He shoved a file folder into Jack's hands. "Toxicology report on Gibbs. Booze was .028, no drugs, prescription or otherwise. Death from massive trauma to head and neck. Repeated blows with a blunt instrument. Their soft X-ray turned up traces of iron, like a crowbar or something."

"And nothing like that at the scene."

"No bottles, either." He thrust another file at Jack. "And this one's the preliminary on the Hell's Angel type. No ID, but those guys, you know, they never have any identity. They come and go and nobody knows."

"Prints are going to be kind of messy too."

"Nothing on that so far. They raised some partials."

"I drove around the campground here and didn't see anyone I know. Think I'll go look around some of the others. Met a couple people, bikers, who might be able to identify him."

"Take Mel with you. It's his lieu day, but he's around."

Jack shook his head. "Low profile."

"Then at least take this." Rice walked over and yanked a handy-talkie out of its charger base. "Channel four for local, one for the repeater."

Jack didn't argue. He accepted it. He glanced through the biker's file. A living breathing man reduced to a few pages in a manila folder. Someday Jack's mortal remains would be recorded in a file in someone's cabinet. Or possibly to nothing more than a couple electronic signals on a small floppy disk. What does the future hold for someone not in Jesus Christ? Was the biker saved by the grace of God? Probably not. Few such are, except for some groups like the Glory Road Riders or something. And George, this other folder. What was his standing with God?

"Toxicology on the biker?" Jack asked.

"Not on paper yet. The coroner called this morning, said he had a couple beers in him but not intoxicated. No drugs. Say—uh—we were going to have quarters ready for you two, but there's a screw-up. Maintenance got one little trailer up and running, but the other trailer has plumbing problems."

"When do trailers ever not have plumbing problems?"

"Good point." Rice scooped some loose papers off his desk. "So we have a seasonal apartment available for you. We'll get the second trailer up and running and put our winter seasonal in that when she arrives." He handed Jack the housing descriptions.

"Miss Brant in the trailer and me in the apartment?"

"Yeah. Nice little place. One L-shaped room and bath."

"Put Miss Brant in the apartment and me in the trailer."

Rice shook his head. "You rank her. And it's not that nice a trailer."

"Then absolutely give me the trailer. Miss Brant'll be much more comfortable inside four solid walls, and I don't care."

"Tell you what. Stop by up at Cow Creek and take a look at it before you make up your mind. The trailer's down in the lot by the grade school. It's the one they call the Silverfish. Try not to step in the pack rat crap." Rice scooped a key off the desk and handed it to him. "How long you gonna be gone?"

"I expect to return before noon." Jack gave him back his housing descriptions unread. He reached the door before the thought struck him. "George Gibbs was over in the inn, right?"

"Yeah."

"The brochures all promise the inn doesn't open until October one. Why'd the inn open early for him? Why didn't you just put him in the apartment or the trailer?"

"Corla—she's the manager at the inn—said they could handle it, since they were opening anyway in a couple days and had enough staff to do it. George's missus didn't like the apartment and trailer. They had a boy with them, a kid, and the trailer and the apartment are too small. One bed each. Hate to talk about a widow, but she's a royal pain."

"Gladys? Yeah. Charming."

"You met her already? You ain't wasting time, Prester. Hey, wait a minute. You mean she's back here?"

"She sure wouldn't want to lose her ten days' vacation over a silly little thing like George's death, would she? Priorities." Jack walked outside into the bright sun and burgeoning warmth of a perfect first-week-of-October morning. Priorities indeed.

Out in the visitor center parking lot, Maxx stood up on the roof of his wire cage and barked a greeting.

Jack called him to the ground with a gesture. He rubbed the hard, knobby head. "You gonna behave if we go visiting? Come on." He unlocked the cab door and invited Maxx in. The dog leaped up eagerly and settled himself on the passenger side. Jack leaned across and rolled the window down for him.

What a beautiful day. *Yes, Gladys Gibbs, I have been to Glacier Bay. And yes, it rained every day I was there too. And I loved it. But I agree with you, you can't beat this.* He cruised north up the main road. To his left stretched those amazing salt flats with their beige streaks writ so large. To his right, a wall of low, barren hills of endless age sat simmering in the sun. "And the everlasting hills." Was that from Scripture or from some hymn? He couldn't remember. He'd have to look it up.

Maxx belched in hollow baritone and licked his own nose, slurping. He stuck his head out the window awhile and let his floppy ears fly. He pulled his head in and watched through the windshield. Neither viewpoint seemed o satisfy him. The Silverfish. Jack turned right and followed a winding lane back to the Park Service residence area. The asphalt road crawled up the hill beside the creek drainage and disappeared in a green clump of cottonwoods. Beneath those green cottonwoods out of sight, a

49

couple dozen two- and three-bedroom homes lined the looping road, huddled beneath leafy shade. But the shade did not extend down here to the beginning of the sloping bajada, where maintenance sheds and trailer homes baked in the brightness.

To the right down here on the flat stood the open playground of the grade school. The kids were all inside now. Beyond it a couple rows of rectangular trailers housed seasonals, VIPs, intermittent personnel, and a few concessions employees. Most had awnings; all had lawn chairs and those clamshell barbecue grills on a stand. Death Valley is an outdoors national monument.

Jack didn't have to ask anyone which trailer was the Silverfish. Beyond the other trailers, off by itself, sat an eighteen-foot aluminum tear-drop travel trailer. No awning. No barbecue. No chair. In fact, no front stoop. A couple of cement blocks formed the steps to the front door. He got out and tried the key in the door. It opened.

He liked the inside immediately—the kitchen/dinette at this end, a built-in table and bench seats by a big window, a bathroom about the same size as the narrow, stubby little hall. The toilet and shower stall shared the same corner. A tiny bedroom barely large enough to hold bunk beds and a chest of drawers filled the back half. A small jalousie window between the upper and lower bunks was cracked open to relieve the oppressively stale air in here. Apparently the front door was the only door.

The wood cabinets were darkly and permanently stained, especially around the handles. Black cracks crossed the worn linoleum on the floor. In the closet-sized bathroom hard beside the kitchen/dinette, gray-white travertine dulled the shower stall and lined the sink and toilet.

Jack had no problem with that; the water in Death Valley is as hard as bleacher seats. He flopped down on the bed and stretched out. Considerably softer than the water. He locked the door on his way out.

Jack had looked for an hour already this morning, but he had not found Hippo and his bunch in the campgrounds near Furnace Creek. Possibly they decided not to come because of the accident, or they were in Vegas with their stricken compatriots. No. Jack remembered the enthusiasm in Hippo's face, the lilt in his voice. They were here somewhere. He drove up the valley, basking in the delight of the day all the way. *Thank You, Lord!*

Despite the wooden ramadas and scattered lacy creosote bushes, the freestanding charcoal braziers and the water faucets, Stovepipe Wells campground perches on the brink of hell. Nearby to the southeast, arrowweed clumps form the Devil's Cornfield, aptly named. Behind it, giant sand dunes stretch. Curious, Jack mused. They form such a small part of the Monument, and yet when you think of Death Valley, what do you think of? Sand dunes.

Bikes clogged the campground so completely Jack had to park his truck out by the information kiosk. He stuffed Rice's radio back under the passenger seat so he wouldn't look like a ranger. He left his hat on the truck seat—he sure didn't want to be wearing anything that could get knocked off—and motioned Maxx out of the cab. Maxx bounded off to do his duty beside a saltbush, then rolled in the powder dirt of the parking area.

Bikers were watching him, and they did not look friendly. Many bikers. Hundreds of bikers. They gathered in clusters around morning fires, or just sat, lounging against their bikes, smoking heaven knows what. A smorgasbord of smells assailed Jack's nose—of unwashed bodies, burned food, campfire smoke, and things Jack was happier not knowing the identity of. Music blared from boom boxes here and there. Rock mostly. A little country. Jack walked fifty feet back the road, weaving among motorcycles, and stopped.

Numerous eyes followed him. Casually, deliberately, he unbuckled Maxx's collar and stuffed it in his pocket. He slapped his leg. *On guard, Maxx,* the gesture said.

Maxx usually treated obedience as an option and not always an attractive one. But when the situation looked like business, old Maxx always came through. He came through now. He swung around behind Jack and fell in beside his left knee, at heel. It helped that he enjoyed this on guard business. Things he didn't enjoy usually went undone.

They walked another fifty feet. When Jack stopped to peer about, Maxx plopped down to sitting. But it was not a casual seat. The big dog vibrated with anticipation, his bottom barely touching the asphalt. His ears worked like radar dishes, perking, flopping, tilting.

Jack sought a familiar face, any familiar face. Nothing. He tried to pick out Hippo's hog, but they all looked alike. He abandoned the road and moved in among the crowds of campers and bikes and empty bottles. He could feel his neck hairs bristling. Finally he just stepped up to a group at random.

Six scruffy gents and four post-pubescent girls sat around a fire. The girls were wearing sweaters and jackets on this warm day. Must be from California. A blackened porcelain-steel coffeepot perched atilt on the edge of the coals. They stared at Maxx.

The farthest of them, a balding geezer in a leather vest, waved a finger. "What's that dog gonna do?"

"That depends on you. I'm looking for Hippo."

"Ain't here." The fellow's eyes never left the dog.

"So I see. I need him, and he can use me. Spread the word he should talk to Jack, will you?"

Jack moved on. Maxx hopped up and strode alongside, basking in the attention. All these campground odors aside, this was starting to smell like a bad idea. OK, so he had told Rice where he was going. But the nearest ranger was almost half an hour away, even if he could summon help promptly. No one except a flock of hostile hippies was within striking distance of him this morning (a phrase not to be used casually, "striking distance").

And they all knew he was there too. What had once been scattered groups and clusters was beginning to become a congealing mass of menace, thickening to block his way. And no way out.

"Isn't he cute!" a sultry girl's voice exclaimed. She called, "Here, doggy!"

Jack perceived she wasn't complimenting his own good looks and charming personality.

"Have some bacon, doggy."

Maxx darted away.

"Maxx!"

Too late. Oblivious, Maxx closed in like a ten-week-old puppy on the tidbit. The jerk.

"What did you say his name is? Max?" A girl in teal sweats and stringy, mouse-colored hair sat by a huge tank of a Harley. She tore off another piece of bacon and fed it to the dog.

"Yeah. Two X's." Jack moved in close behind his dog. If Maxx would not heel, Jack would.

"He's pretty. And so glossy. Does he have papers?"

"Did once, but he ate 'em."

"What's his name really? I mean officially?"

"Hall's Maximian Luxembourg. That's Maximum Licks and Burps."

She giggled, totally at ease. Maxx's tongue, never idle, flicked forward and enveloped her hand clear up to her wrist.

"You must have owned a dog with papers, or you do now."

"My ex-husband raised English setters. They didn't have a great personality like this. And they're scrawny compared to him. Look at that chest and barrel. He's so bulky and solid, and friendly. I bet he wouldn't hurt a flea, right?"

Maxx began avidly licking her exposed forearm.

"Depends on the flea. I'm looking for Hippo. He around?"

53

"He with the bunch that got hit with the truck? They're over that way somewhere." She waved her hand toward the south, leaving her face unprotected. Maxx used the chance to lick her nose and cheek. She yanked her head back and laughed aloud.

From behind Jack a deep voice droned, "Whatcha want with'm?"

Jack turned, trying not to look worried.

The guy was a youngster as this mob went, probably thirty-five or forty. He was dressed in jeans and a tank-cut undershirt. He was not into laundering undershirts.

"Oh, come on, Reef," the girl whined. "Not this early, huh?"

Jack kept his voice low and casual. "You can listen in while I talk to him. If he wants you to."

"I don't think you're gonna talk to him. Know what else I think? I think you're in the wrong place." Reef took a step in closer, blocking Jack's way.

"Know what I think? I think you're making the wrong move." Jack put some bravado behind his voice, but he didn't feel it. He couldn't be sure Maxx's attention was on business and not bacon. And he dare not turn his eyes away to see what his dog was doing.

Reef grinned. He wasn't into laundering teeth, either. They were grayer than his shirt. "Cannibal." He flicked a finger toward Maxx. "Pigs eating bacon. That's cannibalism."

"Five syllables in that word. I'm impressed. Yeah, I guess we're pigs sort of. Hey. Did George Gibbs ever pay you jerk-offs that hundred and fifty bucks he was supposed to?"

The unwashed Reef raised his hand, a gesture of some sort. It wasn't a threatening move as such, but Maxx, bless him, was back to business. With a snarl the dog came hurtling. Reef tipped back, ducking, and tumbled. The dog snarfed with those cavernous sinuses that made his growl sound like a lion in a bucket.

54

The girl twisted to her feet. "I'll go find Hippo." She ran off southward. Experimentally, Reef arched up onto one elbow.

"You stay down." Jack waved a finger. Now what? Walk off south and leave him? Jack had just humiliated this guy. Reef wasn't going to take it lying down, literally.

Plowing a swath through the camp, here came Hippo. He must have been zeroing in on the action like everyone else, because he arrived much too quickly for the girl to have sought him out.

He sauntered up to Reef and kicked his shoulder with a boot the size of a cement mixer. "Whatcha down there for?" He looked at Jack. "Wanna cuppa coffee?"

"Sure. Maxx, heel."

Maxx fell in beside, a bit reluctantly it seemed, and they started off toward the south. Hippo's accolade probably conferred some sort of immunity, but Jack couldn't help but watch for motion in his peripheral vision. Mentally he vowed, *If I ever pull a stupid stunt like this again, I hope Maxx bites me.*

6
Jackpotshot

Walking through this jam-packed campground behind Hippo made Jack feel like a tugboat following an ice-breaker. He simply strolled along in the wide open swath Hippo's bulk cut.

Bikers were born campers, it seemed. No one bothered with wimpy tents, unnecessary in this mild season. Some circled their bikes like wagons. Most used their bikes as furniture. As he tagged along behind Hippo, Jack heard dogs bark here and there and saw a lot of girls. Almost none of them were as old as the men. None of them paid any closer attention to personal hygiene than their biker bozos did.

"How are your buddies doing?" Jack recognized a couple of faces in a group up ahead.

"Still there. Somebody calls down now and then, checking. We sent Barbara home in a box. Cat and Arnie are back."

"Cat! He's the broken leg. How did he—" And Jack stopped because he saw how.

There sat Cat, propped up against his bike, in a walking cast from hip to toe. It was not a straight cast. His encased knee was bent at the perfect angle to ride a bike with, cocked just so.

Cat grinned in recognition. "Came out on my own wheels." He weighed perhaps half what Hippo did and stood a couple inches shorter, cast notwithstanding, but he seemed in some ways tougher. He was certainly quicker and wirier than the mountain.

Jack crossed the camp ring and high-fived him. "Criminy, I envy you!"

Hippo's sleeping bag was draped over his hog. He flopped down and leaned back in his instant easy chair. "Word says you wanna talk to me."

"Word travels faster'n the speed of light." Jack hunkered down beside the fire ring, into the warm, granular dirt.

With a smirk the Hip pulled a handy-talkie out from behind his bike tire. "We ain't all primitive, y'know."

Maxx bellied out at Jack's knee, relaxing by degrees. Good. Maxx could sense hostility long before Jack did as long as bacon wasn't involved. If Maxx relaxed, Jack could. Maxx heaved a heavy sigh that ended in a baritone snarf.

Jack yanked open enough snaps down the front of his shirt that he could get out his photo blow-ups. He passed them across to Hippo. "Need an ID on one of your people."

Hippo stared at the full-length shot. His sunburned face went white beneath the tan. He stared at the photo of the biker stretched out full length. He held it aside and studied the close-up awhile. "I'll be—" His voice trailed off to nothing. His eyes lifted to Jack. "Where'd you find him?"

"Buried out on the flats. Probably died five days ago. As you can see from the photos, pretty decomposed."

"How?"

"Two bullets in the back. They ripped the aorta and inferior vena cava. Clean kill. Almost instant death."

"Bo."

"As in Bo knows football?"

"His name in the world is Chester—uh—" Hippo

stared at the sky. He looked at Cat. "He's always just Bo, y'know?"

"Something Russian. Point Man knows." Cat stretched out his hand. "Bo! Lemme see."

Jack passed the photos from Hippo to Cat. Half a dozen people crowded in behind him to get a look.

Cat glanced up at Jack. "Where's his earrings? You take his earrings off?"

"He didn't have any on, if they're not in the picture. Had a couple gold chains, and a big onyx ring."

"Yeah, I see them."

"What kind of earrings?"

"Big gold loops. Sorta like Mr. Clean, only two of them."

"Tell me about Bo." Jack looked at Cat, at Hippo.

Hippo sucked a couple gallons of air in through his nose. "Bo and two or three other guys are who set this whole thing up. Did the whole thing by phone. He was a good organizer, y'know? He could put something together and have everybody else doing the work, and make it look like it fell together by itself."

"Over the phone, huh? When'd you see him last?"

"Couple years ago, face to face. He came in here about a week ago. No, longer'n that. Maybe two weeks. Anyway, awhile."

"First ones in."

"Hadda be."

"Who was he in the world?" Jack sat forward.

"Cook. Cook at a big hotel. Westin, I think. Westin or Hilton. Only they call 'em chefs, y'know?" Hippo looked at Cat.

Cat shook his head. "Forget which hotel. Mighta been Holiday Inn. Point Man'll know. He was a good cook. Really good."

Jack nodded. "Well regarded here, where it counts?"

"The best." Hippo's voice softened.

"I'm sorry."

58

"Me too."

Cat snapped his fingers. "Robosky. Chester Robosky."

"Nam vet." Jack was guessing, but it fit.

"Yeah." Hippo stretched out his elephantine legs. "Lot of them here." He lapsed into thought, and Jack gave him the silence.

A minute or so later Hippo shifted his bulk and spoke. "Some of us are originals, like Bo and me. We were the real McCoy back then, y'know? Scum of the earth and proud of it. Took nothing from nobody. How many Hell's Angels are there? Not many. Just a few of the real ones, y'know? The ones that were there, back in the beginning. And some wanna-be's. Just a couple guys, but we had a whole nation scared spitless. The whole nation, y'know?! Two hundred million people scared to death of little old us!"

Hippo grinned at the thought. The grin faded. "When our time passed, like everybody's time passes, most of us went establishment. Neckties and everything. If you can't beat em, join em, y'know? A couple of them did what they know best and put together a working drug operation—"

"The motorcycle mafia."

Hippo snorted. "Really overblown in the press, y'know? Not that impressive, believe me. Nobody woulda noticed them at all if they hadn't started out as bikers." He studied Jack a minute. "You look like you don't believe me."

Jack considered this a prudent time to leave his opinions of Hell's Angel drug dealers, with their corner on the illegal methamphetamine trade, to himself. He raised his hands. "An opinionated joker in the same weight class as a Nissan Sentra is not a person to contradict."

The guffaw burst out of Hippo.

Jack pressed on. "So some of you went legit."

"On the outside. I mean, the neckties and the white lab coats, that's all surface, man. Y'know? We're what we were yet, down inside. Oh, hey! Coffee. Mave, get the guy a cuppa coffee. Want some breakfast?"

"Already had."

Hippo continued, "Now a lot of the guys you see here weren't bikers in the beginning. They ain't originals, y'know? Most of em started out establishment. Clean and sober. Most of 'em went to Nam. Most of 'em came back bikers."

"At least down inside."

"Yeah. Yeah! The inside. That's what counts. Bo, he never lost the inside, y'know? He made big money cooking, but whenever he felt like thumbing his nose at the 'stablishment, he did it."

"I understand cooks are pretty independent cusses anyway, at least the good ones." Jack accepted the mug of coffee offered him and wondered about the oil slick on its surface.

"Yeah. Yeah! That's Bo. That might even be why he went into that line of work, think?"

"Any idea who'd do him?"

Cat spoke up. "Two bullets in the back? Not one of us. Count on it." He passed the photos back to Jack. "What caliber?"

"Probably thirty-eight. Slugs are so crumbled we can't get a good ballistics read on them. Really came apart in there."

Cat wagged his head. "Not another biker. Not a buddy."

"Mm. Last night Rice was complaining about all the brawling and fighting in these camps. He mentioned a couple knifings."

"Rice?"

"Chief ranger."

Hippo's eyes snapped. "None of his business! He can keep his flat-hat fern feelers home. We'll take care of our own stuff." And he added a few choice words for emphasis.

Jack pressed on. "Right. So maybe Bo tangled with one of his own? A brawl that got out of hand? An argument turned sour?"

"Look." Hippo waved a finger the size of a bratwurst. "Knives, fists. Nothing, y'know? Your chief ranger complain about any of us shooting our buddies in the back?"

Cat acted just as incensed. "Knife, fists, that's just to emphasize your point, man. Show the guy a little fang. But a gun? You could hurt a guy with a gun."

Jack nodded. "So the brawls and the knifings are surface."

"That's right! You got it exactly right." Hippo bobbed his head. "I might punch out Cat there, leg or no leg, y'know? But you lay a finger on him, and I stomp you."

Jack tried not to take that personally. "And it's always been like that."

"Always."

"But these Nam guys, the new ones, the ones that haven't always been bikers, they might not have the same code of honor you have, you think? For instance, how many Reefs do you have?"

"Reef? Oh. That geek. Most of them. We accept them for what they are, y'know? They're what we used to be, in a lotta ways."

"Lots and lots of anger."

Hippo nodded quietly.

Jack let a minute or so drift by before speaking again. "Somebody from the deep past wouldn't be taking revenge thirty years later."

"We don't work that way. We want to do you, we don't wait. We do you. Finis."

Jack tried not to take that personally either. "Was George Gibbs ever a biker?"

"Who?"

"That accountant whose body turned up on the salt flat."

"You kidding?" Hippo snorted derisively.

61

"Now hold on." Cat squirmed, trying to find a comfortable position. Apparently there was none with an angled walking cast. "Couple guys here are in accounting one way or another. Could be, but I don't know of anyone here ever heard of him."

"What are you in the world?" Jack asked.

"Securities analyst."

"Get outta here!" Jack caught himself gaping. He chuckled, as much at himself as at Cat. "You got too much dirt and fork oil under your fingernails, man."

Cat laughed. "When Hippo here called me, I walked away from my desk and bought myself a bike that same day. Boss wasn't pleased, but what's she gonna do? She filed a formal complaint. Whoop de doo. So I get halfway out here from St. Louis, and I called in to the office and gave them two weeks notice. Then I got her on the line and told her exactly what I thought about her formal complaint."

"That ain't polite, Cat." Jack smiled.

"Neither's security analysis. Bunch of crooks trying to get one up on all the other crooks." His face sobered, took on an almost wistful look. "I forgot too much about this life. Forgot what it feels like—the wind and sun and rain—until this last few weeks, and I remembered again. I'm not going back there. I got enough money stashed, man, I can live on the road for a couple years. Then I'll see what I wanna do, if anything. Rather mule meth than go back to that. At least it's honest dishonesty."

"Where's Bo's bike?"

"Oughta be Furnace Creek. That's where they set up first."

"What was he on, you know?"

Hippo and Cat both squinched their eyes up thinking about that. Hippo mused, "Had that chopper with the chrome fork when I saw him—but that was—think he got a new one since then."

"He ever sell that old Fat Boy? The good one?" Cat squirmed some more.

A couple minutes more of speculation failed to turn up anything helpful. Good. Either these people were acting very, very cagey, or they were straight. They just arrived, and Bo had been dead for days. They shouldn't know much.

"You said about Point Man. How do I find him?"

"Furnace Creek. Or did he go up to Wildrose?" Cat shrugged. "Be nice if he could help you find the guy that did it. He's a Christian, Point Man. Doesn't make a big deal of it, but he don't hide it, either. And that takes guts, man. 'Specially 'round here. He has this outfit just for Nam vets called Point Man International. He don't run it. Some guy up north does. He just calls himself that while he's here. A handle."

"Sounds like a good idea."

"I'm thinking about linking up with it, yeah."

Jack finished his coffee, and his stomach tried to explain to him that you just don't subject a good friend to that kind of abuse. He stood and wondered how he was going to get past Reef the geek. Maxx shifted himself into gear.

"Going down to Furnace Creek?" Hippo lurched to his feet.

"Welcome to come along, if your reputation can stand riding in something with a working muffler. I'm parked by the road."

Hippo yanked his sleeping bag off his bike and dropped it in a heap. "Take my own, thanks. Wanna see if Barbara got home OK. They were gonna ship her air freight. Call Vegas. Maybe look up some of Barbara's buddies at Texas Spring." He kicked his machine to life with one mighty stomp. It roared. He throttled it down, and it rumbled in perfect tune. He looked at Jack expectantly.

Jack swung on behind him. "Sings like an opera star. Do your own mechanical work?"

"Ain't nobody but me tinkers with this baby." Hippo shoved off. They thundered through the crowded camp-

63

ground pretty much straight-line, without regard to life or limb. The lives and limbs managed to all get out of the way.

Jack thought about the millions of clean-cut office types who would look down their noses at the likes of Hippo—tidy, civilized people who didn't know the difference between a timing light and a Bud Lite.

He searched as best he could for Reef. No sign of the man.

Hippo drew up beside Jack's pickup. Jack slid off. Maxx came panting up behind.

Jack didn't bother to shake hands. "Soon as I learn anything more about Bo, I'll let you know."

Hippo nodded. He looked like he was almost ready to say thank you or something. Then his V-twin steed lunged forward, and he was gone, howling down the road with his head held high.

Jack let Maxx in and slid behind the wheel. He leaned over immediately to roll the windows down—it was an oven in here, and Maxx's sloppy panting didn't do a thing for air quality—and got a wet tongue splacked in his ear. By the time Jack drove out to the main north-south road, Hippo was nowhere to be seen.

He passed maybe fifty or sixty bikers going either direction, but not a whole lot, considering the number of people here. They were probably all sitting around camp like the ones at Stovepipe Wells, blotting up the ambiance. Probably stoned.

Toward him came someone on a big motorcycle, north up the valley. But he was not a true blue biker. He wore a full face helmet, gloves, the works. True blue bikers don't wear anything that hinders physical damage should an accident occur.

Passing the Cow Creek turnoff reminded him he had to stop by the chief ranger's office and sign the papers for the trailer. He was getting hungry. Should he take Miss Brant to lunch and touch base on what she found so far, if anything, or should he—

64

The windshield popped and split right across his line of vision. A second slug hit the back of his seat, and a third thunked into the cab outside somewhere. He heard only the third gunshot as the lone motorcycle whipped by.

Intelligence dictated that he floor it and get the blazes out of there. He stood on the brake, pulled to the roadside. His wheels skidded and grated, fishtailing in the dirt. Maxx slammed against the far door. Jack did a pretty sloppy moonshiner's turn and practically went airborne heading north up the road.

There the guy was, way up ahead and pulling away. A Dodge Ram pickup is not the sleekest of pursuit cars, as a basset hound is not the breed of choice if you're chasing an antelope. And Jack didn't want to take time to dig his plug-it-in-the-cigarette-lighter flashing red light out from under the seat.

He roared up behind a camper, and by the time he pulled around the guy, the motorcycle was gone completely. Nothing, as far as the eye could see. He pulled over and shuffled around under the passenger seat, groping for Rice's handy-talkie. He would call Grapevine, Stovepipe Wells, and Wildrose. He'd tell the rangers there . . .

Tell them what? To be on the lookout for a motorcyclist? Ri-i-ight. Could he describe the rider? No. The bike? No. The situation? Not clearly. He stared a moment at the radio, stuffed it back under the seat, and went home.

7

Gladys Changes Directions

Jack scrawled his name across the bottom of the incident report and handed it off to Bob Hodges to sign. Miss Brant was still gaping at those bullet holes as if they were made by laser beams from actual, genuine UFOs.

"Dr. Prester," said she impatiently, "I'm surprised you can't come anywhere near identifying your attacker."

Hodges looked up. "Doctor?"

"I'll hang my diploma up on the wall someday, if I ever get a wall. Speaking of which, Rice wasn't in his office when I got back, so would you let him know I'd like the trailer? It's too late to check out of the inn today anymore, but I'll move over tomorrow morning. Miss Brant can have the apartment."

She frowned. "Mr. Rice said you'd be taking the apartment."

"We can fight over it later if you want. Right now I'm going for a swim to unwind. I hate getting shot at."

Hodges frowned. "I really should impound the truck."

"Then check me out a GSA car. And we'll have to transfer over all my stuff in the drum box—I guess a sedan trunk will hold it all—and Maxx's stuff. Maxx tends to make sedans smell funny, but you can air it out then."

"I hear ya. I don't have time to impound it anyway." Hodges waved it off airily and walked away.

"I haven't eaten yet. Have you?" Jack pulled his door open and flopped onto the seat.

"Yes." She stood there a few moments beside his door. She opened her mouth, closed it, opened it again. "I found something strange this morning. A drug, I think. Beta something. It was attached as a rider to an unrelated item billed to the administrative general fund." She dug into her skirt pocket for a slip of paper. "I wrote it down." She handed it to him.

He scowled at it a few moments, and nothing that he could remember of his organic chemistry courses told him what it was. He fished out his pocket notebook. "Here's Gus's number. He's our pharmacology expert. He'll know." Jack copied the drug name, or whatever it was, into the notebook, then jotted the phone number onto her piece of paper and handed it back.

She nodded grimly and stuffed it into her pocket. "I dislike the way you keep slipping away incommunicado. How will I get hold of you if I need something?"

"I'll try to be better about that. Leave word with Rice."

She seemed vaguely dissatisfied with that. "Are you going to eat before or after your swim?"

"During, if they'll serve at poolside. You in the office this afternoon?"

She dipped her head, yes.

So did he. "See you later, Miss Brant."

It didn't take him long to kennel Maxx and get into his swim trunks. He ordered a reuben and a cola, no ice, and slid into the tepid water of the outdoor pool.

The only other swimmer was a boy of six or seven at the shallow end. With many moist motor noises, he piloted a gaudy plastic boat about six inches long. *Breaaaa brrr brrr brrraaaaa.* He was kind of a funny looking little kid, a bit husky, with a round, moonlike face and a head shaped something like a potato. His hair was a nondescript light brown. That young woman on the lounge over there reading a book must be his mother. She looked young to be a mother. Jack must be getting old.

He floated on his back out to the middle. For the millionth time he ran the incident through his head. The rider was neither big nor small, though you don't notice such things much when one of those huge globular helmets is part of it. It couldn't be Hippo. But it didn't have to be. Hippo had nine hundred ninety-nine friends who would do his bidding, Reef not the least of them. Do the deed, ditch the helmet, get lost in the crowd. But was it a Harley? It didn't quite sound like one. And a non-Harley is hard to hide in that bunch.

A strong, familiar voice broke into his idle speculations.

He twisted around.

Gladys Gibbs.

She came lurching across the pool apron. Her inability to move well shocked Jack. Her legs, the knees bent so strangely, were permanently crooked in two directions. Her spine curved. Her elbows kinked out at a funny angle as she staggered along. She changed directions every time she moved. She plopped onto the lounge next to the young woman's.

Instantly the little boy clambered up the pool steps and ran to her. "Look, Mommy. Look, Mommy. Look, Mommy. Look, Mommy." He said it twenty times at least. She ignored him as she talked to the girl about when they should be ready for dinner.

Finally Gladys turned to the boy. "What?!" She groped in an oversized black leather bag and fished out some cigarettes.

"My boat. I'll show you." He ran back to the pool steps, but by the time he got down into the water she had quit looking his way. That woman had the attention span of a butterfly. She tossed the pack back into her bag and lit up.

"Mommy, look! Mommy, look! Mommy, look!" The litany resumed.

Jack walked to the shallow end and waded up out.

Gladys smiled as he approached. "Jack, right? Jack Preston. Weston. Something like that."

"You have an excellent memory. Prester. I heard you had a son, but somehow I didn't anticipate he'd be here."

"That's Gregory. Our only child."

"Seven years old."

"Last month."

"You're aware, Mrs. Gibbs, that I'm an investigator looking into your husband's death, among other things."

"I didn't know that."

"I would like to interview your son in the morning. Would that be convenient?"

"My son? What could Gregory possibly tell you? I think not."

"When would be convenient?"

"No time."

"As you wish. But I do want to talk to him. I'll put the appropriate legal wheels in motion."

He nodded to the young woman, bade the scowling Gladys a good afternoon, and hustled back to his room. He'd approach her again later and ask to talk to Gregory in her presence. He could always get a court order from the federal magistrate if she kept balking. But first he had to do some shopping. City shopping.

He got back from Ridgecrest past seven thirty that evening. He had forgotten how far away it was. No matter. The Dodge dealer had his windshield in stock, and they took him as an emergency case. Auto dealerships, a law unto themselves, sometimes didn't do that, and he appreciated it.

He stopped by the military surplus store. Now blessed with a stove and fridge, he also stocked up on groceries. He picked up some stuff for Ev, since she'd be moving into the apartment, and he bought a separate sack of

69

goodies to replenish Cheryl Ashley's refrigerator. Impromptu bag lunches for perfect strangers call for a reward. The toy store there had what he needed, too—a couple of motorcycles to add to his play bag, and some other things.

He greeted Maxx, gave the mutt a dog treat, and headed for the dining room.

Half a dozen bikers were eating in the restaurant. That's not a high proportion out of a thousand, but Jack doubted a thousand were here. Six or seven hundred at most, he'd guess. Maybe eight, at the outside. The bikers sat in lordly isolation, a sort of a big vacuum bubble, with the few other diners in the room squeezed into corners and crannies, as far away as possible.

Jack was about to accept the table the hostess offered him by the door, but there sat Gladys and her crew by the window. He engineered a table directly across from Gladys, leaving the hostess only mildly confused.

Gladys's nanny, or whatever the girl was, sat with her back to Jack, with the boy to her left. Gladys, facing directly Jack's way, would see him every time she looked up, a gentle reminder that he was out to talk to her kid.

It worked. She was finishing her coffee when his salad came. She stood up abruptly, scooped up her oversized leather bag, and came lurching over. He realized as she moved that she did everything abruptly. He plucked his napkin out of his lap and stood as she approached.

She plopped into the empty chair across from him. "What exactly do you want, Mr. Preston?"

He sat down and arranged his napkin. "Prester. To talk to your son. You've already discussed it with your lawyer. He said Gregory probably can't say anything damaging, and even if he does, it won't hold up in court."

"How did you know that?" Her eyes, enlarged with make-up to start with, went compact disk size. "Wiretap!" Her voice rose. "You're tapping my phone! Getting the switchboard operator to listen in. That's illegal, Mr. Preston."

"Prester. Which is precisely why I don't do it."

She glared at him.

"Deduction." He shrugged amiably. "You just seem the careful sort who would check with a lawyer, is all. And that's what lawyers always say about child witnesses."

The glare loosened up a little, but it was still a frown. "I have already spent hours and hours with investigators. I can't think of a thing you'd gain."

"I read your statement and summaries of the interviews. You freely admit you did not love your husband, nor he you. That it had become a marriage of convenience, and you both agreed to remain as a family for Gregory's sake. OK so far?"

"You have a good memory too."

"You have no alibi for the time of your husband's death, and don't feel you need one. He weighed well over two hundred pounds, and you are partially incapacitated. You could not have perpetrated a murder."

"I have an alibi. I was walking. It's just not verifiable."

"I stand corrected. You make yourself walk a minimum of two hours each day, to maintain your strength and mobility as best you can. Your health problems include cerebral palsy, scoliosis, and a mild epilepsy which you control with a minimal, low-dosage drug regimen."

Her frown had become a smirk. "Do you remember every word of everything you read?"

"I don't have total recall, if that's what you're asking. I remember what interests me. You interest me very much. You and this case."

"I suppose I'm flattered. When you're over forty-five, any interest is welcome."

Jack continued, "George Gibbs's financial affairs were ordered well enough that you and your son will be able to live comfortably though modestly. George has no close living relatives save a retired cousin in Peoria, Arizona, and the wife of his deceased brother, now living in

71

Michigan. You have no idea who would want to harm him. He gave no indication of finding anything in the books he was examining, although he never discussed his work at home. He was not worried or unduly nervous. At no time did you see him make contact with motorcyclists, nor do you know of anything that would link him to them. Your testimony is consistent. No reason to question anything you said." Jack spread his hands and resumed eating.

"So what do you think you're going to get from Gregory?"

"I don't know." He finished his mouthful. "Mrs. Gibbs, why didn't you love your husband?"

The question caught her off guard. She watched him eat for a few moments, studying his face. "What difference does it make?"

"None. As I said, you interest me."

"He wasn't lovable. I was infatuated with him when we married. The infatuation faded when I came to see him as he really is. Was. By then Gregory was two, so we decided to stick it out. At least until something better came along."

"And nothing better came along for either of you?"

"I think George had a lover or two on the side, now and then. Nothing serious. I didn't find anything."

"That surprises me. You're very good at flirting."

The smirk came back. "And you're very good at subtle flattery. Married?"

He parroted her question of the minute before. "What difference does it make?"

"It may also surprise you, Mr. Prester, to know that it does make a difference. Yes."

"As it does to me. Was George your first marriage?"

She studied him a long, long moment. "Yes."

He finished his dinner without hurrying and crossed the flatware on his plate.

She broke the silence with, "What time tomorrow morning?"

"Ma'am?"

"I changed my mind. What time do you want Gregory?"

"Is eight all right?"

"Fine. I'll give Meghan the day off." Those overly made-up eyes studied him. "You interest me too, Mr. Prester."

8

Truck Jack

When men are late, it is an unavoidable delay. When women are late, it's female nature. Jack remembered his father stressing that point. He also remembered that his father was never on time for anything. Dad became superintendent of Hawaii Volcanoes six months ago, and as a result of his pervasive influence the whole park was now late—the season's tourists, unpredictably, were being slow to arrive, the feral goats that were supposed to be eradicated in March were still there in September, and Dad was trying to get HAVO switched from the regular October 1 fiscal to some weird accounting schedule starting a month later. Even a predicted eruption occurred months past due. "You can't rush Mother Nature," Dad philosophized. No, but apparently you can sure slow the old babe down.

Gladys obviously treated Greenwich mean time with a similar cavalier attitude. Like Dad, she was unavoidably delayed. She said so at 8:17 the next morning as she met Jack by the inn's gift shop/drug store/news agency.

Gregory followed her, pressing as close as he dared to a mother who lurched in several directions at once as she walked, and fear filled his little eyes. Disproportionately little eyes. Beady eyes. Jack had seen pictures of the living George Gibbs. Gregory had his father's two-raisins-in-a-pancake face.

"Sorry to get you up early on vacation," Jack proffered.

She smiled, and her face softened. The wrinkles looked like they ought to be there. "I'm usually up. Besides, I'm out of cigarettes. I told Gregory I'd get him some chewing gum. It'll just be a minute." She staggered into the gift shop with Gregory at her heels. Her bulky leather handbag flopped against her hip. If Jack were Gladys, and he had to carry a handbag, it sure wouldn't be that one. He followed her to the counter.

She told Gregory to pick out the gum he wanted. But he was too slow making his choice, giving so momentous a decision over twenty seconds, and she grabbed a Juicy Fruit for him. "And a pack of cigarettes," she told the girl behind the counter.

The girl, a rather sullen redhead, reached behind and pulled a pack of Dorals off the shelf.

"Not those. Virginia Slims!" Gladys snapped impatiently. "There!" she added as the girl's hand reached the Slims.

The girl glared at Gladys, and Gladys glared back. And the top of the morning to you, too, Jack Prester.

Gladys relegated Gregory to Jack's care with a perfunctory "You behave, now" and turned her back on them. She had her cigarette lit before she reached the hall door.

Gregory tagged along behind Jack silently, just as he had tagged along behind Mommy, all the way outside. He stopped and looked intently at the truck. Then, obediently, he climbed into the seat as Jack held the door for him.

"Buckle up."

Jack motioned Maxx into the bed in front of the cage. Maxx hopped in, reached out, and gave Jack's ear a lick.

Next time he was going to get a less affectionate dog.

75

Gregory stared straight ahead at the dashboard.

Jack glanced at him. "Pretty scary, huh?"

Gregory looked at him.

"Riding around in this crazy truck with a man you don't even know, and you don't know where you're going. You're really brave to be handling all this so well."

"The truck isn't bad." His first words. "I like pickup trucks. I never rode in a pickup truck before." Seat-belted in, Gregory could just barely see up over the window sill. He probably didn't see out the windshield at all.

"I like 'em too. Always have."

"Are all trucks like this?"

They were passing the place where the biker shot at him yesterday. Jack practically broke into a sweat. Why be nervous now, for pete's sake? "No. They're as different as cars are."

"Why do you have two of those things?" Gregory pointed to the gearshift knob.

"That smaller one's the four-wheel drive." That launched a fifteen-minute conversation on four-wheel drive, automatic versus stick shift, engine speed, road speed versus power. That in turn led to a demonstration as Jack pulled over, lugged the motor in high at a standing start, and then geared up as they continued on. How much of all this, if anything, was the kid absorbing?

Gregory watched the tach awhile. "I see. Pretend I'm driving down a dirt road in four-wheel, and there's a hill up ahead. So I want to gear down and build up some power, right?"

"Right. If it's a steep hill, with loose dirt in the road, I'd drop to second before I get to it and hit it roaring."

"So you don't want automatic transmission for four-wheel drive. The car can't see the hill until it gets there and starts up it, so it won't know enough to gear down ahead of time."

Jack stared at the kid so intently he almost drifted out of his lane. "That's amazing! You'll be a world class

76

mechanic, whether you do it for a living or not. You pick the stuff up just like that!" Jack snapped his fingers.

A big black pepsis wasp clunked against Jack's windowsill and dropped through the open window into his lap. It got up onto its gangling legs and lifted off. Wings a-whirring and its long legs dangling in a cluster, it rubbed its face along the windshield down the dash to the right. It came back. Gently Jack cupped a hand and herded it toward his open window. With a little coaxing it made the jump from windshield to A post, and from the A post to the open window. Speed swept it instantly away.

Jack happened to glance at Gregory. The kid sat absolutely typing-paper white, open-mouthed.

Jack shrugged. "We sure didn't want to kill it, right? What'd it do to deserve death? It didn't mean to get in. Probably the first time it ever rode in a truck, just like you."

"They sting!"

"They sure can. And they catch spiders. Did you ever learn how they catch spiders?" Jack described how pepsis wasps capture spiders upon which to lay their eggs. He had Gregory's rapt and total attention all the way to the sand dunes. There is nothing like monumental gore and skin-crawling gruesomeness for keeping a small child interested.

He pulled into the parking area. "And that's why I don't like to kill anything. Especially wasps."

Gregory popped his seat belt and got up on the seat on his knees to look around. "Why did we stop here?"

"This is the world's greatest sandbox, and I love to play in the sand. I brought some stuff."

Gregory hopped out, they locked up, Jack leashed Maxx and retrieved his bag of toys from the drum box. He led the way out into the dunes. They ran around. They climbed up. They rolled down. Gregory laughed a lot, ate a lot of sand, and stashed at least two pounds of the stuff away in his short brown hair. Jack was going to need an industrial strength shower tonight himself. Maxx barked and rolled, joining in as much as his leash allowed.

Jack sat down near the crest of a dune. Maxx bellied out beside him and began noisily licking his private parts. Jack poked him, and he switched to slurpily licking his front paws.

From his bag of toys, Jack got out the motorcycles, a pickup truck, and his six-inch action figures—men and boys and women. "What else do I have in here? Here's a black dog, like Maxx. And a car—and another truck. We can each have one."

Gregory was totally into the program in moments. He adopted the boy action figure as his own, so Jack took a man action figure. Gregory ignored the dog figure. Jack took it. They ran the trucks up the hills and piled bigger hills. Gregory made motor noises and announcements: "This truck isn't a four-wheel drive truck." Looking at Jack, he paused. "What is it?"

"Two-wheel drive."

"This truck's a two-wheel drive truck, and it has to get up the hill. *Rowrrr rrr rrr rrr.* It can't get there. So I'm gonna fix it. I'm the fixer person." He waggled his boy figure back and forth in front of his truck. "There, it's fixed. Now it's four-wheel drive. *Rowrrr rrr rrrrr. Rrrr.* There it goes up!"

Jack rowr-ed his truck up beside Gregory's. "Hi. I'm Jack, and my truck isn't working right. Will you fix it for me?"

"Sure." Again the boy figure did its little dance in front of Jack's truck's radiator.

Jack took off and did some wheelies. "Hey, this is great! Thanks, fixer person. Do you fix your mother's car?"

"No. She doesn't live here."

"Where does she live?"

"Down the hall."

"*Rowr prt prt prt.* Oh-oh. Can you see what's wrong with my four-wheel drive, fixer person?"

Fixer person was on it instantly as Gregory wiggled his action figure.

"What do you mean, fixer person, 'down the hall'?"

"When Daddy went to work she went down the hall. She didn't live there or watch television. So I don't fix her car. There. You're all fixed."

"Rrrr—*rrrr.* Works fine again! Do I owe you money? Here, fixer person. Here's five dollars." Jack's action figure approached Gregory's. They touched stiff, clumsy arms.

The play continued, idly, it seemed, and at random. Jack looked for wedges, for openings, for signs. He noticed none. Careful to stay in the play context, his action figure drove around asking questions of the fixer person and got short, cryptic answers. Was there meaning concealed in Gregory's seemingly mindless replies? Or was Gregory actually so wrapped in the play he wasn't thinking about unrelated topics?

Gregory picked up the motorcycle and ran that around awhile. Unlike the truck, the cycle could carry his action figure.

Jack roared his truck up along side the bike. "Wow! Fixer person! That's a really great motorcycle!"

"This isn't fixer person anymore. Fixer person went home."

"Oh. *Rrrr rrrr rrrr.* That's OK, because my truck works well now. My name's Jack. So what's yours?"

"Bo."

9
Jack Fell Down . . .

If Evelyn Brant's genes had been the genetic inheritance of her pioneer foremothers instead of the other way around, the United States would still be the Thirteen Colonies. The woman was an instant and complete loss whenever she was not surrounded by fast food joints. As an outdoorsman she made Woody Allen look like Tarzan. She took on a scowling, defensive, and intensely irritating attitude the moment they got in Jack's truck and headed north up the highway, away from the simple vestiges of civilization at Furnace Creek.

It had all started innocently enough. Jack had stopped by Rice's office to tell him he was going out to sniff around Chloride Cliff. Considering the road out there, he wanted someone to know in case he broke down and got stranded. In a happy flurry of affectionate slurping, Maxx got dog spit all over Rice's class A uniform trousers. Miss Brant, sitting there in Rice's office, looked disgusted.

Out of the blue, Rice suggested Miss Brant might like to go along, Jack invited, she accepted hesitantly, they stopped at the inn long enough for her to change her shoes, they got two sports bottles filled up with iced tea, and now here she sat in his truck, the scowl permanently implanted on her pretty phizz.

"So you see—" Jack waved a hand for emphasis "—there's a connection. Bo and Gladys. Gregory obviously overheard something or saw them together—enough to make an association between the name and motorcycles. I don't think it was more than a chance meeting, if at all, because Bo has no real form in Gregory's mind. Gregory didn't know him, therefore he probably never met him. It was a name he came up with, triggered by the motorcycle."

"Aren't you attaching a lot to a few random comments by a child at play? You weren't even asking him real questions. You know—interrogation."

"Interrogation gets nowhere with a child that age. Their fantasy is just as true to them as their reality. They don't separate fact from fiction well."

"I had a boyfriend like that once. He was twenty-seven. Apparently that's something they don't outgrow."

"So I've heard. Truth is what they think you want to hear. They're not being deliberately devious at that age. They just want to give the answer that will best keep that big powerful adult off their case. They have an intense fear of the power, the potential to hurt, that adults possess."

She glanced at him. "Your doctoral dissertation."

"Right. But in their play, they're processing the information they're getting about the world. They don't have the verbal skills or depth of vocabulary to think it through cognitively, so they play it out. Dramatize it. You watch a kid at play long enough, and you'll know exactly what's going on in his life."

She sipped at her iced tea. The bottle was nearly empty. She soaked the stuff up like a sponge.

Jack kept on. "I got some other interesting information from him while we were ripping around in the sand. I made sure I had an action figure to represent his father. He kept putting it aside. My play character asked him about it now and then, and he told me Daddy was always away on vacation."

"Which means. . .?"

81

"Gladys claims their marital relationship was intact but sterile. Gregory's play suggests that either George had moved out or simply never came home."

She studied him a moment and turned her attention back to the road ahead. Mirages made temporary puddles on the highway all through the distance.

He let the silence ride awhile. Then, "A penny for your thoughts, or has inflation struck there too?"

"You won't like them."

"Don't let that stop you."

"I don't think you're real, Dr. Prester. I don't think you have a doctorate. I don't think you know what you're doing. I don't think you're competent to conduct an investigation." She turned again to face him squarely. "I'm going to complete my arm of the investigation and go back home and sit down with Hal Edmond. I'm going to tell him what I think, all of it, and request a more thorough background check on you."

"So I'm not for real. Interesting."

"You look and act and think goofy. You even dress goofy."

"Oh, come on. Remember you're in the great American West. Blue jeans are de rigueur."

"Really. I didn't know cowboys wear running shoes."

"I'm not a cowboy. I'm a criminologist."

"Criminologists wear cowboy hats?"

He pondered this whole inane conversation a few moments. "Why are you being such a jerk?"

Her head snapped around, and she glared at him. He let it roll off. The glare softened. She went back to staring straight ahead, looking without looking at a dozen miles down the endless road to nowhere.

A couple minutes later she spoke. "I apologize for sounding hostile. It's what I think. I can't help it."

"Apology accepted." He hesitated. "If I'm reading your behavior right, you're scared spitless. Of me?"

"Scared! Hardly. I'm a grown woman, perfectly capable of handling anything here. You better go back to books and quit trying to read behavior."

The methodical minutes assembled themselves into a quarter hour of silence. "I'm sorry you're uncomfortable. I hope it will ease up as you get to know the place better."

"That's the second time you said I'll like it here. Well, I won't."

"I didn't say 'like.' I said when you know the place better. You don't have to like the place to feel more comfortable in it."

"I wish the place weren't named Death Valley."

"Yeah, I guess that's a little negative. Lurid, even."

"A little negative! Death Valley? What—" She stopped and frowned as they turned off onto a narrow, unpaved side road. "Where did you say we were going?"

"Chloride Cliff." He slowed as a roadrunner popped out of the low scrub, paused on the road shoulder, and darted away.

"So there actually are roadrunners. It really does look vaguely like the cartoon."

"Acts like it too. If you think I'm goofy . . ." All along the primitive road, motorcycle tracks laced the dirt. Bikers had been up here recently. That came as no surprise. According to Gregory's random commentary, so might his father have been.

Jack's action figure had asked, "Where's Daddy?" now and then. Either Bo the biker or the fixer person replied, variously, "Daddy's on vacation at Chloride Cliff. He went there." "Daddy's on vacation at Wide Roads." Wildrose? They were the only two geographic references made in that play session, and Jack decided to look at both of them from, he hoped, George's perspective.

The truck bucked and yawed as it heaved itself up the dirt road. The track hadn't been graded for a while. Jack took the trouble to shove it into four-wheel drive and thought again about the mechanically astute Gregory. They wound through creosote bush and low rabbit brush, skirting washouts, and finally topped out on the broad, rolling ridgecrest.

Jack parked it and turned Maxx loose as Miss Brant slid down off her seat and locked the passenger side door.

Here and there on the essentially bare ground, skeletons of little rectangular buildings stood topless against the sky. They had been built dilapidated over half a century ago and had deteriorated from there. When you're out digging for gold, building an edifice to stand against the ravages of time is the last item on your list of things to do.

She looked around apprehensively. "This is a ghost town."

"Right. Chloride City. Once a thriving little mining town. There are a lot of these in this area—places that started up for a few years, sometimes just a few months, and died. There was plenty of gold fever around here, but not much gold to feed it." He scanned the ground as they wandered over to the trail.

"Why did Durwin ask me to come here?" She crowded close despite the fact that they had the whole western United States to walk in.

"I don't know. Show you the best view of the valley that there is. Let you get the feel of the place. You're not going to do it holed up in the administrative office."

"Dr. Prester, I do not want to get the feel of this place. I'm not the least interested in another view of the valley. Durwin said—naturally I thought you two had some professional reason for bringing me. Business."

"Must everything be business?" Now this was interesting. One of the bikers, the one out most recently because his tracks were fresh and on top of the others, had run his bike out here among the scattered, abandoned walls of the forgotten little town. In fact—Jack squatted down and poked at the tracks with a finger.

"What?" she asked.

"Made today." He stood erect. "Maxx! Find!"

The dog had been wandering about aimlessly, sticking his nose down in bushes and small animal holes. He began deliberately circling, ranging out, moving faster.

"Find what?"

"We won't know till he finds it."

Maxx disappeared behind a building for a few moments and popped out the other side. He sniffed around a weathered freestanding wall. He disappeared again.

Jack walked over to the brink of a steep, steep slope and looked out. White-throated swifts with their slim, pointy wings swept wide circles in the trackless sky out beyond the cliff. The white salt flats, miles away and below, glistened in the sun.

"This is the best view of the valley?" She sounded derisive.

"No. Out that way a short distance. We'll go look at it then. Miss Brant, you're an accountant. George Gibbs was an accountant. If you were to come up here, what would you be doing and where would you go?"

"I wouldn't in a million years come up here on that terrible road. I seriously doubt he ever did either."

"Play the game. Assume he did. Where would he go and why?" Where was Maxx? There he was, way out beyond the last building. Jack started off that way, a roofless corrugated-tin shack on his right and the bluff falling away sharply to his immediate left. He liked the feeling of airy openness up here, the wind, and the vivid, glowing sky. A white-throated swift zipped by them and swooped out into the emptiness to their left.

"It's not a game." Her voice rose. "I can't imagine him coming here. Not everyone is as morbidly fascinated with vast wastelands as you seem to be." She trailed along twenty feet behind him, obviously and dramatically dispirited.

"He drove a rental car. I presume he could get it up here. Road's not that bad."

She snorted derisively. And then she screamed, a terrified sort of soprano yelp.

He wheeled to face a flurry of motion behind him. Then the world exploded in his face, and he was falling.

85

10
. . . And Broke His Crown

Don't move! Please don't move!" Her voice sounded far away, like maybe in Oregon.

His head howled. His face ached. He started to take a deep breath; pain stabbed across his back. He tried again to raise his hand, but it wouldn't rise, as if it were tied to the ground. So he retired from the fruitless task of attempting to move or think and just floated awhile.

"Jack?" She was closer now, probably inside the state line.

The right arm wouldn't move, but he could raise his left one. When he did a small, cool hand grasped his. He grasped back, grateful for any little contact at all with reality. He smelled doggy odor and doggy breath. A coarse, wet tongue splashed across his face. Her voice reprimanded Maxx. She probably didn't realize that telling Maxx not to lick was like telling mud wrestlers not to get dirty.

He was looking at blue sky ahead and rocks to his right. Maxx's tongue slurped one eye shut again momentarily.

"How do you feel?"

How could she ask such a stupid question?

It took him a few long moments, and a couple of false starts, to get his mouth in gear. "This is the absolute worst headache I've ever had in my life. Including when the moose kicked me."

"The moo—. This is no time to be funny."

"I'm not joking." He tried a deep breath again, but his ribs in back wouldn't let him.

Her face hovered above him, a little left of center. It was smudged and dirty and tear-streaked. She looked beautiful. But it wasn't all dirt. He let go her hand and reached up to tip her face aside slightly for a better look. A broad, nasty scuff on her cheek, up by her right eye, oozed drying blood.

He got his head cranked around to look at his right hand. Her pantyhose were knotted to the base of a sturdy bush. One leg tied his right wrist to the bush. The other leg, stretched tight, looped through his belt, anchoring him. "What's all this?"

"You were trying to get up. Moving. I was afraid you'd fall off accidentally. I still am."

"Fall off—" He rootched his head around left. The world dropped away. He was sprawled out on a narrow, sloping ledge. Crumbling rock and dirt formed a wall up one side and fell away on the other. The shimmering expanse of Death Valley, quite picturesque if you're on flat, stable ground, spread out beyond them. Between Jack and the mountains on the west side of the valley stretched nothing but air. Miles and miles of bare, uninterrupted atmosphere.

She shuddered. "I don't know how we're going to get off here. Wait until someone comes, I guess. I don't know what else."

"How did we get on here?"

"He knocked you over the cliff. I mean, he hit you, and when you fell you just kept sliding. And he knocked me down. Then he got on his motorcycle—it was right there—and rode away."

"A biker—"

"A motorcycle. Yes. Maxx came up and licked my

87

face. Then he jumped down over the side after you. I could see you down here, about—I don't know—three stories, I guess. Maxx reached you quickly, so I figured I could. I almost slid right past this ledge getting here. I almost fell off the mountain, Jack."

"But you didn't. You got here."

"But I can't climb back up. I'm sure I can't. I don't know how I did it, getting down here. I was so frightened. There isn't much of a ledge here, and you were moving around. I was afraid you'd slide the rest of the way to the bottom. All I could think of was you falling clear down the cliff." She shuddered.

"He. What'd he look like?"

"He had one of those dark round helmets on, so you can't see anything. Black leather. One of those bikers, but I couldn't see his face. It was all too fast."

"Big man. Real big man."

"No. A regular size person. He was waiting there for you."

"Or busy with something else, and we surprised him."

She frowned. "That could be. He hit you with some tool."

"What tool?"

"I don't know. I'm not into tools. It was green."

Green. Now that was helpful. Jack closed his eyes and tried to relax. Green, for crying out loud.

What if his back was broken? He drew in a long slow breath and assayed the pain it caused. Probably not his spine. Definitely one rib, possibly two, a couple inches below his left shoulder blade. What else? He flexed his legs. All there. His hips and shoulders, OK. If his right arm weren't chained to a tree it'd be all right. His neck? No pain or tingling. His head? Another matter altogether. It refused to do any thinking, but other than that it seemed to function all right.

"Did he hurt Maxx?"

"No. The dog got there as the man was riding off."

88

Maxx started licking again. Jack shoved the big hard head away. "I don't know why I bother to buy you dog food. Where were you when we needed you?"

Slurp.

Incorrigible mutt.

"Untie me, huh?"

She tried, but the knot at his wrist was too tight. He loaned her his pocket knife, and she sawed through the nylon. They left the safety line on his belt intact. His arm free, he could perform a few simple experiments in sitting up. One of them worked, eventually. His ribs were going to render his left arm pretty much useless when it came time to crawl up out of here.

He perched, sitting, on the ledge, and she perched hard against him. On impulse he wrapped his right arm around her shoulders and drew her in. "I had a low opinion of your value in an emergency. You just proved me as wrong as wrong can get."

"I didn't do anything. I should have brought some water, or something. To drink, and wash with. If Maxx hadn't licked it off, your face would still be covered with blood." Her dark flyaway hair tickled his nose as she shook her head. "That's disgusting. So gross when you think about it."

"You kept me from falling into the Keane-Wonder mine. Which is about a hundred stories straight down, if you want to measure cliffs that way."

"Still, I can think of so many things I should have done."

"Easiest thing in the world, hindsight."

"I suppose." She twisted around and looked at his face. Gentle fingertips drew his chin around so she could see better. "You're a mess. He hit you in the face with whatever that thing was—that tool. There's a cut above your eye and a bruise on your cheek. I hope your eye doesn't swell shut. And your nose was bleeding. It quit, though. All the bleeding pretty much quit."

"Sounds like I'll live." He said it with more conviction than he felt.

"Scared." She let her head lie on his shoulder awhile. "You were right on the button. I'm so scared."

"Of this country. Miles and miles of miles and miles. Out of your element."

"Yes."

"And of me. Because I'm not scared out here."

Her head bobbed against his arm, a nod. "And because you—you're so superior." She took a deep breath. "For instance, when we were walking back to the parking lot that first day, after digging up the body. Miss Ashley said something about God, and you said something, and you both laughed. Inside joke. It feels like everything in this miserable Monument is an inside joke."

"And you're not inside any of it."

"Yes."

"You'll remember when Miss Ashley first arrived on site, when she was distributing the lunches—"

"And you prayed over yours."

"Right. She identified herself as a believer. Miss Ashley is a Christian, as am I. Let me think—" Jack racked his brain a few moments until it came clear. "Miss Ashley was talking about digging up remains from the other end of the time scale, remember? Freshly buried instead of centuries old."

"I remember something like that, yes."

"Then she said, 'That didn't come out right,' and I mentioned Romans eight in the Bible. It says that because we don't always pray the way we ought to, the Holy Spirit butts in and redirects the prayer. Edits it. Basically, it's 'Hear what I mean and not what I say' on a cosmic scale."

"She caught on to a reference that vague?"

"Actually, it's not that vague. It's one of the first things you learn about the way God works. Anyway, that was the crux of the in joke, as you call it. The reference." He waited. No response. "Believe me, I'm not superior."

"When Hal Edmond said he was sending me, I thought I could do it—just come out here. And then when I saw what the country is like—so bleak. And you weren't like the men I'm used to at all. Not urban. Not—I don't know how to explain it. You're not like Eastern men. Anyway, I went paralyzed. That's the only word for it, especially at that accident Monday. Paralyzed. I couldn't move. I couldn't do anything."

"You did this, when it counts."

"Not well enough. It's so alien."

"I understand the feeling. I felt that way the whole time I was in Washington. Even the cherry trees looked alien to me."

She lifted her head and twisted around to stare at him again. "You're kidding."

"No joke. I'm a country boy, born in Colorado, and raised in New Mexico." He looked at those huge dark eyes and almost got lost again. "Maxx." He reached out and gave the mutt a cursory scratch behind the ears. "How do we get out of here?"

Maxx the Wonder Dog tilted his head, perfectly content to sit and be scratched.

Jack leaned back, settling into the sun-heated dirt, and closed his eyes. Even lying down he was still half sitting. The slope had to be at least seventy degrees.

"Do you know what we should do?" she asked.

"Give my nerves and muscles another half hour or so to reconnect and calm down. Yours too. Then we'll climb out."

"I don't think we can." She lay back too and snuggled in tightly against him.

"You can. Maxx can for sure. Once you reach the truck you can drive out for help."

"I never drove a stick shift before."

"Never?"

"I never really figured out the gears on my bicycle. I just put it in the middle and left it there."

This lady definitely needed Gregory.

Eventually Jack convinced himself that if they didn't climb out pretty soon, thirst was going to start becoming a problem. Besides, it would be dark in a couple of hours, and the last thing they needed was a night on bald mountain here.

His left eye was swelled clear shut now. Just what he needed. A fat face. He got his belt untied from that bush and retrieved as much of the pantyhose as he could, in case they would need them. Heaven knew what for. But then, he would never have thought to use them for a belaying line. Clever lady.

He scanned the wall, picking a route, choosing a way with what looked like dependable handholds and rest stops and as many shrubs as possible. Not many. "OK. The rules of the game are, you make sure you're anchored on three points before you move the fourth. Always. You move one hand at a time or one foot at a time. Never two at once. Test every purchase before you trust your full weight to it. If you doubt it, pick another one. Go patiently, don't hug the wall, take your time, rest whenever you have a convenient place to do it. Slow and steady will put you on top. Here's my truck keys. You'll get there before I do."

"I don't have a pocket in this skirt. Never mind. I'll put them in my shoe." She jammed them down inside her instep. "What do you mean, don't hug the wall?"

"If you've ever seen pictures of rock climbers, you notice that they don't belly up to the surface they're climbing. They keep their body free. It's safer than snugging in too close."

She didn't look convinced.

He coached her ten feet up the slope and reminded her she was a third of the way already. He got five feet and had to rest. She did the next ten feet on her own. He made it another three. She almost froze, and he had to talk her up, handhold by handhold. "Grope around with your right hand. What do you find?"

92

"A bush. Here's a bush."

"Can you rip it out?"

"No."

"Grab on. How about your left foot? What can you find?"

"Nothing. There's nothing around, Jack."

"So leave it where it is. What about your right foot?"

And up she went, inch by inch. With a plaintive, grateful little cry she disappeared over the top.

Big talking man. He was going to bog down. His ribs had rendered his left arm completely useless. No strength of grip, no stretch. He was seeing out of one eye only, and that not too clearly. He wedged one hip in a chink in the rotten dirt and felt the sweat pop out. He was getting dizzy. Not a good time for that. And nauseous. Not a good time for that, either.

He heard Maxx bark somewhere. Was the dog stranded too? Old Maxx could come down places like this a lot easier and faster than he could scramble up them.

Something brushed his shoulder. A rope! His old goldline dangled beside his arm.

"Tie it around you!" she called.

It took him a minute. He had to snug it in up high under his armpits, lest it ride across those sore ribs.

"I can't pull you up, but I can help you." Her voice called down from on high, but he couldn't see her.

With renewed vigor he reached for a handhold and dragged himself up. The rope drew tight, would not let him drop back. Another foot up. Another. Firmly belayed, he could compensate for the loss of one arm without worrying about tumbling. It took him twenty minutes to make fifteen feet. Or was it that long? He lost track. It seemed like hours.

He was scrabbling out onto the rounded crest now, and now he could crawl on one hand and knees up to level ground and safety. She sat twenty feet up the hill, her feet wedged solidly in a small outcrop, the rope wrapped around her waist. Perfect belaying position. He crept up over the brow of the hill until he could flop onto his back in level dirt. *Aaah.* He closed his eye.

Then it hit him like a thunderbolt. In all this long ordeal, he had not once appealed to God for help. It had never even occurred to him to pray. The one resource he was supposed to tap into first and he thought of it last, after the trouble was over. He apologized to God right there, but apology seemed like a cop-out. He had just flunked the faith. And Miss Brant had just passed Crisis Control with flying colors.

Maxx came bounding over and started licking sweat off his face. He shoved the dog aside.

She was hunkered here beside him now, with a sports bottle of no-longer-iced tea. He raised his head, and she held the bottle for him while he dragged in long, cool, delectable gulps. He dropped back onto the stones, incredibly grateful in mind and in silent prayer that this had all turned out so well. Praise the Lord who delivers even when you forget to ask Him!

"Do you think you can make it to the truck?" She sounded worried.

"Miss Brant, it's all downhill from here. Yeah."

Silence. He opened his eye and looked at her.

She appeared almost embarrassed. "Somehow, 'Miss Brant' doesn't seem appropriate anymore."

"You're right. Evelyn."

"Friends back home call me Ev."

"Rice doesn't."

"Durwin's not that kind of friend."

For some reason, her comeback tickled him. He sat up and motioned Maxx in beside him. "Sit." Inch by inch he went over the dog, checking for scrapes and lumps. Maxx had come through this better than anyone.

He spent another fifteen minutes examining the ground where the attack occurred, studying tracks, seeking any bit of evidence at all. A good forensics team would probably pick up anything from hairs to fibers—solid evidence pointing the finger at specific people—but there was no way to get that kind of investigative expertise up here.

He looked for signs of digging or any other use of tools. Zip. The tool, whatever it was, apparently was intended as a weapon. That means it had been brought up here for the purpose of attack. Unless he and Ev surprised the guy before he could start digging or whatever he intended.

Finally, unable to think of anything else to do, Jack leaned back against the wall and hung his thumbs in his pockets. Why did that guy jump them? What was he doing here? It was almost definitely the same one who tossed a few slugs at him, but he didn't know that. Thoughts came all ajumble. Nothing made sense.

He lurched erect. "I was going to say, 'Ready to go?' but I caught myself in time."

"Good. That would have been absolutely stupid." She moved in beside him. She had relaxed remarkably in the last half hour. "Did you really get kicked by a moose?"

He headed toward the truck at a casual stroll in keeping with his giddiness and the miserable headache. "Grand Tetons. We tranquilized this lady moose to fit her with a radio collar. She woke up before we expected her to, and I thought I could bulldog her, like you wrestle a steer down. Moose don't bulldog worth diddly. I guess moose and steers are built different."

"You tried to wrestle a moose." She was looking at him with all the disdain a fool notion like that deserves.

He wanted the conversation shifted—and the sooner the better. "Where'd you learn how to belay a climber?"

"Remember you asked if I saw pictures of rock climbers? There was a television special once, and after you reminded me I remembered seeing how they did it. Are you sure you can drive?"

"Yeah. If I start to feel woozy I'll pull over."

They walked in silence the rest of the way. She was pondering something, her lips pressed into a thin line, and he was wishing he could ponder anything at all.

He stopped by the door. "You have the keys."

"Yes, I do. And I'm going to drive. Do you want Maxx in his cage or on the box back here, the way he came?"

"In the cage with the door hooked open. You're not going to drive my truck if you never worked a stick shift before. I value my transmission."

"Your transmission may look like your face when I'm done, but at least your truck won't be demolished at the bottom of a cliff." She unlocked the passenger side. "Hop in."

"Miss Br—Evelyn. Ev. Whatever. I don't w—"

"Stop arguing! You talked me up that impossible cliff, and you can talk me through this." She was glaring again, but it wasn't the same as before. Hostility had given way to concern.

Besides, she had a point. What if he faded at the wrong moment? Or had to react quickly in some simple emergency, like a deer bolting out into the road? Her welfare was at stake here too. He placed his transmission in the hands of the almighty God he had just injudiciously neglected and crawled in the passenger side. He wedged himself in a corner and closed his eyes. The truck jiggled. The driver-side door slammed.

He spoke without moving. "Dry run before you start the motor. Clutch in. That's the left pedal. Shift to first. Upper left. Clutch out slowly. Clutch in, shift to second —lower left—clutch out slowly. Slower. When in doubt, clutch in. Always. Your automatic response if you see trouble is both feet hit the pedals, clutch and brake together. Here we go."

She stalled it only twice getting out to the paved road. He kicked it back into two-wheel. And when he dozed off, she made it on her own to Cow Creek just fine.

11

Point Man

The Silverfish had a phone. Jack knew that because it was ringing. But where was it? Stiff as a crutch, he wrenched himself to sitting and tossed his legs one by one over the side of the bed. Maxx came galumphing in and mashed up against Jack's legs in happy greeting. The mutt squirreled around, bumping into him, whining that weird little whimper that meant, "My legs are crossed, and you wouldn't want me to do unspeakable things."

Jack staggered down the miniature hall. Every single body part he owned ached. Even a few he was renting. The phone rang again right next to his ear, a wall phone beside the sink.

He dragged the receiver off the hook. "Hello." His jaw ached. His neck refused to bend at all. And his jaw and neck had not been hit directly. If only pain had the decency to stay where it belonged.

"I'm sorry to get you out of bed, but it is almost nine."

"Good morning, Ev."

"You sound like you're asleep yet."

"I am asleep yet. Nine? Really? I never sleep this late."

"I found some things I want to show you. I'll bring

the printouts to you. Did you get word about the luncheon?"

Maxx stood expectantly beside the door.

Jack scratched his itchy scalp. "The luncheon?"

"The superintendent and his wife invited us to luncheon. Noon at their house. How about if I come by around eleven, show you this stuff, and we can go up the hill from there?"

His day just began, and it was shot already. "No way out?"

"You don't like luncheons?"

"Hate 'em. Destroys the image, right? Like Smokey Bear raiding garbage cans when no one's looking." He kicked his brain into gear with difficulty. "I have business down in Furnace Creek. I'll pick you up there around eleven. How's that?"

"Durwin said you went to see a doctor," she said. "Did you? Or was he just saying that to get rid of me?"

"Mel Forrest drove me in."

"Where?"

"Semiretired fellow in Beatty. Nice enough guy."

Long pause. "So what did the doctor say?"

"Nothing I didn't know already. Two cracked ribs—probably hit a rock falling—and various medical terms occurring to my face. He wanted to keep me overnight, but I decided to come back."

"You shouldn't have. Didn't he explain to you about the serious nature of—you know?"

Jack snorted. "Did he ever. I'm three hours short of a master's degree in head injuries. I wanted to come home."

"Yes, but what if—"

"I don't let 'what ifs' govern my life. Eleven?"

"Yes." She bade him good day and hung up.

He snapped the long line onto Maxx's collar, let the pooch out, and looped the nether end of the leash over the doorknob.

Now, about his daily Bible reading. Thanks to oversleeping he was already three hours behind. He could give it a cursory quick shot now or wait and settle in for some serious work tonight. He voted for postponement. He made his bed and laid a fork, tines up, on his pillow. That would remind him Bible study came before sleep. In less than half an hour he took his famous thirty-seven second shower, shaved selected portions of his mutilated face, dressed, ate some toast, and drove the five miles to Furnace Creek.

Here he went again with this on-guard business, taking Maxx's collar off and wading into a nest of bikers. But this time it didn't seem so bad. Furnace Creek felt more civilized than Stovepipe Wells, the rangers closer, the accoutrements of fine living nearer at hand. Besides, he was getting to understand these people a little better. That helped.

"Point Man." He asked a couple camps and wondered whether the new arrangement of his face wasn't somehow winning him points with these people. They seemed friendlier, more tolerant. They directed him to the group camp. It was jammed full.

"Point Man."

"Full beard and black T-shirt over there. You ain't no vet."

"You'd be surprised."

Point Man was Jack's height, five eleven, a little heavier than Jack, about his coloring—mouse brown hair and beard—and a whole lot brighter and happier just now. When the gent smiled, his beard bunched up in interesting ways. When Jack smiled, his face hurt.

Point Man extended a hand. "Bet you're Jack."

"You win. Who introduced me?"

"Hippo was by, right after he heard about Bo. Tuesday morning, I think. Bo and the girl named Barbara. The deaths hit him a lot harder than he's willing to admit. And he talked about you. Cat mentioned you too."

"Chester Robosky. Bo. Cat seems to think you can provide me with helpful information."

"I don't know about that. Hippo said you were investigating his death. You're with the feds?" Point Man waved in the general direction of his cold campfire ring.

Jack sat down slowly, gently, stiffly. Nothing in him had quit aching yet. "Trying to find a connection between Bo and a man named George Gibbs, an accountant from Washington, D.C."

Maxx sat down beside him, nose high, checking out the area for bacon.

Point Man stretched out like a Roman reclining at dinner. "Bo worked in D.C. for a while. A chef." He said it more to himself than to Jack. "He claimed he could have poisoned every senator in the city and often regretted out loud that he didn't. Moved to Seattle. No—as I remember, Tacoma first for a while and then Seattle. Anyway, he got involved with Point Man International there. He wasn't ready to embrace the faith, but he was close. I'm very sad to hear he died when he did. I'm afraid he's lost."

"You knew him in Seattle, then."

"No. I'm from California. Our man up there called me when he learned Bo was coming down to this rally."

Maxx curled up close beside Jack and began licking his pants leg. He shoved the dog away. Insistently Maxx pushed his big head up under Jack's arm. *Pat me, you jerk.*

Jack thought a moment. "Point Man International is a church outreach, right?"

"No. We aren't affiliated with anybody. Our only purpose is to meet the special needs of Nam vets. Faith in God is one of those needs, and the most important one. But it's not the only one by far. Bo was hurting. Our people were there for him. When he came down here they let me know so I could maintain the support at this end."

"He organized this rally."

"Cleverly, too. 'We can't say it's a rally, or that we're organized,' he said. 'We just all show up. We're just a bunch of people who got the same idea at the same time.'"

"Yeah. A thousand of you."

Point Man squirmed around to sitting upright. "He set up the dates, called around some, had them call others, and the idea was off and running. Great opportunity for Point Man International to make contact with a lot of the very people we're out to help. I've made contacts here, got several chapters going already."

"So you have your own agenda here. And Bo was involved in it. Was George Gibbs?"

"I never met a George Gibbs by that name. But then, so few people use their name here." Point Man sat forward cross-legged and propped his elbows on his knees. Jack wished he were that flexible. "Yes, we have our own agenda. Nam vets are special people, you know. Our divorce rate is in the ninetieth percentile. Ninety. The national average is fifty. Three times as many vets have died of suicide since the war than ever died in the war itself. I could spout statistics all day, but look around here and you'll see what the statistics don't tell you. Booze and drugs. Anger. Frustration. Depression. Fear."

"Paranoia." Jack's headache was growing.

"Guns and tripwires. Yes. That's why Point Man exists. To be there, to help, to reverse some of that if possible, at least in individual cases."

"Through understanding."

"And God. What is your relationship with God, Jack?"

"Thought you'd never ask. Saved by the blood of Jesus Christ."

Point Man nodded. "So what does that mean in English?"

Jack had to think a moment. Nobody had ever asked him that in that way before. "Because we've done wrong, human beings can't be children of a sinless God. So Jesus paid the bill for our wrongdoings with His death—His blood. I accepted that; God accepted it; and now I'm His."

Point Man grinned. "Not bad. I ask everybody that, sooner or later." He studied his fire ring a few minutes.

"Why do you assume a connection of some sort between Bo and this Gibbs?"

"Their bodies were found close together."

"Gibbs was a park employee."

"No. A government employee on special assignment here. General Accounting Office. Not Park Service."

"Bo was at the stage prior to salvation you'd call defiant. He kept trying to shock me. Generate outrage. Resisting, defying God. What he was doing, he was defying his concept of what he thought God is. He boasted a passionate affair with a park employee's wife. I don't think she was an employee herself."

Gladys. It had to be Gladys. "No names."

"No. Bo didn't kiss and tell. In fact he didn't boast generally. Just to me. As I say, he was defying God, and I was the contact point between them—between Bo and God."

How should he phrase this next question? Jack mulled two or three ways and none worked, so he might as well just out with it. "Any chance his affair was with a male Park Service employee or spouse? There are several female employees here whose spouses are non–Park Service."

"No."

"Defiant. Any chance the affair was fictitious, and he was just trying to get under your skin with a lie?"

"Possible. But it's God he was defying, not me, and he knew you can't lie that blatantly to God. I'd say, if he claimed he was doing it he was doing it."

Jack tried to sigh and couldn't. His ribs still wouldn't let him, and his lungs were negotiating a mile a minute for a little extra oxygen to work on. "Who is Gladys?"

"Gladys." Point Man frowned, and his eyes, his face, his hands all suggested that he was being honest and forthright in his reaction. "I know a Gladys over in Pomona. No way Bo would. And a friend of mine in San Diego married one. Different one. It lasted a couple years. Again, no possible connection to Bo. I have no idea where the

San Diego Gladys is or what her last name is, but I can give you the Pomona Gladys's address."

Jack shook his head. It rang with pain. "How about Myrtle?"

"No Myrtles at all." Point Man smiled. "It's not a name you hear often in my generation."

Jack spent another fifteen minutes trying to find any connection between Bo and George other than Gregory's innocent name, between Bo and Park Service, George and bikers, Gladys and anybody. He even worked on possible Durwin Rice, Em Leighton, and other employees' connections awhile. Zip. The dialogue fizzled. His headache, now a howling monster in this bright sun, prevented clear thought.

Point Man gestured toward Maxx. "Well behaved dog."

"He's showing off for you. He's usually not this good."

"Doesn't even need a collar or leash, huh?"

"Collars are for control. When we're working like this, I take his collar off so the bad guys can't grab it to control him. When we're in the world, he leashes up like any other tourist."

Point Man chuckled.

Jack took one last flyer. "Six days ago, at least two people went walking out to those salt pools, 'way out on the valley floor. I'm looking for anyone who might have seen them. A casual observation. Anything. Can you help me?"

"No. The park rangers have been asking that for days."

"How do we find Bo's motorcycle? The rangers and FBI haven't been able to turn it up."

"A bike isn't a machine. It was a personal part of Bo, and his friends regard it that way. It may never turn up, just as a lot of his friends won't talk about him. I'll see what I can do."

"Appreciate it." Jack began the painful and complex job of getting back up on his feet. Maxx lurched to standing and, bored with Jack's slow progress, wandered over to lick Point Man.

"You might ask Slim's Son too. He seems to see everything." Point Man rubbed Maxx behind the ears, permanently imprinting himself as a worthy human being in the mutt's mind.

"Where do I find him?"

"I have no idea. He's not one of us. He's apparently the son of a local character, now deceased, called Seldom Seen Slim. He has mine workings somewhere in the hills near the park here. Does 'Ryan' mean anything?"

"Ghost town on the south end. I'll check it out. Thanks. Maxx, heel."

Maxx continued currying Point Man's favor.

"Hey, you!"

Reluctantly, the dog fell in beside his knee. Jack took his leave and walked out to the visitor center. The walk loosened him up a little and soothed a few of the greater aches, but considering the sheer number of aches he started the day with, that was like dipping a bucket of gravel out of a full dump truck and calling the truckload "reduced."

People stared at him, most openly, some discreetly. It occurred to him as he shoved through the glass doors of the VC: Why didn't Point Man ask something about his face?

The girl on the desk, a bright-eyed blonde named Karen, stared just as hard as anyone else. She wagged her head. "I heard about you getting shoved over a cliff, Dr. Prester. I always wondered what it would look like. Now I know."

"And that's not to mention what it feels like. I don't recommend it. How do I go about finding Slim's Son?"

"You don't. He finds you, if he wants to. No phone. No address."

"Where does he hang out?"

She giggled. "I wouldn't think of using the term 'hang out' when you're talking about him. It doesn't fit somehow on an old fellow with a beard like his. He looks like 1880 on the hoof. He's so prospectorish he has a burro. He makes a couple hundred a day during the height of the season posing for tourists."

"He's gotta pay the Internal Revenue Service, surely. No post office box number?"

"Why pay them? I bet they don't know he exists."

Jack pondered this ultimate freedom a moment. "Well, if you see him, tell him I'd like to talk to him. Mention money, if you think it'll help, but don't promise too much."

"Where will you be?"

"Around here, after luncheon with the superintendent."

"And Myrtle." She smiled grimly. "Enjoy." Her whole tone of voice told him it was definitely not to be anticipated as an enjoyable experience. He walked outside into the brilliance and the vivid heat. No bird sounds. No natural sounds at all.

If it weren't for people, Death Valley would be perfect.

12
. . . And Pulled Out a Plum

If there's more than one fork beside your plate, leave the table and go buy a two-piece dinner at the Colonel's. He don't care if you lick your fingers.

Sage advice that, proffered by Jack's Uncle Fred. This was supposed to be lunch, for pete's sake. Jack shook out his napkin—cloth napkin, of course; none of this gauche paper stuff—as he studied his place setting with misgiving. Two spoons, two knives, three forks, and a silver-plated Something arrayed themselves around his ornate china plate. Once upon a time Jack's mom gave him a lecture on fancy table manners, which she ended with "But don't worry about it. Normal people eat like normal people."

Myrtle Leighton was not normal.

By any measure.

At their first meeting, Jack had garnered the impression that as Emery strolled through life all laid back, Myrtle jogged, frenetic. This home confirmed it. The house was the standard three-bedroom WODAC floor plan from the sixties. Living room with a foyer, a dining room elled off to the side, the kitchen, and bedrooms down the hall. Bath and a half. Nothing snazzy.

But her house was spotless, her windows so clean they looked open, her furniture straight out of the showroom—the inside of the furniture store, mind you, not the Bargain Days tent in the parking lot. Like so many park families, they had decorated their walls with tasteful photos of their former park areas. They'd served in Mammoth Cave, Arches, Mount Rushmore, and Kings Canyon, that Jack recognized.

Another first impression, an impression Jack had doubted out in the harsh glaring sun of the salt flat, proved itself true. Myrtle was blue. A lot of older women tint their graying hair blue, but Mrs. Leighton tinted her eyebrows too. Or maybe drew in extra hairs with a blue pencil. Either way it made her look like a fugitive from a four-year-old's coloring book. She smiled a little more than the occasion warranted, tried a little more than you wanted her to to make you feel comfortable. It made Jack feel distinctly uncomfortable.

At least he'd had the foresight to grab his sport coat.

"A sport coat and jeans?" Ev had asked critically.

"The coat's denim, right? Matches the pants."

"First denim sport coat I ever saw. It doesn't quite make the same statement as tweed, believe me."

He would probably have felt even more uncomfortable had Myrtle not displayed one tiny stroke of human fallibility. Her guests arrived before she did. Emery ushered Ev and Jack into the spotless house, and Myrtle came boiling in five minutes later with the tomatoes and fresh mushrooms for the salad, extolling the life-saving virtues of the convenience store at Furnace Creek.

Now, her propriety restored and formality solidly bricked into place, Mrs. Leighton smiled at him across the table and her pudgy cheeks folded into interesting globs. "Your father's at White Sands, isn't he?" She tackled her appetizer, some sort of stuff in a stem glass, topped with itty-bitty pink shrimp far too young to be sacrificing their very lives for a formal luncheon.

"Hawaii Volcanoes, six months ago. He wanted to see what wet looks like." Jack's jaw still hurt when he spoke or chewed.

"Oh." She frowned at Emery as if he'd been holding out on her. "Then where did Gene Peter go?"

Emery Leighton shrugged and finished his Shrimp Something.

"Early retirement," Jack offered. "John Connors took White Sands behind Dad, but I don't know who went to Mesa Verde."

Emery spoke for the first time since greeting the guests. He passed a soup tureen to Jack at his right. "Scuttlebutt at the superintendent's conference says Bill Walton's leaving region. They might stick him there."

"Or Rocky Mountain. I hear ROMO's opening up." Jack ladled himself some soup. Broccoli soup. Great, if you're into broccoli. Jack was more of a green peas and corn man himself, neither of which makes into soup worth anything.

Nor does broccoli.

For the next five minutes they cast speculations around about actual moves and potential moves of the Park Service old timers they knew in common. It was the game every group played whenever Park Service people got together. Jack grew up listening to Dad second-guess all the park superintendents and regional offices who authorized the personnel shifts.

And it dawned on him that only three of the four at this table were talking. Ev sipped at her soup, casually and effortlessly employing perfect manners. She wasn't saying a word.

Table talk died as the soup ran out and Mrs. Leighton served the next course, some kind of casserole that did not contain cream of mushroom soup. Until this moment Jack had never guessed you could build a casserole without cream of mushroom soup. What she made it from escaped him, except for the diced ham which he recognized almost right away, but there wasn't a telltale miniature gray chunk in it anywhere.

She launched conversation in a new direction. "So

108

how is your investigation coming? Durwin can't imagine that you'd find enough to do to stay busy, but apparently you're doing so."

Jack smiled. "Some things to look into." This New Mexico farm boy was having a hard time figuring out which fork to use. He took Ev's lead, placing the smaller fork in his tossed salad dish and picking up the big one. Jack had trouble with the wealthy end of the social spectrum.

Myrtle was rolling along. "Really! Just what do you look for? Do you ask all those questions they ask on television?"

"Yes, ma'am. I even tried wearing a rumpled raincoat for a while, but I've never been able to match Columbo's style." Jack smiled noncommittally.

Ev's mouth was on the verge of smiling. Her vast eyes flicked from face to face.

Mrs. Leighton wagged her head. "No one ever interrogated me. I would love sometime to be interrogated. I don't think I'd like to be an actual suspect, of course—"

"But be able to participate."

"Exactly."

Jack took her subtle lead. "Very well, Mrs. Leighton. Please be advised that anything you say can and will be used against you in a court of law. Now, where were you last Thursday between the hours of five and nine?"

She played the game instantly. "Oh. I was home, but poor Emery has no alibi. He left the office early and drove into Lone Pine. He didn't get back until nearly midnight."

"Ah. Sorry to hear Mr. Leighton has no alibi. Did anyone see you at home here or call you?"

"Oh, dear. That means I have no alibi either, is that right?"

"That's right. So I'll just have to add you to the list of suspects." Jack tried to read her face. She was obviously getting a monstrous kick out of this silly game.

Except that it wasn't silly.

109

Ev grimaced, almost ashamed. "I'm very sorry, but may I be excused a moment?"

"Of course. Down the hall on the left." Mrs. Leighton airily flapped a mitt.

"Thank you." Ev laid her napkin aside and disappeared into the back of the house. Women pick the strangest times to powder their nose. Even with nearly eight years of marriage behind him, Jack didn't understand women's arcane biological functions.

He learned in passing that George Gibbs and his wife and son had sat in this very dining area not two weeks ago. Mrs. Leighton dwelt at length on the irony of all this— you know, entertaining both the man and the investigator probing the man's death. He learned that Emery enjoyed woodcarving in his spare time but hadn't carved any wood in the last year. Too busy. He learned that of the Leighton's four children, none seemed destined to enter government services. With his military service, Emery had almost forty years under his belt.

Next came dessert, a fluffy something with plums, much too sweet, a blob of whipped cream, and a maraschino cherry. It wasn't a complete loss; Jack loved maraschino cherries. Then they repaired to the patio out back for coffee. Not just coffee—that vanilla-flavored coffee you're allowed to pay double for in the specialty stores.

Embarrassed, Ev asked to be excused again. Jack wondered about her. Maxx paid less attention to trees. Or maybe all that iced tea she drank yesterday was finally surfacing.

They talked about camping for a few minutes, a subject Jack was finally comfortable with, and he wondered if Ev went camping much. The Leightons did frequently, Myrtle said. Jack's family spent most of his boyhood vacations camping. Where did Navy families go? Sailing?

"Have you traveled much in Mexico?" Mrs. Leighton asked.

Jack nodded. "Colima, across from Big Bend. Dad

110

took the family down around that country a lot. We'd go camping in the Boquillas. And Dad speaks Spanish like a native."

Ev returned and perched herself demurely in a patio chair.

"Not much use for Spanish in Hawaii." Mrs. Leighton sipped at her coffee. "Em and I took the Copper Canyon tour in March. Amazing. I see why they call it the Grand Canyon of Mexico."

Ev forced a smile. "It must have been lovely."

"Oh my, yes! Excuse me!" Mrs. Leighton leaped up. Emery looked pained. In moments she was back with a fistful of photos and travel brochures. She handed them to Jack.

He leaned over in his chair toward Ev so that she could see them too. His aching body griped anew.

Some of the brochures were in Spanish only. There were several flyers about the guided tour of the gardens in Mexico City—some duplicates, in fact—and a whole lot of flyers, one each, about other tourist meccas. The snapshots looked like they had been taken from a moving train. They were. The train is how you tour Copper Canyon.

Interest in Mexico waned presently. With one ear Jack stayed with the conversation, and with the other he analyzed what was happening here. Mrs. Leighton, the perfect hostess, kept things going. She seemed to have a store of topics ready. The moment talk flagged, she'd trot out the next item. An inordinate number of items bore directly or indirectly on the investigation.

Emery spoke only when spoken to. He maintained that vacant distance he'd had at the crime scene.

Jack skated around the edges, trying to stay friendly while spilling nothing pertinent. He was pleased to see Ev was being circumspect as well. She never mentioned anything remotely close to the fact that she was uncovering some very strange and suspect expenditures in the maintenance budget. And some in the ranger budget. And a few funny items in special projects.

111

This morning Jack had gone to her immediately after he left Point Man. She had shown him the unusual entries. It was Einstein explaining relativity to a reindeer herder. Jack hadn't the foggiest how she found the stuff or why she considered it out of line. And it wasn't that she hadn't tried to clarify it, either. Jack's idea of balancing his checkbook was to stay within fifty bucks of what the bank claimed. He wasn't made for this stuff.

Now Jack sat on the main man's patio, beneath the shade of rough, yellowing cottonwood leaves that warned him in a stage whisper, "Autumn is here. I'm dying now." He wondered how Emery was cheating Uncle Sugar out of thousands, and why he would. Or was it Emery? It could be someone else with access to the ONPS and special project budgets. The administrative assistant. The budget specialist. Chief of maintenance. Secretaries. The chief ranger or chief naturalist. Some computer hacker in Schenectady, New York, who loved to break into systems a continent away.

And then there was the missus. What was the basis of her extreme curiosity about the case? A simple hunger for juicy gossip or something more? Amid layers and layers of additional staid formalities, Jack and Ev made nice, thanked the lady and praised the luncheon, and beat an elegant retreat.

She saw them to the truck, made Maxx's life complete by scratching him between the ears, and returned to the house.

Jack peeled out of his sport coat. Ev shed hers too. It was much too warm for these formal shenanigans.

Maxx stood around wagging his tail as if Jack were returning from a three-month absence. Dogs have no sense of time.

"I thought that would never end," Ev muttered. Her sense of time was just as bad as the dog's.

And Jack stopped. He was blocked in. A lady in a beater station wagon pulled into the drive and parked behind him. Here she came at that rolling gait that seems built into older women.

She paused and stared at his mangled face, but all she said was a muttered "Oh my." She brightened. "You're leaving, aren't you? I'll just be a moment, and then I'll be out of your way. I have to deliver this make-up to Mrs. Leighton. She wasn't here when I dropped by before. I'm the Avon representative here, you know. I have quite a large territory. Beatty, here, and Death Valley Junction. And Wildrose, of course, but the women there don't really buy enough to make the side trip worth it. I'll just be a moment. I would have left it in her door, but it wasn't paid for yet, and I hate to leave anything that hasn't been paid for. Very bad business. Sometimes I'll forget whether it's paid for and have to ask, or the customer forgets and I have to request payment. This way, when they get their products, they pay the bill and that's that. I'll just be a moment."

Jack looked at Ev, and Ev looked at Jack. He leaned on the fender, since his truck wasn't going anyplace for a while. "You fit into this dinner-at-the-White-House scene easily. I envy you." He lurched erect, opened the passenger-side door, and dragged the seatback forward. He stuffed his coat down behind. Good riddance. He dropped the seatback into place and held the door for Ev like a proper gentleman. If they were going to be The Elegant Folk, they might as well go whole hog.

Elegantly she settled in and hauled her seat belt down. "For a man who hates luncheons, you did just fine."

Elegantly he motioned Maxx into his cage, but he left the door hooked open. He climbed behind the wheel and shut the door. Privacy. He could let his voice rise to normal volume. "I just did whatever you did. Except go to the bathroom over and over."

"Here! Wait till you see—no, better leave first." She sat back. "We don't want to look suspicious."

"Heavens, no. Suspicious how?" He watched the

Avon lady flap her hands wildly as she engaged in a lengthy conversation with Mrs. Leighton. Emery sidled past them and crawled lackadaisically into his white GSA car. He was blocked in too, but he didn't show any sign that he cared.

Ev ignored his question. "I borrowed a GSA car to bring my belongings up here this morning. It's a cute little apartment, sort of. Wonderful view."

"You can see most of the valley from up on the hill there."

"And yet from the main road you'd never guess there's a whole complex of houses back here."

"Keep the natives hidden. From perusing financial records, you know that most parks maintain their own residential areas."

"And I always thought it was a waste of taxpayers' money. The residences usually don't pay for themselves. Until just now, I thought all park personnel ought to find housing out in the community. But there's no community here. Nothing for a hundred miles."

"Correction. There is a community, and you're sitting in a parked truck in the middle of it right now. The Park Service provides housing in most areas because there's nothing in the surrounding civilian area. Even when there is, we tend to band together. As a result, parkies are a very close-knit bunch. In this little residence compound of—what? A couple dozen houses?— there are friendships being forged that will last a lifetime. When we were talking at lunch about people transferring around, we were talking about friends and friends of friends. That's why most of us have a Christmas card list three hundred names long."

"Living in the Washington office, I never guessed."

"Don't feel bad. Living in the Washington office warps just about anybody. Especially congressmen."

Finally, finally, Mrs. Leighton took her bag of war paint inside, and the Avon lady came waddling back down the drive.

She paused at Jack's door so he pretty much had to roll down his window, however reluctantly. "Thank you so much for waiting," she gushed. "I try never to make extra trips outside my regular schedule. The time and expense. Here's my card. Here's our latest catalog." She passed a vivid pink business card and a small, colorful booklet in through the window.

Another booklet came through the window. "And here's the sales campaign before this one. You can still order from that catalogue. You might want to note the specials on page twenty-four. If you or your lovely wife there see anything at all, just give me a call."

"Thank you. Here you go, wifey." Jack glanced at the card as he passed the stuff to Ev. "Pleased to meet you, Mrs. Roye."

The lady glowed at the sound of her name, and Jack was afraid she'd burst into another interminable explanation of some sort. But she didn't. She apologized for being in such a hurry, but she had so much distance to cover and it was getting late—oh my, almost two thirty already!—and with a series of convoluted good-byes she left them.

Jack was breathless just listening to her.

She started up her station wagon on the third try and backed out into the street. Jack backed out then and drove down the hill, from dappled shade spot to dappled shade spot under the fading cottonwoods.

Ev began babbling like a man in mid-life crisis who has just discovered the joy of model railroading. "When I excused myself there it wasn't just to go to the pot. I went through their medicine cabinets. Both bathrooms. And you remember when you were all out in the patio, and I came inside again? I sneaked a quick look in the kitchen cabinets then. People often keep medicines in a kitchen cabinet, you know."

"Looking for that Beta stuff?"

"Any stuff." She dug into her elegant tweed pockets.

"I wrote down everything I found. Prescription numbers, the works. Here! See?" She held up several slips of paper.

"Impressive. You pulled out quite a plum there. Let's stop by the trailer, and I'll copy them."

"You have a Xerox at the trailer?"

"No, a pencil. Low tech, but adequate for this job."

She smiled, sort of. Actually smiled. For her it was a first. "I feel very—very—detective-ish. This investigation business—I didn't realize it would be so much fun."

"It wasn't any day at Disneyland for Gibbs. So be careful."

"You think there's danger?" She studied his dashboard. "Of course. You very nearly died. That cliff. Do you think that was connected to this? He seemed to be after you, not me. And Hal said there wasn't any real danger."

"Hal had only the outside to look at. We're looking at the inside. Besides, it's not Hal getting green tools in his face."

Jack pulled left into the trailer park and cruised at five miles an hour past the big rectangular tin boxes with their barbecue grills and lawn chairs. The kids at the grade school were yelling and chasing each other around the yard.

"Inside. You were inside again, and I wasn't." She grimaced. "You and the Leightons were talking about people transferring. Not only did I never hear of any of the people you talked about, I've never heard of most of the park areas."

"We left you out again. Sorry." He nosed his truck in by the propane tank of the Silverfish. "I keep forgetting you're Navy folk, not Park folk. Next time I'll try to bring the conversation around to aircraft carriers or something."

"This is where you're living? Durwin seemed so apologetic about how old the mobile home is, and he's right. It's so primitive, and—" Words failed her as she gazed upon the sorry, dulled-aluminum trailer.

Jack watched her a moment, bemused. This old country boy didn't consider anything with a working flush toilet under the same roof to be primitive. "Here's the key. Go on in. I'm going to tie Maxx up. He might decide to go play with the kids, and teachers don't appreciate him."

Ev headed for the door as he motioned Maxx out.

Maxx's outside leash was twenty feet of old climbing tape and a carabiner, tied to the trailer hitch. He snapped the 'biner into Maxx's collar and scooped up the dry water dish on his way to the door. A whole day of being out and about, and he was still as stiff as a frozen garden hose. His ribs, his face, his jaw, his neck—falling off a cliff ain't all the fun it's cracked up to be. He heard the screen door creak.

It wasn't a boom. It was more a muffled, thudding *fwoomp!*

Ev flew backwards, propelled straight off that cement block, away from the door. She lit inelegantly on her back in the dirt six feet from the trailer.

A poof of dark smoke rolled out of the trailer. Fire! Jack must put out the fire in there! Every second counted. He must—

But all he could think of was Evelyn Brant in the dust.

13
Iron

A twenty-four-inch exhaust fan howled in the doorway of the Silverfish, blowing smoke and powder out into the previously unsullied breeze. It was practically sucking the furniture out the door. The kitchen curtains, ripped off the walls, lay outside in the dirt, their hems charred. White fire extinguisher powder coated the scorched wall by the stove, the scorched closet door across from the stove, the dinette and the sofa cushions. And the stink, the pervasive stink of smoke . . .

Jack stood by his kitchen sink surveying the execrable mess. "I suppose this means I forfeit my deposit?"

Engulfed by the intricacies of still another incident report, Durwin Rice stood scowling in the middle of the floor, clipboard in hand, absently scrawling away.

Jack poured a tumbler of tomato juice from the can in the fridge. "You realize, if we were working regular hours, and that door had opened at five-thirty instead of two-thirty, the propane would have had three hours more to build up. They would've heard the boom in Riverside."

If Rice realized, he made no sign.

Jack plopped ice cubes in the juice and walked outside, side-stepping the exhaust fan.

Ev reclined in a chaise longue under a cottonwood

by the neighbors' trailer, thirty feet away.

He crossed to her and handed her the glass. "You don't look quite so much like a stewed tomato with your face washed. But your eyebrows are frizzled. You'll need Mrs. Roye's Avon eyebrow pencils for a while. Draw them on until they come back in. Go through her Avon catalogue, wifey, and we'll get some out of Hal's slush fund."

"Thank you for the juice." She sipped.

He perched on the end of the chaise longue uninvited.

Her huge eyes rose. "I'm getting a little bored with stepping into the traps they're setting for you."

"I hope you know I appreciate you taking the heat off me. Nice gesture to make for an acquaintance you hardly know."

She shuddered. "Is it official? A trap, I mean?"

"The pilot lights were turned off and the stove burner opened. The trapper duct-taped a match to the screen door so it'd strike along the floor as the door was pushed open. Not original, but it shows thought. I doubt it was intended to be lethal."

"Then someone with access to a key is responsible."

"The door was forced. You can cut your way into the Silverfish with nursery school scissors."

Here came an eager-beaver intake ranger named Someone White with another clipboard. The guy had to be six-four, and if he weighed one seventy that was ten pounds Jack didn't know about. His grin was sort of built into the musculature of his mouth. The name badge loomed close enough to read. Aubray White.

White crowed exuberantly with a Southern accent thick enough to caulk windows. "If you hadn't gotten on it instantly with the fire extinguisher, this thing woulda been gone in a minute."

"Almost lost it anyway. I would've hated that. That's my only toothbrush there in the bathroom."

White's face turned red. "Uh—you're staying here?"

"Yes. Miss Brant was merely slumming this afternoon. She lives in the lavish apartment up on the hill."

White frowned. "Now 'cording to housing, Miss Brant is assigned to the trailer here. You have the apartment."

Ev scowled. "How did they mess that up? I signed for the apartment. If you want confirmation, go look in my closet."

"Or her bathroom," Jack suggested. "She has an affinity for bathrooms. Does some of her best investigative work there."

White held his hand up hastily. "No suh, I believe you." He shrugged and brightened. "Want to sign off the incident report?"

"If this is the incident report, what's Rice sweating blood over inside there?" Jack took the clipboard.

"I do fire reports. This was a fire. I better check." White left his clipboard and jogged away, all lanky legs and elbows.

Moments later, here came Rice. Unceremoniously he shoved his clipboard at Jack. "When did you two switch quarters?"

"We didn't. I told you folks I'd take the trailer. Verbal. Unlike Miss Brant, I haven't signed in yet. I guess you didn't get the word." Jack scanned the report, which was correct in most details—better than average for reports— and signed it off.

"You live right up the hill there, Durwin." Ev frowned at Rice. "Surely you saw Jack's truck parked here."

"That don't mean nothing." He squatted beside them.

Rice's offhand comment irked him. Jack handed the clipboard to Ev. "Miss Brant has scruples, Rice."

"Well, sure. I mean—I didn't mean to offend you, Evelyn."

"No offense taken." She signed it without reading it. You'd think a hotshot accountant would know not to sign

120

without reading it. On the other hand, she had watched Jack read it. He appreciated that she would trust him after getting blown out his door.

Rice held Jack's eye a moment and stood up.

Jack excused himself and followed the chief ranger out to his car.

Rice studied the loose dirt at his feet. "Say—uh—you and Evelyn. You two an item?"

"Not that kind of item. Co-workers is all."

"No wife mentioned in your dossier."

"Not anymore. No."

"I hear you. Mine decided she didn't like it out in the weeds." His eyes flitted away. "We were at Wind Cave. She got her master's. Pretty soon she's staying in town, and I'm out in the park. Iron will, Marg. Sets her mind, that's it." Rice heaved his shoulders, a gesture of hopelessness. "You know how it goes."

"I'm guessing it went."

"It went. Now I always sort of wonder what would've been if I'd put in for the New York City group or something."

"In a big city? Kind of hard to handle, if it were me."

"Me too. This—" he looked out across the miles-long expanse of the valley "—nothing like this. Nothing. Space to move. Peaceful. Marg had already filed the papers. Figured I had nothing left to lose, so I put in for this position. What's Evelyn like? I get a feeling she's city."

"Very."

Rice snapped back to gruffness. "Just wanted to be sure you two weren't a couple. Doesn't pay to trespass on a GS-12's turf. Later." Rice crawled into his car and drove off.

Jack wandered back to Ev. Trespassing? Why did that bother him so? Ev and Rice were adults. Let them work out whatever they decided to work out. None of his business. He smiled down at her. "I'm going out to the crime scene. Back around dark, I think."

"You're going out there?" she asked. "But it's so hot."

"Only in the low nineties. Hot is a hundred and twelve." Jack paused. "The evenings are nice."

"Yes, they are. I noticed that." She watched him expectantly, with bated breath as it were, as if awaiting an invitation. This was the lady who hated hiking, not to mention disinterring things, the city girl terrified of the wide open spaces.

Jack tested his hunch. "You—uh—are welcome to go along if you wish. If you feel up to it."

"If you promise your dog won't dig up more bodies."

"No promises. I bought a metal detector in Ridgecrest when I got the windshield fixed. No telling what we'll dig up."

"Why?"

"The weapons. The crowbar or whatever it turns out to be. It might be out there yet, probably buried somewhere. Possibly even the gun. Maxx's nose won't serve this time."

"He smells iron?"

"He smells who buried it. But a week later in dry weather, no dog can really follow a scent trail. Best scent-tracking in the world is moist woods right after a rain. Which this definitely ain't."

"Why do you think it's out there?"

"I don't. You can hide a lot of lethal iron in a campground full of Jolly Rogers. But the weapon wasn't with Gibbs or Bo, and it's probably not a pocket item. Why carry it back to Furnace Creek and maybe get seen? Someone might notice that when they wouldn't notice an empty-handed hiker."

"One of those backpacks like Cheryl Ashley's."

"Or stuffed in a belt under a shirttail. I'm basically just covering one more base. Making certain it's not out there. Sure you feel up to it?"

"I'm sure."

It was almost five before they got on the road. Jack counted at least three cans in his cupboard suitable for

122

late supper—chili, beef stew, and chicken chow mein—so he loaded his daypack with apples and soft drinks for snacks. They could eat a real meal when they got back.

While she changed her clothes, Maxx wolfed his dinner and magnanimously accepted his doggy treat.

They drove down to Furnace Creek in silence. The visitor center parking lot stood vacant. Jack crawled out absently.

She frowned at him as she locked up and fell in beside, her footsteps matching his. "You're preoccupied. Or are you simply fading out from all the stress?"

"You've got seven or eight hundred surly, burly bikers in your park. And possibly more yet to come. You have maybe five or six law enforcement people: a couple district rangers and some seasonals. What's the first thing you do?"

"Five or six isn't very many if there's trouble, is it?"

"Right. You beef up your force with a call to some neighboring areas for more rangers. Yosemite's right over the hill, if you don't mind calling one of the world's great block-fault granite ranges a hill. And the Grand Canyon's a day away if you drive fast. Why no SET?"

"SET?"

"Special Events Team. Why isn't Rice bringing in backup?"

Ev was pretty good at hiking if you didn't call it a hike. Everyone knows walking is easier than hiking. "Did you ask him?"

"Not yet." How should he explain that he considered Rice as much a suspect as anyone else? And that—because diplomacy was such a big part of this experiment with Hal's pals—he didn't want to appear to be calling the chief ranger on a matter that was not directly his concern? Or . . ? Nah. Let her guess. He cranked up the metal detector so hard it could find the grommets in his running shoes.

He spent fifteen minutes of the walk explaining how

a metal detector works. She spent another ten explaining again how she uncovered the suspect entries because they had been moved from one account to another. Jack thought number crunchers did that all the time. They nibbled apples.

Carefree and unburdened by such things as work and duty, Maxx rolled in the creek bed and investigated alien aromas around the few scraggly weeds.

On a map in his mind Jack sketched a wide circle around the crime scene and headed out cross-country to search it to its perimeter.

Maxx started limping. He lost a little of the joyous air with which he started this excursion.

Jack waved the metal detector about, uncertain what, if anything, it might pick up.

Ev looked back toward Furnace Creek in the distance. "I'm trying to remember why I consented to come out here."

"You like fresh air and long walks."

"Not it." She stumbled along beside him in silence a few minutes. "Why didn't they just leave it beside the body, whatever it was? The iron thing."

"I don't know. Traceable, I guess."

"If it were me, I'd just throw it as far as I could. Do you suppose that's what happened?"

"Could be. If Hal weren't the Ebenezer Scrooge of the Department of the Interior, we'd have some money to hire a chopper with infrared and metal detectors and just overfly this whole basin. Find iron, find the gun maybe, though I doubt it, find more bodies. Who knows?"

She shuddered. "Why not the gun?"

"Guns are hard to alter so they can't be traced. Also hard to let go of. The killer could have disposed of the gun, but when you're larcenous it isn't easy to give up such a dandy ego link. We'll look for a gun, but I'm betting we won't find it."

She studied the ground awhile. "Why kill one person with one thing and the other person with another thing?

124

Why not murder them both with the iron something or both with the gun?"

"Excellent question."

"And why leave Gibbs out there for all to see and then carefully bury the other one?"

"Why not bury the iron with the biker if neither are meant to be found?"

The sun floated low against the mountains. It dipped behind Wildrose, plunging the flat valley into shadow although Chloride and the mountains to the east still glowed gold. Jack loved this time of day.

Ev apparently had her misgivings. "Do you think we'd better start back soon?"

"Not many muggers out yet. It's OK."

"Just bears and pumas."

"Nah. Just scorpions and spiders. And rattlesnakes."

"Really?" Those doe eyes filled her whole face.

Jack grinned—disarmingly, he hoped. Really. A whole zoo of creepy-crawlies. But he wasn't about to let her know that.

Maxx and the metal detector beeped within a minute of each other. Jack let Maxx do the digging. It was about six inches down in a clump of not-too-hard dirt. Solid iron bar, fifteen inches long, flat at one end and chisel-shaped at the other. The iron lode lay absolutely in the dead center of nowhere. Not a chance in Helena, or anywhere else in Montana, that a casual trekker would ever find it.

"What is it?" Ev stared as Jack gripped its edges by two fingers and lifted it out of Maxx's diggings.

"Tire iron. You use it to pry a flat tire off its rim."

"Is that dried blood on it? It's too dark to see."

"I think so. No rust or salt corrosion. It hasn't been down there very long at all."

"Do you think there's fingerprints or something?"

"Almost certainly not. The killer was so smart in other ways, I doubt he'd mess up that way. But we treat it like there are, of course."

125

He bagged it and took a little extra time document-ing it. This was one piece of evidence he didn't want to lose by some axle-grease defense lawyer managing to get it declared inadmissible. He marked the spot with a yard-long strip of surveyor's tape. He'd start here tomorrow or the next day and continue his sweep. This find pleased him immensely, but there was still the gun to look for. He swung Maxx up onto his shoulders and started straight back toward the creek.

For a while as they walked, Jack reflected on the things God was doing in his life, prospering this, prosper-ing that—this investigation not the least of them. He was nowhere near a solution, but things were popping up. If Jack were a better Christian he'd recognize all the little fa-vors God did him and be properly appreciative. He regret-ted he failed to notice so much. The sky glowed. He loved this time of day.

Thank you, Lord!

"Know what we forgot?" Ev's voice dropped to a hushed murmur. "A flashlight."

"Not really. I have my pocket light. But if we use it it'll ruin our night vision. If we just sit around and rest awhile, the moon will be here. Half an hour or so."

The sun gave it up for the night about the time they reached the dry creek bed, but that didn't matter. Jack chose a soft spot, relatively speaking, from the hundred miles of creek bed available to lounge in. He laid the day-pack and the dog aside, stretched out flat on his back, and laced his fingers behind his head.

Ev did so too, lying so close to him that their arms touched whenever somebody inhaled.

He watched the sky turn from pink-orange to purple. The first stars came out. Silence. Peace. You could still hear the traffic—the cars, RVs, and motorcycles—roaring up and down the distant road to the east. It all seemed remote over there, though, a world apart. This was reality over here, this separateness.

126

"You can't see stars in D.C. most of the time," she mused.

"Too many city lights."

"This is beautiful!"

Beautiful. Yes. He watched Vega, Deneb, and Altair hang just inside infinity toward the west, and he thought about the year he and Marcia learned the star names. They would lie on a blanket in the front yard at Joshua Tree on nights like this, a piece of red cellophane over a two-cell flashlight, studying the sky as they referred to the Golden Nature Guide to the stars. In ten months they knew all the constellations and the stars down to third magnitude, and then he transferred to the Grand Canyon.

After looking up at the stars awhile, they would make love while the stars looked down at them. Rich days. Happy days. Gone forever. His eyes welled up all hot and spilled over.

He glanced at Ev. She was watching the heavens, rapt. Her cheeks were not tanned, and tears would not have been visible on her face in this faint light, so they probably weren't visible at all on his darker skin. He had an image to uphold, the Man of Iron, the Law Enforcement Officer, and getting mushy wasn't the least bit ferric. He breathed through his mouth so he wouldn't have to blow his nose, and waited for the tears to dry. There are distinct advantages to a climate with two percent humidity.

Marcia.

Three years, almost, and he still came apart sometimes at the thought of her. He forced his mind to the puzzle at hand, to figuring out who had wielded the tire iron in his daypack. His mind mulled the question as Marcia kept intruding, and he got nowhere.

The eastern sky turned silver and waxed bright. The moon oozed up out of the black skyline, looking bigger than it was, as it always does when near the horizon. Two days past full. Its voluptuous brightness bounced off the white salt and the beige dirt. They had ample light to walk home with.

He stood and stretched mightily. Every muscle in him squawked in protest. But his headache, thank the Lord, was abating from a constant background howl to nothing more than a dull thickness.

He ought to hand carry this iron to the forensics lab in Vegas. He hated to spend all that time on the road. What he needed was a helicopter. Whisk over there. Whisk back. Would Hal spring for air time?

Do hermits shave?

Upon request, he gave the metal detector to Ev. They began a casual stroll back toward civilization, away from the peace and silence.

On the way back she played with the detector and managed to detect a couple of vintage tin cans. The find really tickled her. A few minutes later she came up with a rusty harness ring.

You would've thought it was the Holy Grail.

14

Son of Slim

The sign sounded like a military installation:

No Unauthorized Personnel Beyond This Point

Jack tried his M-1 key on the lock. It opened. He drove his truck through the wire-and-pipe gate and locked it behind him. A quarter mile farther down this ugly little dirt track he hit another gate in a barbed-wire fence festooned with "Private Property" and "No Trespassing" signs.

From that gate still another sign spoke. This one shouted, in all capital letters:

NO UNAUTHORIZED PERSONNEL BEYOND THIS POINT

Pity it lacked an exclamation point. Jack jammed his M-1 key up into the lock. Nothing. He hated picking locks. He wasn't good at it. He sat down cross-legged in the dirt and spent five minutes getting the stupid lock to drop open. Maxx sat casually in the passenger side, watching Jack with the supercilious air of someone who could have done the job faster.

Again he closed the gate behind him, but he didn't lock it.

The bare, dark brown hills scooped up sun heat and tossed it at Jack from all directions. In October the heat was fairly gentle. In midsummer these hills acted like a huge toaster, as the sun burned down from above, and they bounced and rebounced its heat on you from all sides and below.

Somewhere off to the north, to his right, Death Valley lay shimmering and white, like an empty smile on the blonde they make all those jokes about. Here at his immediate right, the dark hills frowned with gullies and vales like wrinkles on a puckered brow. No trees, not even the ten-foot shrubs desert people grace with the exaggerated epithet "tree." He drove perhaps a quarter mile along this dusty path.

The road split into two, one winding, level, along the hillside and the other climbing it. Jack got out of the truck and studied the ground. Neither road had been used recently. Someone must be taking the warning signs at face value.

Ten feet along the level road, a burro's fresh tracks angled across, the footprints close together. Not in a hurry. Browsing, probably. In theory, Death Valley had been cleared of feral burros some years ago. In fact, the pesky little critters were just as common as ever. Was this a feral burro or Son of Slim's personal animal?

Jack slid into his seat and drove slowly, cautiously, out along this level road, not because it promised more than the climbing road did, but because he had to drive on one of them and he chose this one just for kicks. When it came to random movement, old Jack was right up there with the amoebas under a study slide.

A narrow foot trail came snaking up the hillside and angled into the road. The trail, well used with deep powder dust, must be Son of Slim's way in. It followed one rut of this road.

Maxx started barking. On the brown hillside to the right, a browsing burro raised its shaggy head to look at

130

them. What did the thing eat anyway? Jack saw no grass, and scant bushes. It answered his question for him by grabbing a mouthful off a little rabbitbrush and placidly chewing.

The burro, the dark gray-brown-almost-black that some burros are, had a small bald spot on its near shoulder, a rub spot. Chances were excellent that this docile little guy was Son of Slim's burro, one of the most photographed animals in California. Accustomed to the stares of his admiring fans, the burro placidly resumed browsing, here a nibble and there a nibble. Now that's star quality.

A few furlongs farther Jack approached a tin shack a hundred feet off the road. The powdery foot trail led directly to its front door. Jack parked the truck on the shoulder, not that this faint and misbegotten road could be accused of having a shoulder, and slid out. Maxx hopped out behind him and trotted off, nose low, exploring what had to be a highly odoriferous hillside, what with the burro dung, a ripe outhouse beyond the shack, deer droppings, creosote and incense bushes, and a couple of whitened beef bones. Essence d' burro hung heavy in the warm air.

Jack stood a minute beside his front bumper. "Hello! Anyone home? Son of Slim?"

His voice echoed off a hillside and returned to him empty.

With a joyful yowl, Maxx took off across the hillside to the east, flat out. Like the charge of the light brigade he thundered away out of sight, barking madly. The way he ran, he was chasing something impressive. Jack just hoped it wasn't Son of Slim.

He started up the path to the little shack. The house wasn't more than fifteen by eighteen feet, with a slightly sloped, flat galvanized roof to match its galvanized iron walls, and a cockeyed tin-pipe chimney sticking out. No smoke in the chimney. Jack paused to marvel at the trash all over—broken bits of leather harness, a thoroughly dead lace-up boot, half a sheet of galvanized tin, a washtub you could see daylight through the bottom of, a big rusty gate hinge. Nothing combustible. No doubt every bit of paper and wood Son of Slim laid hands on went into his stove to cook with.

No tin cans or beer cans were scattered about, either. Not that there were none at all. Rather, they formed an impressive pyramid in the front yard, the most faded on the bottom and the brightest on top. Obviously, Son of Slim tossed all his aluminum cans out the door onto that pile. Its sheer size anointed Son as the King of Beer Drinkers. Any recycler would give his eyeteeth for that trove.

The thunder of hooves to the east grabbed Jack's attention. The outlaws? The posse? Here came Maxx across the hill at a dead run, his tail between his legs. And hard behind him clattered the burro, its ears plastered flat against its neck, dead set on reducing Maxx to a little black spot. Clearly burros can run like thoroughbreds when they put their heart in it.

Without slowing, Maxx made a flying leap for the truck bed. He reached the bulwark and scrambled in. Jack heard his toenails screech and his hundred-plus pounds slam against the far side of the bed wall. The burro executed a hard left and galloped around the truck a full circle, hoping perhaps that the dog had leaped over and come down on the other side.

If the burro exercised malice aforethought toward the dog, did that mean this was a watch-burro, an attack burro, and Jack's own hide was in danger? Jack froze in place, studying the burro and, most of all, its floppy, expressive ears. The burro knew Jack was there—its broad range of vision surely included him—and one ear flicked his way occasionally. But the burro's heart and mind were focused on the eradication of that nasty dog.

Jack saw movement to the south, halfway up the hillside, barely in time—a hat and a plaid shirt, ducking and weaving through a field of boulders.

"Down, Maxx!" Jack bellied out on the hot brown

caliche, scuffing both elbows, and grabbed for his revolver at the small of his back. His sore ribs calmly announced, "We will not put up with that sort of thing for one minute," and quit working. His stiff neck threatened not to bend at all.

A rifle shot, probably a 30-30, echoed off three peaks simultaneously. A bullet rattled the pile of cans. If Jack hadn't seen the hat he would never have guessed where the shot came from. He returned fire in that general direction, with no idea whether the hat and the rifleman under it were still amid the boulders. Two shells gone.

The burro tolerated gunfire even less than it tolerated Maxx. It's bulbous nose high, it trotted briskly forward —hesitated. Jack fired again at the boulders. The burro broke and ran, up and out, following a steep gully to the west.

Jack scurried zigzag to the truck and slammed against the door. He was sweating, and it wasn't that warm out. He gripped his gun with slippery palms. His hands shook. He tried to gulp air, but his ribs were still out on strike.

If that was Son of Slim up there, Jack was not just outgunned, his .45 versus that rifle and quite possibly a sidearm. He was outgunned in the advantage department. Son had to be a superb outdoorsman, and he was on his own turf. Jack had never seen this parcel of ground before.

Son wasn't shooting the tires out. That meant he intended that Jack should hop in his truck and leave, didn't it?

Jack opened the passenger-side door and grabbed his carton of shells from under the seat. He flopped down by his front tire, close under the bumper where he could see the boulder field, and reloaded his three spent chambers. He jammed another handful of shells in his pocket.

A distant voice yelled, "Get out," or something.

"Stay, Maxx. Down." Long down was not Maxx's best trick. Jack applied to the only Person who could really make Maxx do what he ought, God Himself. He took a few moments to let the hand of God calm him, the patient voice of God to remind him he was safe regardless what happened here.

Jack's ribs finally relented, back on the job. He inhaled enough air to fill a balloon in Macy's Thanksgiving parade and bolted forward, away from the safety of his truck, straight up toward the boulders.

Barely visible, a hat rose up behind a creosote bush west of the boulder field. Jack fired in that direction, and the hat disappeared. Son, or whoever it was, had to be lying flat. There simply wasn't all that much bush to hide behind.

Jack took the boulder field and started working up toward the last sighting. The hat popped up; its wearer started running. Jack stood up and ran toward the guy as fast as he could.

He almost froze in his tracks. What if there were two or more out here, and the hat was merely decoying him into the open?

The hat dropped down behind a small quartz outcrop. Jack bellied out again in the hot dirt—carefully, this time, lest he rile his cantankerous ribs anew.

"Maxx! Come! Here!"

Good old Maxx with his superior dog senses could see everywhere at once, smell someone behind them, hear noises too faint for Jack's ears. He needed Maxx now.

Of course the mutt took his sweet time coming when called. Jack laid his gun down long enough to remove Maxx's collar. "On guard, Maxx. Guard!"

The hat sent a random shot over Jack's head, jumped up, and zigzagged down the hill toward the road.

Jack took off running, cutting the corner, running the hypotenuse of the triangle while the hat scurried down the leg.

Jack yelled as the figure reached the road. The hat paused, hesitated, turned enough to glance at Jack, and threw the rifle aside. He flopped face down in the ancient dirt, thereby single-handedly saving Jack from the chagrin of losing this duel.

Most would spread their arms and legs out when they went down under the muzzle of a gun. This guy grabbed his scalp in both hands, his elbows poking out.

Jack and Maxx reached him together. Maxx, his beak high, was doing his job. Jack stomped his foot down on the guy's neck and patted him down more roughly than he had to.

Here was a skinny fellow, incredibly sun-browned, with a scraggly beard and a bush of salt-and-pepper hair. His clothes were pure stereotype prospector, with suspenders on his duck pants and long red underwear sticking out from under his shirt. His dried-out, scuffed lace boots were a good match for that rotten one in his front yard.

"I enjoy a joke as much as anybody. So. Any good excuses for shooting at me?" No other weapons save a pocket knife. Jack pocketed it. He lifted his foot off the guy's neck.

The man never moved. "Y'r an alien spy."

"Says who?"

"Am I wrong?" The pronunciation came out "Aam Ah rah-awng?"

"Yep. Why the fireworks?"

"You got no call to be here. Hit's posted."

"OK. If you're a prospector, I'm a cello player for the Philadelphia Symphony. Why is the land here posted? It's not to protect some gold find."

"Cuz Ah don't like smartmouths. Ah see through you."

"I can blow you away right now for opening fire without checking my authorization. Let's—"

"Ah'm the only one does the authorizing around here, and you ain't authorized. Didn't hitcha, did Ah?"

"And next you're going to tell me you never miss unless you want to." Jack placed the man's accent as some-

135

where in Missouri or Arkansas. "And then you tell me your burro sprouts wings and soars when the moon's full, and I'll believe that too."

Jack circled the pseudo-prospector widely enough to stay clear of a lunge and picked up the rifle. He hefted it. "Nice little carbine. The kind of gun I'd expect from you. Traditional caliber and style. Fits the image. But hang it, man, you ought to know its range is nothing to write songs about. You weren't nearly close enough to do much damage." He broke it open and emptied its two remaining shells into the dust. He double checked that it was empty, snapped it closed, and dropped it by the fellow's hand.

He hunkered down eight feet away and tucked his revolver in his belt. "You're Son of Slim, right? So what's a good old Arkansas boy doing out here in the barren wastes of California?"

Son wrenched around to stare at Jack, his face twisted into a knot as if he'd sucked in a string of acid spaghetti. "Who are you, boy? Ah mean here in California."

"You said I was a spy."

"Ah mean besides that."

"Park Service investigator. Why aren't you in Arkansas?"

Son turned his head and watched Maxx for a long, long moment. Cautiously he rolled to sitting and gathered in his carbine. "Why should Ah talk to you?"

"Your pending arrest, for one thing. Assault with a deadly weapon. Assault with intent to kill. Resisting an officer. And that's just your burro."

"Ha! You *are* a guvment man!"

"Glad that's settled. Now talk to me."

Son sat there, just sat there, and Jack dreaded to think what all must be going through that mind. If Jack spent some time here stacking this guy's stovewood, would he be a couple sticks shy of a cord? Or was this man much sharper than he looked and sounded? Contrary

136

to stereotype, you don't get much past your typical savvy Arkansas backwoodsman.

Son shifted his attention away from Maxx and turned narrowed eyes on Jack. "You was supposed to hightail out when Ah fired at you. Why'd you come at me like that? Stupid stunt. Woulda 'spected smarter of someone as high up as you are."

"Want to talk to you."

"'Bout what?"

"One thing when I came up here, but now that we've had this little falling out, so to speak, two or three things. Your hooch any good? Or are you cooking meth?"

The eyes narrowed further until they were crackling slits in the bushy eyebrows. "Jest for curiosity, why'd you say that?"

"You have to be defending something. The cabin doesn't really look all that lived in. For example, there ought to be dish towels drying on that line out back or something like that. Your accent gives away your origins, and some of the best moonshine in the country comes out of the Ozarks. Perfect place up here for a still, and the harness rub-mark on your burro suggests how you'd transport the stuff, right under the nose of the law and no one the wiser. You pack it out on your fearless attack-burro there." Jack shrugged. "Deduction. So is it hooch or methamphetamines?"

"Drugs is a curse on the human race! Ah wouldn't never stoop so low as to make drugs or sell 'em."

"And moonshine liquor is a blessing on all mankind."

"Done right, hit is. Defending?" He blew a couple expletives past Jack. "Jest trying to keep the rays off. You go away, and Ah won't be plagued so much." He put his hands back on his head the way he had before, his gaunt fingers laced through his hair.

"What rays? You concerned about the ozone layer?"

"You get 'em yourself. The thought control rays."

137

"Why does anyone want to control your thoughts?"

The steely eyes narrowed further. "Don't play dumb."

"If alien spies were so smart, they wouldn't bother infiltrating a planet with such big environmental problems."

Slim digested that a moment. He glanced again at Maxx. Maxx was looking a tad bored with all this.

"Maxx, sit." Jack might as well let him relax a little. Maxx's butt plunked into the dirt.

Slim leaned forward and dropped his voice to a conspiratorial whisper. "Ah can recognize the aliens. You ain't no alien. But he is." Another suspicious glance toward Maxx.

Maxx curled around and began licking his nether regions.

Jack studied the mutt. "That would explain a lot."

Slim nodded toward Jack—more specifically his battered face. "Glad to see you put up a fight there, even if y' lost."

Jack pondered the situation a moment. Either Slim was as loony as a Canadian lake or savvy as a Philadelphia lawyer. If he was faking this insanity bit, he'd recognize that Jack was pulling his leg and play the game or not as he chose. If he really was a couple sandwiches short of a picnic, Jack could earn some bonus points here with a little shuck and jive.

"Bad headaches, right?" Jack pressed fingers to his temples. "Here especially, where the bone's thin and the rays penetrate."

"Terrible ones. Blinding. You too, huh?"

"Used to, but I learned how to beat 'em. The rays, I mean. Filtering them with your fingers helps a little. You know, homemade booze can give you a brain-buster even if you don't get drunk on it. The congeners do it. All the chemicals besides the alcohol, that is."

"My stuff is pure."

"Nobody's stuff is pure. Aldehydes—furfural—all kinds of fermentation byproducts."

"You see?" Slim sneered. "They're controlling your thoughts, trying to use you to turn me against my own shine. Leave more for them. Well, it won't work."

"When we get back to the truck, I'll show you how to escape their rays. Tell me something. Thursday a week ago, three people went out for a walk across the salt flats west of Furnace Creek. What did they look like?"

"Them murdered folks."

"Them murdered folks. And at least one other."

Again the slits crackled like anthracite. "That why you come here?"

"That's why. I'm investigating the deaths."

"You try to tell me you ain't out looking for a still, and Ah'll tell you my burro does too fly."

"And Tinkerbell will steal the gold out of your fillings if you let her. What'd they look like?"

"Ah tell you everything Ah know 'bout Thursday, and you climb in your truck and drive away without looking around none nor talking to other people 'bout looking around here. Deal?"

"You tell me everything you know about Thursday, no holding out, and we'll both walk over to that truck and drive away. You go along as far as the Park Service gate, so you don't decide to protect your interests by putting a bullet in my back."

"My word's good."

"Just making a good word better. And I won't mention anything to anybody about suspicion of a still. I'll let them figure it out for themselves, if at all. Deal?"

He sat for the longest time. Jack was afraid Son wasn't going to buy in, but he finally nodded. "Deal."

"Why the Arkansas drawl?"

"Come from there."

"Seldom Seen Slim lived here nearly his whole life, as I understand it."

139

"Ain't no closer related to him than Ah am to my burro. Ah liked his name and decided to whatcha call—capitalize on it. He ain't around to object, and Ah'm the kinda son he'd like to have if'n ever he had one."

"Pride of any daddy's heart." Jack watched the hills around, as much for that burro as for possible colleagues of Son. "Tell me about Thursday."

"Ain't as much as you might think. Most years, the Inn opens up on October first. This year, though, they opened one wing up a little early to accommodate some people from the Park Service. Some other folks staying there too, Ah opine. And the campgrounds were starting to fill up with them bikers."

"Describe the people in the Inn."

"Jest heard. Didn't see. A lot of retired people with travel trailers and RVs come through this time of year. They're the ones take the pictures. So Ah'm down at the visitor center a lot. Harmony Borax Works is a favorite place for the picture-takers."

"You're saying you can't distinguish people in the Inn from people in the trailers and RVs."

"Right. All their cameras click the same."

"How many people walked out towards Salt Creek? Lots?"

"During the day, maybe fifty, sixty. Ah didn't watch close."

"Close of day. Evening."

"The retired-oes, they're solar powered. Sun goes down, they disappear into their fancy RVs."

"You're saying nobody went out there after dark?"

"Saying Ah doubt the retired-oes did. But there was three, like you say, who walked out when the moon come up."

"What phase was the moon?"

"Jest coming full. Couple days short of full. Plenty of light. Two people walked out there, and Ah wondered what they thought they was doing since they was drunk as

140

a skunk in a berry patch. Then twenty minutes later or so, a big fat guy walked out there."

Jack sat. And waited. And waited. "Well?"

"By that time Ah was up by the date grove, so Ah jest kept going, back into Breakfast Canyon and set up at that group campsite there. Do that, usually. The tour bus operators like it, with the local flavor, and Ah make some nice bucks."

"The prospector in camp with his little greasewood fire, cooking pancakes."

"And salt pork. Don't forget the salt pork."

"McDonald's and their eggs McMuffin are really losing sleep over the competition, I bet."

"The flapjacks taste like burro chips." The beard shifted. Probably Son was grinning. "But y'r average city tourist, he's about one step smarter than a cucumber and twice as green."

"About the three people out by the creek—?"

"Don' know. Tolja. Ah went my way and never seen 'em again."

"Describe them."

"Not close enough. The couple: one was kinda burly and the other kinda slim."

"Couple. Man and woman?"

"Couldn't tell. Didn't see faces or nothing. If one of 'em was a woman she sure didn't have no figger that's gonna be in a calendar worth anything. Both kinda square built."

"Hear any shots?"

"Nope. Jest them blasted motorcycles roaring around."

Jack pondered this a few moments. "You yourself were the third person. You saw not two but one walk out across the flats. The moonlight is good light up close, but not from a distance. The flats were deserted, with all the retired visitors snug in their cocoons. No one to see what's happening. You followed the drunk out, mugged him, and had to shoot the big bozo because you couldn't handle him otherwise. Then another fellow came along, a fat guy, so you beat him to death and left him in a salt pool, weighted down with chunks of travertine. I know from recent experience that you aren't at all chary of pulling a trigger."

Son came back immediately. He was working with a full cord and maybe a few sticks extra. "Ah'd be a fool to do something like that out in the open. Not when so many rich couples go walking back in the canyons. If'n Ah wanted to mug folks, Ah'd do it in the close places, not out in the main arena, and not with all the spotlights on me." He dropped his voice to a level purr. "Ah ain't no fool."

"Oh yeah? Albert Einstein wouldn't have opened fire on me."

Son cackled. "Nope. He woulda set there and discussed whether the bullets would go the speed of light."

The comeback robbed Jack's tongue for a moment and reminded him how easy it is to underestimate someone just because he speaks with a rube accent. "Every now and then I miss an important piece of information because I fail to ask the right question. I might be doing that now. What question should I be asking that I'm not, and what's the answer?"

"You should be asking me if'n Ah got a still."

"I don't give a hang whether you do or not. You're not worth trying to prosecute. This is a private inholding. All you'd have to do is set the county and the park rangers and the treasury boys against each other and sit back and watch the dogfight. Your case would never see trial for all the jurisdictional hassle."

"'Bout how Ah see it too. Still, you said you'd keep your mouth shut."

"You didn't give me much."

"Gave yuh all Ah got. Whut y'ast for."

"And I shall." He really should take this joker down. Shooting at people, authorized or not, is clearly a no-no. But Son here must see and hear everything going on. Jack

142

would be foolish to poison this well of information for the sake of making an arrest he probably couldn't prosecute anyway. It was Son's word against his. Neither Maxx nor the burro would take Jack's side on the witness stand.

Slowly, stiffly, Jack stood up. "My ribs are killing me. Let's go home."

Son shot Maxx another glance and hopped to his feet, remarkably spry for someone with salt-and-pepper hair. He started back the road toward the shack. "What about your ribs?"

"Cracked a couple. Where—"

"Wouldn't have something to do with the way your face looks, would it? Mule-kicked?"

"What? Something wrong with my face?"

Maxx ranged out, still guarding, technically, but not really working at it. He jogged along the hillside, sniffing the air, sniffing the ground, looking around.

Jack asked a couple more questions, little details he'd thought of, but nothing came of it, probably because he was expecting nothing. They arrived at the truck. "Stop here." Jack motioned Maxx inside the steel mesh cage and hooked the door open. "Clever, huh? That metal wire cancels out the alien thought rays. I don't think he realizes I have him foxed, or he wouldn't go in there like that."

He opened the passenger door and cocked the seat forward. From below his camp stove he fished out the roll of aluminum foil, keeping an eye on the alien-besieged prospector. "Ever try a pomum Adami? It works for me." He ripped off a length of foil and squeezed it into a rope. He drew it up under his chin and hooked the ends over his ears. "Redirects the thought rays down to your glottis. Know how aluminum blows out a microwave oven? Same principle." He took it off and handed it to Son. "Where do you hide your motorcycle? In the shack, I suppose."

"Never ride them things."

If Son was covering up, he was using a clever blanket Jack would never get past. Carefully, cautiously, Slim

143

tucked the foil under his beard and drew it up over his ears. "Bought me one a few years ago, thinking hit's the perfect thing for up here. Cross country, tight trails. Weren't. All the time coming apart, shedding bolts, conking out. Sold it to some pipe jockey from Edwards when hit dumped me in a cactus onc't too often."

"How many times in all?"

"Onc't."

Jack took him along out to the Park Service gate. Son was even so nice as to hop out and hold the gate for Jack, closing it behind him. Jack watched in his side-view mirror as Son snapped the lock shut and headed home. Jack waited until all he could see moving across the hillside was a glint of aluminum foil that caught the light just so.

15

Burro Control

Noontime in Death Valley is like living inside a 300-watt light bulb. Brilliant sun washes across the dazzling white landscape, almost all of it bouncing off the ground and back into your eyes. The vault of rich blue sky looks almost as big as Montana's, for, at several miles across, the valley is wide enough that its encompassing mountains recede, particularly on the east side.

One little part of Jack's mind reveled in the raw beauty. The rest of it dwelt on the puzzles at hand. He could think of a dozen questions he needed answers for, and those answers would surely generate a hundred questions more. Maybe Hal was wrong to assign only one person to a job like this. Sure, local law enforcement was working on it, but even by taking the fringes and the leftovers, Jack felt overwhelmed.

This was as good a time as any to spend a couple hours with the reports and supplementals filed so far, to get caught up on what everyone else was doing.

He drove into the back lot of the administration building and parked at the far end. Maxx hopped out, trotted over into the dirt, and dropped onto his back. He wiggled and squirmed, getting dusty. He oiled the tire of a GSA pickup and reluctantly came back at Jack's call. For

145

an alien spy he obeyed reasonably well.

Jack motioned him into the cage and took an extra couple minutes to secure the canvas tarp across the top as a shade cover. He left the door hooked open. When he turned his back, Maxx was rotating inside, finding a comfortable spot to lie down.

Jack stepped from 90 + -degree sun into 75-degree air conditioned chill. He had to stand in the administration building hallway a couple of moments until his eyes adjusted.

Ev was diddling around with her tableful of printouts and notes. She must have drawn colored lines through a hundred entries here and there. She was a real go-getter with those Magic Marker highlighters. Her computer monitor glowed amber.

She saw him almost before he spotted her. She left her work and came over, capping, this time, the blue pen.

She brushed at his shirt. "You've been rolling in the dirt, it looks like."

"Picking up some of Maxx's bad habits."

"They say a dog and its owner start to look alike after just so long. Why were you rolling in the dirt?"

"A jerk was shooting at me. Twice in my life I've been shot at and both times on this case. I dunno."

"Again!" Her mouth moved. Obviously she was picking through things she wanted to say, trying to find something appropriate. She ended up with, "Who? I mean—"

"I'll tell you about it later. Or file a report."

"So are you going for another swim?"

"Nah. Actually, I'm sort of getting used to it by now. Ready to break for lunch? We can compare notes over a sandwich."

"Sure. Let me get some stuff to take along." She hastened off to scoop up printouts Jack couldn't care less about. That, besides airports, was another thing he disliked. Self-important computer printouts that got in the way of actual knowledge.

146

Ev stuffed a bunch of papers, a notebook, some pencils, her beloved Magic Markers, and heaven knows what else into a big plastic grocery bag, slipped her purse over her shoulder, and away they went.

"Nice briefcase." Jack nodded at the plastic bag.

"I have an overnight bag just like it. Matched luggage." It was her first-ever attempt at wit and, eager to encourage her, Jack chuckled appreciatively.

Maxx raised his head as they came out, but he didn't bother to stand up. Getting chased by that watch-burro sure left him pooped. His chin was back down on his paws and his eyes closed by the time Jack had snapped his seat belt in place and glanced over his shoulder out the back window.

Should he describe what happened? She was watching him, expecting something. He didn't know where to start and ended up saying nothing—for miles.

She stared thoughtfully at the dashboard. "I never thought I'd say this, but your place or mine?"

Jack let the double meaning slide by. "That depends on whether you have mayonnaise. Without mayonnaise, lunch is a hollow cacophany of bologna scraping against bread, full of noise and furor and signifying nothing."

She was staring at him, but whether her feelings be awe or irritation, he could not tell. "I have that salad dressing stuff. And sour cream."

"My place. Hey, wait a minute. Where'd you get Miracle Whip? Not in the bag of groceries I brought you."

"That little store by the museum. They had Lite too. You watch your cholesterol, I hope."

"Never let it out of my sight."

As they pulled into the Cow Creek turnoff, Myrtle Leighton came driving out. Jack slammed on the brakes and rolled down his window.

She touched a button and let the wonder of electricity roll down the window of her white Lincoln. The car's hood was a soccer field, its tail end stretched into another

147

zip code, its front seat looked like a living room sofa. How did she get that road monster parked in your average space, Jack wondered. She probably needed a class 2 license just to turn corners with it.

Myrtle bubbled over with the usual social niceties and comments on the excellent, reasonably mild weather.

He changed topics. "I'm gonna call Dad sometime soon. He did the Copper Canyon trip about three years ago, in the fall. I'll tell him about you and Emery. When did you say you went?"

"Third and fourth weeks of March. We just missed Easter week, on purpose. Emery needed peace and quiet."

"Don't we all. I'll tell Dad your trip went well."

"Oh, yes! Emery just loved Copper Canyon." Those blue eyebrows shoved together in a frown. "Durwin says someone tried to blow up your trailer yesterday."

"Right after we left you, yeah."

"He says you were very lucky it wasn't worse."

"That place is a firetrap, all right."

"I don't know why they didn't scrap it years ago. Durwin says one of these days they're going to, as soon as they get some more decent units for the seasonals. Well. I'm meeting Emery and Durwin for lunch. I'd better get going."

With a barrage of further pleasantries they parted company.

Jack pulled up at the Silverfish. Beyond the trailer pads, the maintenance sheds sat simmering, their tin roofs reflecting bright sun. A dozen pieces of heavy road equipment sat out in the yard. Death Valley looked prepared for blizzards with all the dump trucks, graders, and front end loaders. What they were prepared for was washouts and drifting sand. Maintaining roads in Death Valley is an exercise in futility oftener than not.

Jack put Maxx on his outside leash. The water dish was dry again. Ev hung back as he shoved the screen door open.

She asked, "Don't you lock it now?"

"Why, when whoever wants to break in can do it using a few simple tools easily found around the home?" He crossed to the kitchen sink to refill the dish. "Sorry for the mess. Got a running start and didn't have time to clean up breakfast."

She wrinkled her nose at the bacon pan and scowled at the dried egg on his plate. "What's your cholesterol reading?"

"Hundred and seventy-eight."

"There is no justice."

He took the dish out to Maxx. The thirsty dog practically drained it.

Lunch. While Ev settled at the table by the window and sorted through the mess in her fancy briefcase, Jack dug out potato chips, mayo, bread, and bologna. Should he open a can of soup, too? Nah. Too warm out for soup.

The kids over at the grade school broke for lunch. Happy soprano screaming blasted away the silence.

"Where did you go this morning?" She danced her printouts on end, trying to straighten the pile.

"Got up at five, shower and all that, Bible study for half an hour, drove to Vegas, gave the crime lab the tire iron and picked up the lipstick-and-cigarette results, came back, went out to Son of Seldom Seen Slim's, exchanged gunfire with him, talked to him awhile, and met you at the office."

She looked like she was having a little trouble absorbing all this, starting with the five A.M. wake up. "Son of—who?"

"Seldom Seen Slim was a local character about thirty years ago. He and Panamint Annie and a couple others. They're gone now, and this Ozark boy sort of took over the name." Jack added a couple of lettuce leaves to the sandwiches, just to show off. Personally, he hated lettuce, but he ate it anyway, and it made sandwiches look more festive than bologna looks plain.

"And he shot at you?"

"I was trespassing."

149

"Still—"

"That's what I told him." He brought lunch over and flopped into the seat across from her. He lowered his head and closed his eyes to ask a blessing. Then, "What do you have so far?"

"I called that number. Gus the pharmacologist. He overnighted. Out here it's not overnight; it's second day air, if you're lucky. He sent this pharmacology manual. I've never had any chemistry. Have you?" She hauled out an eagle envelope and from it dragged a book heavy enough to anchor a tugboat.

"Yeah, some." He took the book from her. As good a place as any to start was that Beta stuff in his notebook. He began thumbing through, acting like he was not totally confused. It was an Oscar quality performance.

"I asked Durwin what one of the suspect entries was, just casually. He said it was a drug you use to tranquilize and capture wild burros. Burros! Does that sound sensible to you?"

"They're a constant problem. Muddy up water holes, ruin the bighorn sheep habitat, overpopulate like crazy. Yeah, the Monument might be doing some burro control." He abandoned the search for the Beta stuff and looked up. "Which entry did he identify as the burro tranquilizer?"

"This one." She shuffled printouts. "Here. I marked it."

She sure did. A bright pink highlight line ran through the entry. Jack scowled at it a moment. "I've been in on some major taggings and relocations, but I never heard of that stuff."

"You mentioned wrestling a moose, I believe."

"Yeah, like that." He paused a moment, his mind on the book. "And culvert-trapping bears in Yosemite. Boy, can I tell you some bear stories. Here it is! The stuff Durwin was talking about."

She rose and leaned by his shoulder, craning her neck.

"Nothing to do with animal control. It's not even a tranquilizer. It's an experimental drug for slowing cell growth."

"Slowing cell growth." She stood erect, frowning. "Cancer?"

"My first guess."

"It originally appeared in resource management, then in the rangers' budget. Would that be consistent with burro control?"

"Doesn't sound like it. Why move it? Resource management is where you'd expect it. No clue on why it moved."

"No. First it's here, then it's there."

"Can you backtrack this to the original requisition or purchase order?"

She shrugged. "I tried, but I can try again."

"Interesting!" Jack gathered up the glut of paper and the book and plopped them on the floor. "Let's eat."

Ev wanted to clean up after lunch, but Jack nixed the idea.

They had more important places to be than scullery. He shooed Maxx back into the cage, and they hit the road. The kids were still yelling out in the school yard.

They were passing the parking lot of Harmony Borax Works on the way back to the office when Jack spied a familiar figure. He ducked aside into the parking area.

Ev frowned. "Gladys Gibbs, right?"

"With Gregory and the sitter, admiring the picturesque ruins. I want to find out what brand of lipstick she uses."

He slid out without locking up and headed for Gladys. Maxx whined piteously. *Oh, all right.* Jack snapped a leash on him and let him out. "Heel." Maxx strained ahead. "Heel!" Reluctantly, Maxx pulled a little less. Miserable mutt.

If Maxx attacked the tilting, lurching Gladys with the same emotional enthusiasm he tackled everyone else, he'd bowl her over. Jack left him tied to the low rail by the parking lot and continued on out the paved trail.

Gladys watched him come, her son at her side. Gregory's grin was so wide his face could get stuck in a door.

"Jack Prester. Good afternoon." She shifted that ungainly leather bag from one shoulder to the other and extended her hand.

So he shook with her. "Mrs. Gibbs. Delighted. Interesting area, isn't it?"

"Very. How far is it from the visitor center—two miles?"

"Just about exactly. Quite a walk for you."

"An hour. I average pretty close to two miles an hour. We'll be leaving Monday morning. I'll hate to go. There are a lot of nice walks here. Much better than back home."

"No danger of getting mugged."

"Panhandled, yes. Mugged, no."

"Panhandled?"

"That prospector type. He's very subtle about it. Doesn't say it. But he makes it clear he needs to feed his burro."

"That's a no-no in your national parks. I'll talk to him."

Gregory wandered on out toward the parking lot. Good. Jack would just as soon the boy wasn't in on this. "Mrs. Gibbs—"

"Gladys, remember?"

"Of course. Gladys, I'd like to check out your lipstick, if I may."

"My lipstick? Well—"

"If you prefer, I can get a search warrant faxed out of Independence. Keep it formal."

"No. No, I don't mind showing you my lipstick." She rummaged through that bag, dug out a gold tube, and handed it to him.

He took a couple minutes to document it clearly and smear a sample across a paper. He tucked it into an evi-

152

dence bag. It was neither the brand nor the color of the lipstick on that cigarette butt. "And what brand of cigarettes, may I ask?"

"Cigarettes! I suppose you want one."

"To put in a bag, not to smoke."

She hauled out her pack. He held out a bag, and she dropped a cigarette into it. Virginia Slims. The butt buried with Bo was a Doral. Dead end.

From out beyond the adobe ruins of the borax works, here came Son of Seldom Seen Slim. He trudged purposefully, his attack burro in tow. A frying pan, a canteen, various mining tools, and a nose bag hung from the burro's packsaddle. Son himself was all dolled up in his Ancient Prospector costume with the long underwear (and it's 90 degrees out?!), the duck pants, the battered hat. Picture perfect. In the trail thirty feet from Son, a lady tourist in a floppy straw hat flicked a camera up against her face, so Son literally shifted into slow motion, providing what is popularly known in show biz as a photo op.

"Gladys, I appreciate this immensely. Thank you." Jack nodded toward her left ear. "Striking earrings. Pure gold, I'd bet. You can't beat plain loops for elegance."

"Thank you. I like them. A gift from a friend."

Here it came. He fired a big, big shot in the dark. "I admire how well you're handling all this. I realize it's none of my business, but I'm very curious—"

"You mentioned once you found me interesting."

"And I still do, even more so. Forgive my rudeness, but tell me, whom do you miss more, George or Bo?"

If looks were knives, Jack would have been chopped up like stir-fry pork, right on the spot. She was either so irate or so frightened she was rendered momentarily speechless. Jack braced himself for the inevitable barrage.

Then the burro spotted Maxx.

The burro jerked its head aside, yanking the rope out of Son's hands. With a bray to waken a dormant cactus, the burro aimed itself at Maxx. Over at the parking lot rail,

Maxx peeled out, from zero to sixty in nanoseconds. He would have been out of there in no time flat had he not been tied. He probably would have remembered he was tied had he not taken off so hastily. He hit the end of his leash. His head stopped, the tail kept going, and he slammed on his back in the dust.

Jack was too far away. There was no way he could reach the dog in time to somehow deflect the burro.

But Jack's was not the only body in motion. Gregory—dumpy, overweight little Gregory—came bucketing toward Maxx at a stubby, bumpy run. He waved his arms shrieking and literally threw his body between the burro and Maxx. Startled, the burro veered and galloped off, its lead line flying.

Jack got there then and planted himself between Maxx and danger, shielding little Gregory as well. He noticed somewhat abstractly that his gun was out. He leveled it with both hands on the burro. He yelled as much to cow the burro as to address Son. "Control him or lose him, Son!"

Son ran not toward the burro but toward Jack. He got between Jack and the burro. Jack swung his revolver up, aiming hastily at God lest a tragic misfire happen.

The burro charged again but slowed and trotted off to the side, perplexed by the wall of bodies between him and his nemesis.

Son moved forward smoothly, purring vile, filthy epithets in a loving croon, and managed to grab a handful of leadline. He gave it a quick double wrap around his fist.

Jack holstered his gun.

Gregory, in the 90-degree sun, stood shaking.

Jack watched the burro a few moments. Son of Slim was leading it away, chewing it out in terms any grizzled old prospector would appreciate. Safe again. Jack untied Maxx and brought him to heel, then dropped to a squat, the better to talk to Gregory eye to eye.

Talking didn't seem to be the thing to do, though.

Jack looked a moment into the terrified eyes and gathered the kid into a tight, engulfing hug.

Gregory melted against him sobbing.

Jack mumbled, "You were magnificent, kid! Real guts. You saved Maxx, probably from getting killed. Those little hooves would have cut him in pieces."

Gregory clung like duct tape, so Jack held onto him until the snuffling stopped. This tubby little child had just been used by God, he reflected. The Lord used whoever was handy, whoever allowed himself to be used, whoever He chose to use, without regard to worthiness. Or, the other way around, He gave human beings worthiness by making them His allies. Curious.

Finally it seemed OK to loosen up.

Gregory moved back a step. "I was afraid he'd get hurt."

"You should have been afraid you'd get hurt."

"I was. It was so big."

Of course. When you're Gregory's size, a burro is as big as a fire engine.

"Why'd you do it?" Jack didn't let it sound accusing or impatient. He kept his tone of voice upbeat and curious.

"Remember that wasp?"

"No. Oh, yeah. The pepsis in the truck."

Gregory bobbed his head. "You coulda got stung, but you didn't want the wasp to die. I wasn't gonna do it, but I didn't want Maxx to get hurt. I couldn't let him get hurt if I could help it."

"Do me a favor, huh?"

"Sure."

"When you're president of the United States and leading the country through dark times, don't forget to drop me a Christmas card, OK? I'll be really proud to be able to tell all my friends, 'Why, I knew the president when he was just a little squirt, and he was magnificent then too.'"

155

16

Jack and the Bean Soup

What is this mystique about bachelorhood, anyway? Why did millions of young American men of otherwise normal intelligence resist marriage so passionately? Sure, you can play the field, assuming the field lets you play, which it often doesn't, but you sit alone most nights, wash your own socks, vacuum your own floor, and stand in front of a kitchen cabinet staring at cans and wondering which one to open for dinner.

Not to mention that these days the dating scene is a huge, dangerous, tension-laden stress situation.

Jack stood at his kitchen cabinet and morosely pondered the bachelor's first question, "Which can shall I open?" He didn't even want to consider the bachelor's other question, "Is it worth the hassle and possible rejection to look for a date tonight?"

Soup and sandwich? That bologna sandwich this noon wasn't all that bad. He pulled down a can of bean-with-bacon soup and opened it, then gouged and prodded its contents with a table knife until they reluctantly slid into his only saucepan. That was one question answered.

A halting, timid knock on the door set Maxx to barking. A beautiful woman stood on his cement block, a woman who only yesterday had been blown off that very cement block.

He swung the inside screen door open as wide as it would go. "The other question answered. Come in."

"What other question? Good evening." Ev stepped inside, and Maxx slammed into her, tongue-first, in greeting.

"Don't ask. Maxx, lie down!" Jack dragged the dog back and pointed to the floor.

Maxx flopped down, his tail still wagging.

"Good evening. I see you have your laptop with you, and your elegant brief case. Can't you forget work?"

"You asked if I could trace any of those strange entries back. I want some help on this."

"Sure. Ate yet?"

"No." She said it in a guarded sort of way, as if uncertain whether the answer would force her into some sort of sticky situation. Dating is stressful, all right.

"Rerun of this noon plus bean soup, or I can heat something in a can from the selection you viewed last night."

"Soup and sandwich sounds fine, if you don't mind me just dropping in like this."

"I love you just dropping in like this. Saves me pondering unanswerable questions. What do you have there?"

She glanced at him warily, perplexed, and shined his nonsense on through. She popped open her laptop. "I just loaded everything I thought might be pertinent. It's all README. We can't change anything, but all we want to do is read it, anyway."

She scooted over in the booth seat, and Jack slid in beside her. He nearly had to stick his ear up against hers to read the screen straight on. It faded quickly when viewed from an angle.

"Premium pays. Holiday and overtime, mostly. One hazard, to Durwin. A little high but not enough to be suspicious." She rolled a series of entries down her screen. "Ad-

157

ditional funding and special projects. Emergency exhibit rehab, but I can't find any subsequent paperwork on it."

"They assigned the funds but didn't do anything with them?"

"The funds are gone. But I can't find exactly how."

The soup boiled over. Jack bolted to his feet and made a dive for the stove. Too late. Soup really stinks when it blackens on a burner. While he was up he finished building the sandwiches, ladled out the soup, and brought supper to the table. He closed the venetian blind against the brilliant evening sun.

"It looks like they prepared some preliminary estimates for construction and equipment. But that's as far as it went."

"Any 10-237 and 10-238 proposals? I C investigations?" He gave her a paper napkin and took one himself. He paused to ask God's blessing on the food. When he looked up she was watching him self-consciously. He smiled. "It's OK. I asked Him to bless yours too."

She turned red. Was this an appropriate time to open the topic of salvation? Probably. So why wasn't he? He could be gently drawing her closer to God. He hated himself when he failed to speak boldly. The soup tasted like it came out of a can.

Then she changed the subject. "All the motorcycles roaring around. I hate to drive. What if I broke down or something?"

"Hippo said something about a big rally tomorrow night. Maybe they're practicing finding their way to Furnace Creek."

"They give me the willies. This whole case does."

The phone rang.

Jack got up and went to the stove, pulled the receiver off the wall, and greeted it.

"Mr. Prester? This is Angela Roye."

He rotated toward Ev. "It's the Avon lady, wifey."

She wagged her head peevishly and rolled her eyes

158

ceilingward, no doubt at Jack rather than at the Avon lady.

Mrs. Roye plunged forward. "I thought I'd call and see if you or your lovely wife would like anything in the catalogs I gave you. I got your number from the office today."

"Ev is in the market for an eyebrow pencil, but we don't expect any more explosions, so I'm afraid we haven't really looked at them thoroughly yet."

"Eyebrow pencil! What is her color? She's a winter, right? A dramatic winter, I'd guess, so she uses colors from the cool palette. I'll bring samples when I come. You're at Cow Creek?"

"In the Silverfish, yes ma'am. You come into the Valley here on Thursdays, as I remember."

"That's right. Friday in Beatty and Wednesday down around the south."

"Lathrop Wells and that area."

"No. I used to have a couple customers at Lathrop Wells, but that was, oh, maybe five years ago. Shoshone and Tecopa, but the trip barely pays for itself. I do it more as a service for them. One dear old lady, Mrs. Schreiner, is just precious. I'm the only company she has, and she always invites me in for tea. I keep telling her she should move closer to town, but she likes it there, and she owns her place. No mortgage payments, and the taxes are low."

"They ought to be. Yesterday you stopped by Mrs. Leighton's to drop off a package. I take it she was not there when you delivered the week before?"

"With Avon, you call on your customers once every two weeks. Every other week."

"So yesterday was a sales call?"

"Nooo, I'm trying to tell you. I reserve every Thursday for the Valley, and every Wednesday for Shoshone and the south, and every Friday for Beatty."

"Every other week."

"No. I am explaining, Mr. Prester. I reserve—"

He listened to the complete litany again, but this

159

time he pinched his lips shut with his fingers, to prevent himself from interrupting and hearing it all yet again.

She continued, "But very often people aren't home, or my order doesn't arrive in time, or something else goes wrong. So I simply plan to drive the route every week on Wednesday, Thursday, and Friday. Then if, for some reason, I don't have to go out in that direction, why so much the better. A pleasant surprise. But that's rare. I almost always cover the whole route every week."

"I see. Like yesterday. You should have delivered that order the week before, but she wasn't home then so you came back."

"Right. Also the ranger at Grapevine. She wasn't home the week before either. So even if Mrs. Leighton had been home last week, I would still have to come down again yesterday to get Mrs. White's order to her. You see? Out here, it's just about every week. Never fails."

The line went silent. Jack was about to say good-bye when she spoke again. "Exactly where is the Silverfish?"

He explained and mentioned about dinner being ready. Mrs. Roye failed to take the hint that the conversation had ended. It took Jack seven minutes to pry himself loose from the phone.

"Here! Look!" Ev had abandoned her delicious soup and was playing a symphony on her miniature keyboard.

Jack grabbed his tepid soup and squeezed in beside her.

"I found some more! Let me freeze this and this item here." Ev's fingers flew, she paused to study the monitor, the fingers flew again, like an airline clerk making a complex reservation. "Drugs! More purchase orders marked burro control. But they started out in that construction fund and ended up here."

Jack pulled the pharmacopoeia out of her plastic bag and started looking up names. She finished her sandwich.

He borrowed one of her Magic Markers and under-

160

lined entries—it wasn't easy picking a color; he had so many to choose from—and held pages with fingers. Only when he ran out of fingers on his left hand did he look up. And he felt a smug little tickle of discovery, though exactly what he had just discovered, he had no idea. "All either experimental or not used in the U.S. Some drugs listed here have no known use."

He twisted around to look at her, and his stiff neck complained mightily.

She was staring at him. "Could they be ingredients for manufacturing illicit drugs?"

"As in the drug trade?" He shook his head. "Nothing in my courses or hazmat training mentions anything like this stuff."

"Hazmat?"

"Hazardous materials handling and removal. It's a science all its own. A lot of hazmats are created by illicit drug cooks."

"And none of these drugs is useful for burro control projects or anything like that."

He shook his head again and noticed he still had half a headache from sailing off a cliff. "When exactly did those drug requisitions shift from the special fund to resource management?"

She let her fingers do the walking again, as the screen flickered and unfolded readout after recondite readout. "Of the ones I've found so far, two in February —this one was July. Hm—over the Fourth. That's interesting. This one was in the special projects listings in March and in the resource management environmental rehab in April. That was the twenty-fourth—and the latest one was August, the—uh—fifteenth."

"March twenty-four. While Leightons were in Mexico."

"So it's someone other than the superintendent."

Jack sat back and studied the far wall awhile, not hard to do in an eight-foot-wide trailer. "I noticed a curious thing when Myrtle was showing us those folders and memorabilia from that Mexico trip. Whenever Marcia and I went somewhere, we ended up with two each of some stuff. She'd get a self-guiding folder and so would I, for instance. Or we'd both pick up a flyer to send to the parents. Myrtle's goodies were all still in a T-shirt bag—"

"A what?"

"T-shirt bag. You know. Like your brief case there. Handle holes at the top. The folders weren't sorted yet, or arranged. No duplicates except from Mexico City itself." He shifted his gaze to the tabletop a moment and could think of nothing to argue against his surmise. "I don't think Emery went. He probably went to Mexico City, but I'll bet he didn't go to Copper Canyon."

Ev was studying him. "Who's Marcia?"

"My wife."

"Your wife. Of course." She flipped the lid closed on her laptop. "I'll write this up tonight, while it's still fresh, and document as much as I can. I don't know how to start exactly."

"I suggest taking it chronologically. Describe what first aroused suspicion and work from there."

She stiffened, so he slid out to let her up. She gathered her stuff unceremoniously and jammed everything but the laptop into her bag. "I'll see you tomorrow morning, I suppose."

"It's Saturday, but that probably won't stop us. Sure."

With a minimum of pleasantries she made her exit out into the cooling evening air. Jack noted she was driving the GSA car Durwin Rice usually used. Women. He was glad he wasn't dating. He hated having to deal with moodiness, and Ev was one of the moodiest.

Not that he'd ever date Ev anyway.

17
Fire

Jack left the door open with only the screen door closed and opened all the windows. He much preferred natural air to air conditioning, and it was getting very comfortable outside. He hadn't realized Evelyn Brant wore perfume. The slightest hint of it still lingered in his kitchen, minutes after she had left. Maxx leaped up and barked. Durwin Rice, encased like sausage in one of those neon-colored stretch-fabric cycling outfits, doffed his bike helmet and stepped up on the cement block.

Jack kept the screen door closed. "I see those file folders in your hand, Rice. If I let you in, you'll give them to me and expect me to read them."

"Have a heart. You're looking at a man who needs a beer."

Jack swung the door open. "Wrong place for a beer, but I've got orange juice, tropical punch, and an occasional Pepsi."

Rice padded in in his dainty cycling shoes. "One of each." He flopped in the kitchenette booth. "Make that two." He laid the stack of file folders under the window.

Jack popped Rice a Pepsi because that was quickest. He plunked the can by Rice's elbow as the chief ranger pulled off his leather cycling gloves. "Evelyn Brant has your car, so you're reduced to a bicycle."

"Exercise keeps an old man young, Prester." He gestured toward the pile of file folders. "For your spare time."

"Right. When I'm not out exercising." Jack poured a tall tumbler of orange juice, set it beside Rice's Pepsi, and uncorked himself a Pepsi. He settled into the booth across from Rice. "If exercise makes you young, you'll be in diapers in another three days. Your face is the color of a giant, oxygen-rich corpuscle."

Rice stared a moment and burst into belly-laughter. He swilled Pepsi like it was more a key to youth even than exercise.

Jack leafed briefly through the folders. Forms, reports, supplementals. Buried somewhere in this material was the answer to who killed George Gibbs. Or maybe it wasn't. Either way, Jack faced a lot of reading, of analyzing, with no guarantee of fruit.

Rice was looking at him oddly, almost surreptitiously. "You're thirty-four, right? Hal's pals start at—what? GS-12?"

"Us field folk do, yeah. I think that's about where we'll stay too. Doubt there'll be much advancement for investigators."

"Any idea where you want to go from here, careerwise? Small area superintendency? Something like that?"

"Haven't thought about it. If Hal's pals flies, and our success here may determine that, I wouldn't want to go anywhere else. The whole program depends on a couple big early successes."

"That's quite a load on you and Evelyn."

Did Ev fully realize the importance of clearing these cases? Jack rather doubted it. She didn't seem exceptionally eager.

Rice drained his Pepsi and started on his orange juice, so Jack poured him a glass of tropical punch and got him out another can of pop. He stretched out in his booth seat. His ribs hurt.

Rice sat in silent thought a few moments. "So you

164

two aren't an item. But you just happened to notice she's driving my GSA car. Pretty observant." He cast a sidelong glance at Jack.

"Us detectives are trained to observe. I do that with horses too. Notice what people are riding." Jack studied his own can of pop. "I'm an investigator, but not a private investigator. And I'm not really with a specific agency, so I kind of think of myself as a public investigator." He smiled. "A public eye."

"A new breed." Rice wagged his head. "The Park Service has changed. When I first came in, rangers didn't wear guns. Didn't carry mace or anything. We mostly helped little old ladies in hiking boots find the right trail. Find lost kids. Chase bears out of the campgrounds. Not much law enforcement. Now look."

"That's what Dad says. He really misses the old days."

Rice nodded. His voice turned a little misty. "I don't know your dad, but I know of him. I know he pioneered a lot of the soft-sell law enforcement techniques Leighton's pushing here. He wrote the book on low-profile, high-impact drug enforcement. Way ahead of all the others in the parks."

"And that has always surprised Mom and me, because he's constantly late for things. Yeah, I guess he's a legend of sorts." Jack's admiration and pride in his dad burned anew.

Rice sighed. "I envy him. He made a mark."

Jack watched the man's profile a few moments. "There's making marks, and there's maintaining marks. Maintaining law enforcement is just as important as being a legend, and it's harder to do—to hang in with the grind day after day. That's Dad's words, not mine, though I agree."

"Guess so. Still, I wish I'd go out as a legend and not as a maintenance man." Rice snorted. "Just another peon in the field."

What should he say? Jack met the attitude often, al-

165

though not usually expressed quite this eloquently. Men who burn out on the day-to-day drudgery and paperwork. Men who see dreams of advancement fade as they get stuck in some out-of-the-way job. Men who watch promotions for which they qualify go to people they consider less qualified. Men who have seen the Park Service evolve from a woodsy, casual, Boy-Scout agency to a high-tech paperwork jungle with law enforcement specialists, environmental specialists, budget specialists, interpretive specialists, and hardly any old-style rangers. The man beside him was all of those men. Someday Jack, too, would be the old warrior yearning for the simplicity of the past.

Rice drained the orange juice but didn't touch the tropical punch. He made lighter, more casual conversation for a while, donned his cycling gloves and helmet, climbed back on his bike, and began the grinding ride up the hill to his house.

Jack cleaned up his kitchen for the first time in twenty-four hours and settled in for four hours of reading Rice's reports and supplementals. What did law enforcement do before the invention of paper? Just go out, bop the miscreant on the noggin with your club, and go home. Clear and simple. The main thrust of progress, obviously, was complication. He turned Maxx out for one last encounter with nature, called him back in, and latched the screen. He went to bed at eleven.

Was that glass breaking? Now what? Maxx was barking.

"Quiet, mutt!"

The barking escalated.

"Maxx, what—" He rolled over as the dog slammed against his bed, barking like the last trumpet call.

The orange night-light glowed in the hallway.

Except that Jack didn't have a night-light.

The light flared brighter.

Jack leaped from the bed and very nearly tripped

166

over his frantic dog. He slammed the bedroom door even as a gust of flame came whipping down the hall toward him.

The only door, the only way out, lay on the other side of the fire.

The window.

It was a single small, aluminum-frame jalousie window, shoulder high.

Jack yanked a drawer out of the little chest. He swung it at the window, spraying undershorts and socks through the darkness. It bounced off the jalousie panes. He swung it again. The window gave. The drawer stuck in the aluminum. Jack yanked it back and pounded on the window opening, breaking the glass away. The drawer came apart completely.

Despite the closed door, smoke rapidly filled the tiny room.

Jack grabbed Maxx by the scruff and hooked his free hand under the dog's belly. He shoved Maxx through the blue-black hole into the blackness. The dog yelped in pain and disappeared out the window.

The flimsy, hollow door burst into flame. Incredible heat swirled in on the back draft, but no light. Jack thrust his head and arms out the window, angling his body, writhing and twisting, to wedge his shoulders through. Jagged glass or aluminum—who knew which?—raked his right shoulder and sliced down the length of his back as he shoved himself out into the cool night air like toothpaste from a tube. He didn't fit in this window, but that wasn't going to stop him from leaving through it.

Searing heat swirled against his legs. He braced his palms on the trailer's exterior aluminum skin and shoved. He tucked his head barely in time and landed *splat* on his back. The fall stunned him, taking his breath away. He couldn't move, couldn't breathe, couldn't gather his wits.

Maxx, bless him, grabbed Jack's wrist in his mouth and started dragging. Were the dog any stronger he could

167

have towed the trailer off. He turned Jack 180 degrees, pivoting him in the dirt. Jack managed to roll to his stomach. Maxx kept pulling.

"Gimme my hand back!" Jack tried to say it, but smoke in his lungs wouldn't let him speak. It came out as a few feeble wheezes and a cough. Jack squirmed, and the dog tugged, and together the two of them eventually ended up fifteen or twenty feet away.

The fire siren on the roof of the maintenance shed growled a glissade up the scale to a minute-long tenor howl. Maxx dropped Jack's wrist and howled back.

With four limbs to work with, Jack pulled himself to his knees and crawled drunkenly to that chaise longue under the cottonwood, still woozy. He flopped beside it, too stunned to climb up.

A set of headlights came zooming down the hill from the residences. Here came another, and another. At least no one had to tell the volunteer firemen where the fire was.

The trailer's aluminum siding glowed cherry red like a cheap wood stove, the fire crackling in the windows. The metal roof sheets popped and buckled and curled. Ventilated, the fire roared straight up in an earnest effort to singe angelic marshmallows.

The fire pumper pulled in beyond the trailer, its big white floods brilliant in the night. Moments later a spray of water arched up over the trailer and hit the cottonwood above Jack's head. Water cascaded down on him. Of course they wouldn't try to save the trailer. They wetted down the nearby trailer and trees to keep them from catching. The Silverfish was way past saving.

Jack stood up, shaky. Then he dropped to his knees and grabbed the chaise longue as he tossed his sandwich and bean soup in the cool dirt. He lay there a few minutes while artificial rain pelted him. He was headed back toward his feet again when strong hands gripped him and hauled him off, stumbling, into the night.

Eager-beaver Aubray White talked fast and excitedly. "Here you go. This lounge right here. It's safe, this distance. Here—sit." Aubray held one side, and a pretty young woman held Jack's other arm in a grip that would have piloted King Kong away from New York.

Jack flopped into the lounge. Aubray wore his fire turnouts, yellow reflector stripes on the black coat and pants, his white helmet glowing in the light of the distant fire. Jack wore the undershorts that were his usual warm-weather night attire. He grabbed Aubray's helmet off his head and dropped it down into his lap, a fig leaf to cover Adam's wet shorts with.

Aubray and the young woman hovered close, looking anxious. "I'm an EMT," the woman said. "Where were you burned?"

"Wasn't. Give me a minute. Fell. Knocked the wind out."

Maxx shoved his huge, hard, velvet-upholstered head up against Jack's arm. Jack rubbed it. Rubbing the dog's skull set Maxx's tongue in motion, as always. He started licking furiously up Jack's wrist and arm. He snuffled and snorted noisily.

"Call me if you need me." Aubray spoke to the woman rather than Jack. He disappeared back toward the fire.

She wrapped firm, slim fingers around Jack's wrist, taking a pulse obviously. Jack finally gathered enough air for a complete sentence. "Can I have your jacket?"

"Of course!" The woman peeled out of her windbreaker instantly. "You're wet—you must be freezing."

"Nope." Jack tossed the helmet aside and used the windbreaker to cover up with. It served a lot better than that brainbasket. Why should he feel so self-conscious? These shorts concealed more than most bathing suits. Funny what culture does to modesty.

She started laughing suddenly. "Aubray will bring the jump kit over pretty soon, and we'll get a BP and all that. I'm not too worried. You're looking better every second. I'm Diane, Aubray's wife. We live in this trailer right here. I'll go get you a blanket and whatever in a minute. I want to watch you a while yet though. Make sure you don't zonk out."

Her speech was crisp. Aubray might be a good old Southern boy, but he had married a Yankee. What must the family think?

She reached out and wrapped both hands around Jack's head, her fingers gently probing. "Tell me if you feel any pain, discomfort, tingling—anything unusual, OK?" She was starting a secondary survey, a careful inch-by-inch check for broken bones and other injuries.

Jack definitely did not want this pretty lady probing every inch. "What's Aubray's pants size?"

"Thirty thirty-four."

"That'll do. If I promise not to zonk, and faithfully recite all my injuries for you without a secondary, will you bring me a pair of something to wear in public? Any old jeans will do. And a shirt maybe."

She looked off toward the fire, then at Jack. She watched his eyes for a count of ten. "Sure." She stood erect and ran off. He heard the trailer door slam.

She returned in moments with clean, folded jeans and a flannel shirt. That rake down his back still oozed sticky blood. It burned. His cracked ribs ached anew. And all the rest of his ribs objected strenuously to having been dumped into the dirt from six feet off the ground. He stood up despite all the anatomical objections.

Were she a polite lady she would have turned her back. But EMTs are trained to be rude. It's part of the basic instruction course, one of the things you learn first. He slipped into the pants while she steadied him with a strong hand. Good thing—he was still too tipsy to be standing one-legged like a flamingo. She helped him with the shirt and in the process saw his back. She sucked in air and let fly with an expletive.

Obviously it must look worse than it was.

"Just a scratch, ma'am." Jack pulled the shirt over his shoulders. "I heard that line in about two hundred Western movies when I was growing up, but I've hardly ever had a chance to use it in casual conversation. That and 'All right, men, let's ride.' If it wasn't Randolph Scott getting scratched it was Gary Cooper. Or Red Ryder. More falooting scratching than Maxx in flea season."

"You're trying to create a diversion, and it's not working. Let's go in the house. I think a doctor's going to have to suture you up."

"Suture a scratch? Don't be silly. Suturing is what you do to a turkey you're roasting, so it doesn't have to sit in the oven cross-legged." He tucked in his shirttail. His back burned worse than jalapeno juice in your eyes. "Let's go see what's going on. Maxx, heel." He headed off toward the fire truck.

Mrs. White bleated a variety of reasons why he should sit down, but he kept walking, so she fell in beside.

Everyone in the residence area, young and old, stood about on the perimeter watching, a ring of spectators. A guy in T-shirt and cutoffs was putting up a tape to keep the gawkers at bay. Rice stood by the pumper directing the fire fighters—quite capably too.

Jack did a slow turn, trying to memorize faces present, trying to think of who, that he knew, was not present.

From the darkness, from among the onlookers, Ev popped out. She hopped the tape and came running. She latched onto his arm, and her eyes glistened in the harsh lights. "Thank God! I saw the trailer and—" She shuddered. "Are you all right?"

Jack was saying yes when Mrs. White said, "No. The turkey doesn't think he needs trussing."

"What?"

A sudden thought hit him. Jack looked around anxiously. "Where'd my truck go?"

Aubray White crossed to him, smiling. "We rolled it back a hundred feet, get it out of the way. Nice finish on it—we didn't want to see it blister. And thanks for leaving the window open. Saved us having to break it to get in."

"Anytime."

The Silverfish smoldered. It smoked. Gray steam rolled off it, for they were training the water from their tanker onto the trailer itself now. The excitement was about done. The fire had run out of food. Both tires had popped and burned, and the trailer sat forlornly on its rims, with a couple of smoldering piles of ash on the ground beneath where the floor burned through. Licks of fire consumed the last few pitiful remnants of fuel, little hot spots here and there in the dark mess. It stank to heaven.

Aubray stared numbly at the black pile. "Did you hear anything? Smell anything? See anything?"

"None of the above. Maxx woke me."

Diane White crowed, "Your dog saved your life!"

Jack wagged his head. It rang. "Altruism is not Maxx's long suit. With fire blocking the only exit, he needed me to save his black hide." He frowned. "Wait a minute. There was a smoke detector in the hall across from the bathroom. It didn't go off."

"Fire reached it too quickly, probably."

"It surely would have beeped a couple times at least, and I would have heard it. I'm certain it didn't."

Ev piped up, "That soup! It boiled over and stuck to the burner. That should have triggered the smoke alarm."

"You're right." Jack nodded. "'Dinner's ready when the smoke alarm sounds.' I saw that cross-stitched in a wall hanging once."

White shook his head. "We change all the batteries every January first."

Emery Leighton and his wife broke the fire line, and no one stopped them. Superintendents have perks.

Myrtle Leighton stepped in beside Jack and gaped, entranced, at the blackened wreck. "This is horrible!"

"Yeah." Aubray nodded. "He's going to have to buy a new toothbrush."

18

Winds of War

This was, essentially, Jack's first assignment as one of Hal's pals. He could anticipate maybe half a dozen such assignments a year, the rest of the time being devoted to paperwork and collaboration with various prosecutors, assuming he managed to actually catch some perps. So far just on this one case he had a swollen eye, a stiff neck, one each of lacerations and contusions on his face, a dandy of a laceration down his back, and two cracked ribs. Multiply that by six, and he'd find himself in a nursing home by Christmas.

As he pulled up to Ev's apartment, she came out the door and slammed it closed behind her. She opened the passenger door and just stood there. "Are you sure you won't let me drive?"

"I'm fine. Really."

Somewhat dubiously, she climbed in and hauled her seat belt down. He started around the loop and down the hill, beneath the rustling cottonwoods of Cow Creek. The rambling ranch style homes were quiet this morning, sprawled in earth tones beneath the trees, apparently uninhabited.

She glanced at him. "Durwin's right. You really have

to get that looked at. I'm glad you're being sensible about this."

"You're implying that I'm not always sensible about things."

"You are hardly ever sensible about anything."

"Thanks a bunch. You're just sore because my cholesterol count is lower than yours and you eat Weed-and-Feed."

"Weed-and-Feed is a lawn fertilizer!"

"Weed-and-Feed is bread with whole wheat, various seeds, probably some sawdust for the fiber, and weird grains."

"I eat healthful foods, if that's what you mean."

"Life is too short to eat health food."

This Saturday morn was not a real great day in the making. Jack felt irritable, and Ev acted irritable, and two irritables add up to people who may gouge each other's eyes out eventually.

Rice wanted to prosecute the trailer fire as an arson for sure and an attempted murder probably. To make the arson charge worth anything there had to be injuries, and a doctor had to verify them. Being the only one injured in that fire, Jack was "it." He didn't mind the semiretired chap in Beatty, but he hated driving clear out there for a lousy doctor appointment.

And why did Rice send Ev along? Driver? Gadfly? Nuisance? Get her out of the office? At Jack's behest she had copied just about everything in the main computer memory over to floppies. If Rice altered anything in her absence, they'd know it.

But was it Rice? And if so, why?

Jack turned aside into the trailer court. Ev scowled at him.

"I'm hoping the trailer's cooled off enough to dig around a little."

"You're going to be late for your appointment."

"Won't take long. Either it's there or it's not."

174

Aubray White was guarding, so to speak. He had dragged his chaise longue under the cottonwood near the smoldering trailer ruin. Sprawling at contented ease, he waved as Jack pulled up.

Jack slid out and pulled his crowbar from under the seat. "When you works, you works hard."

White hopped to his feet grinning and strode out into the sun. "Duty calls."

"So that was duty. I thought it was a coyote with kidney stones." Jack stepped over the police tape and walked over to the mess that had once been his home sweet home. The burned tires stank. The ashes and debris stank —different kinds of stinks.

Jack measured two paces from the cement block toward what would be the bedroom. The smoke detector would be about—right there. Jack stuck his crowbar in a split in the aluminum sidewall and pried. The aluminum groaned and popped. White licked his lips. "Uh, the fire marshal said it shouldn't be disturbed until he gets here."

"When does he expect to get here?"

"Tomorrow afternoon."

"Did you take pictures?"

"All angles. Yep."

"The fire marshal should be more prompt." Jack widened the split and tried again.

"Whatcha digging for?" White hung close by his elbow, guarding, no doubt.

"Smoke alarm."

It took them ten minutes to find it. The plastic had burned away completely. All that was left was a tiny palmful of scorched electronic junk and a glob of hard black plastic residue. Heads together with White, Jack poked at the remains in his hand.

White grunted knowingly. "You can still recognize the connectors. But no battery."

Ev came strolling over.

Jack straightened and looked at White. "I wish the

175

amateurs would stay out of these trades. If you're going to enter a line of work, get the proper training."

"Why do you say that?" Ev frowned at the crisp remains.

"The battery was removed by an arsonist who knows nothing about fire investigations. A pro would remove one of the terminal connections and leave the battery in, so the investigators poking through the ruins later—that's us—would see the battery and entertain some doubt that maybe it simply hadn't been connected properly. Carelessness. But outright removal tells the whole world 'malice aforethought.'"

Aubray nodded. "Rice and Bob Hodges looked around this morning enough to establish that it was arson. The accelerant smells like kerosene, and a cardboard box of crumpled paper inside the door. But they didn't look at the smoke alarm angle."

Jack dumped his palmful into White's palm. "My warden here is getting antsy. She's afraid I'll be late for an appointment. I'd like to tag along when the fire marshal does his thing—if he ever shows up."

"You'll be the first to know."

Jack offered good-byes and climbed back into his truck. His back hurt, but not like fire anymore.

Ev hopped in beside. "Arson. You said that trap with the gas explosion wasn't meant to kill. I'd say it was."

"You're probably right." He started the truck forward.

There sat the heavy road equipment in the maintenance yard, partially obscured by the long sheds.

"That's it!" Jack slammed on the brakes.

"What's it?" Ev's voice sounded instantly suspicious.

Jack drove not to the road but up into the maintenance yard. Dirty, greasy, looking forlorn, a dozen pieces of heavy equipment stood in rows. The windowless, dark brown sheds on either side sat silent, looking just as forlorn. Even when maintenance people are about, and on

Saturday they rarely are, these places look abandoned. Today was totally empty. The big bay doors, evenly spaced along the fronts, were all tightly closed.

Jack stopped his rig behind a dump truck. "Put it in first and drive to that number four bay and knock on the door. OK?"

"No, it's not OK! What's going on?"

"Testing a theory." He hopped out and motioned Maxx to heel. Man and dog dog-trotted around behind the nearest shed as Ev noisily explored his transmission, hunting first.

By the time she found it Jack was hustling along the back side of the old shed, seeking the exit door that once upon a time led to the outhouse. Exterior facilities had long since been replaced by genuine flush fixtures ("Gorsh, Reuben, hit's even indoors!"), but the old way out was still there. Was it locked from the inside or the outside?

Outside! Hah! Carefully, as quickly as he could, Jack tried masters until one fit. The sun bounced off the rough shed side, its heat radiated off the dark wood. It felt like inside a toaster. Quietly he turned the knob. He could hear Ev diligently pounding on the bay door.

He wasn't going to be able to open this door silently. He could not enter the bay undetected anyway, for opening the door would let bushels of bright sunlight into what should be near total darkness. But he'd try.

Cautiously he lifted as he shoved the door in a bit. Ev was knocking louder. He slipped, sidling, into the darkness, leaving Maxx sitting outside, and closed the door behind him.

Only it wasn't dark in here. The overhead fluorescent lights were all on, merrily creating their substitute sunlight. Every head was turned toward the bay door on which Ev was pounding, and there had to be over a hundred heads present, all attached to husky ranger types. Oh, true, they were dressed in civilian jeans and T-shirts with statements

("I survived the AlCan Highway"; "Life is too short to drink cheap beer"; "RangerFest 92—Yellowstone"), but a ranger is a ranger, identifiable from a mile off.

One of the hundred guys nearest this door wheeled. "Hey!"

All one hundred heads flipped around in this direction.

Jack motioned toward the far bay door. "Would somebody over there let Ev in, please?"

No one moved. "Who are you?" the guy blurted.

"Clue number one. I'm not wearing black leather." If they wouldn't get the door, Jack would. He threaded among them toward the bay door. He reached for the handle, but blocking his way stood a big, burly guy who could give Hippo a ride for his money on any teeter-totter.

"Nobody opens the overhead doors," the mountain snarled. "Rice's orders."

"Ev?" Jack called. "Go around back to a small unlocked door and come in that way. Bring Maxx in with you."

"What's going on, Jack?" she shouted.

"I'm lining you up a date for tonight. It's Saturday, you know." He lowered his voice slightly and turned to the roomful. "OK, guys. She's gorgeous, and she's not spoken for. Bidding opens at a hundred bucks. Who's first?"

The big man frowned. "You aren't normal."

"Nobody in the Park Service is." Jack dug into his pocket. "I'd love to show you my ID, but it burned up last night. Here's a badge I borrowed from Aubray White. Will that do?"

The man's eyes went wide. "You were in that trailer fire?"

"Not for long. So Rice is planning a big surprise party for the bikers. You're still outnumbered eight to one, you know."

The guy grinned wickedly. "Do we look worried?"

"Neither did Custer." Jack extended his hand. "Jack Prester at your service."

178

"I heard about you. Walker Tayes." The man shook with a grip that could crush walnuts. "Hal Edmond's special task force."

"'Task force' is such an ugly word. We like to think of ourselves as 'Hal's noble experiment.'"

"Jack?" A familiar voice called from twenty feet away. Here came Ernesto Morales, grinning. Jack and Ernie had gone through ranger training together, the dual bane of the training center director's existence. Good times with Ernie, good memories.

Jack grabbed Ernie's extended hand and wrapped around him in a one-armed hug. Ernie, unfortunately, hugged too. Jack's ribs and back registered a stabbing protest. Jack pretended to smile. "How's it going?"

"District Ranger at Mesa Verde, since June." In the five years since Jack had last seen him, Ernie had put on maybe twenty pounds, all within five inches of his belt.

"Great! What's Craig up to?"

"Still at Zion."

The crowd of rangers parted silently, like the Red Sea before Moses. Ev appeared, walking through the gap, and beside her Maxx heeled as if he were an obedient cop dog.

She stared, puzzled, all around. The light came on. "You're all rangers!" Her doe eyes flicked to Jack, startled. "Jack?"

Her head snapped around to look at Walker Tayes. The elfin flyaway hair followed belatedly. "It's going to be a war! If all you go out there, it's—" She took a deep breath and frowned at Jack. "How did you know they were here? Did Durwin tell you?"

"All the machinery that's supposed to be inside here is standing out in the yard. I was wondering why the buildings should be emptied." Jack turned to Tayes. "She's right. It's going to be a war. I hope you guys have troop transports and army tanks. You're going to need more than flak jackets if the bikers are really feeling cranky. And most

179

of them have hangovers by now. The outlook isn't good."

Ernie looked from Jack to Ev to Jack. "They brought us in last night in a grocery distributor's semi. We haven't had a chance to see anything yet. What's out there?"

"Eight hundred antisocial misfits roaring down memory lane on V-Twin Fat Boys."

"Eight hundred!" Ernie snarled at Tayes, "Rice said three hundred, maybe three hundred fifty."

"Then that's what it is out there." Tayes snarled in turn at Jack. The whole place was getting kind of snarly. "What are you up to, Prester?"

Jack moved in closer to the bruiser. "Ernie and I go way back. Seasonals, training center together. I'd hate to see Ernie cash in just because Rice can't count straight."

Ernie picked it up. "Yeah. I don't mind this gig, but I want to know what I'm up against."

Jack spoke to Ernie, but he raised his voice enough to fill the shed. "You're up against guys who have been making their living as methamphetamine salesfolk for lo these many years, and they know which end of the AK-47 to point toward the cops. And a flock of Nam vets who never quite fit in, and are getting kind of used to being hated now, and have been polishing their attitude for maybe twenty-five years. These aren't college kids on Easter week at the beach, folks."

"Firepower?"

"I don't know. They're keeping it under the camp tarp for now. Knives and such, but so far they're only entertaining each other. You show them a line of solid gray-and-green, you're going to see some heavy artillery."

"You don't know that, Prester. You admit you haven't seen anything." Tayes was past snarling and into yelling.

"Hey!" someone interrupted. "Rice said keep it down."

"Just one thing—" Ernie moved in and lowered his voice.

"What?" Jack watched the pudgy Morales cheeks, big globs, move around on Ernie's face.

180

"This chick here." Ernie turned to Ev. "He pegged the 'gorgeous' right on. You really open for a date tonight?"

She gaped at Jack. Her mouth formed the word, *What?* but her voice didn't do anything.

Jack grabbed her elbow. "Tell you what, Ern. If I decide to stay home and watch videos, she's all yours."

"How come you always get first choice?" Ernie whined.

"Because Mommy always liked me best." Jack got serious. "These guys are here for a few days, and then they'll be gone. A week's worth of bikers is nothing to die for. Walk carefully."

One of Rice's army, a kid who had to be a decade younger than Jack, spoke up. "Hey, it doesn't matter how many are out there. There's a bunch at Wildrose, a bunch at Texas Spring, another bunch up the way at Mesquite Spring. We mop them up in little groups."

"Starting when?"

"Tonight after dark."

"Jack?" Ev's voice took on an edge of unmistakable terror.

"What?" Ernie was picking up the concern.

"Big rally tonight at dark. They'll all be in one place at the same time." Jack turned to Tayes. "Start your mop-up tomorrow morning. They'll be soft then—and divided back up."

"I take orders from Rice."

"Domino Pizza takes orders. God gave you a brain. Use it." He grimaced to Ev. "Let's go talk to Uncle Durwin."

She nodded and turned away.

Jack started after her, back through the crowd, but Tayes grabbed his arm. It was Maxx's turn to snarl.

"Maxx, sit. Down." Jack stopped, lest Maxx think he was being attacked and take out Tayes.

"Keep out of this, Prester." Menace dripped in Tayes's voice. "This is a police matter unrelated to your investigation. You got no jurisdiction and no business with it."

181

"I think the classic line is 'Unhand me, you cad.'"
He waited.

Tayes let go and stepped back.

Silently Jack walked Ev to the back door, and silently the roomful of horse marines watched them go. Silently he and Ev stepped into blazing brilliance. He closed the door behind him.

Ev stared unseeing out across the bare hillsides. "Durwin didn't tell them. They don't know." She wagged her head. "When I think about it, I can see you're right. If they must go after bikers, go after them tomorrow morning when they're in their camps and not expecting it. Why is Durwin trying to start a war?"

"I don't know."

It was the truth. Jack didn't know. But he had a couple of ideas. Rice could be seeking legendary status. He'd talked about that. It would be a negative legend, more Charles Manson than Mother Theresa, but any legend might be better than no legend at all, in his mind. Or—and this thought intrigued Jack more and more as he pondered it—could Rice be setting up a diversion?

An all-out war with the bikers would grab major media attention, not to mention the eye and mind of the powers that be in region and the Washington office. It would be the kind of world-class diversion needed to deflect scrutiny away from the embezzlements and, most of all, the Gibbs murder. Gibbs would become, at best, a side issue in the shadow of the big war between the rednecks and the bikers. History books for years after would mention the biker war just as they mention Kent State and sometimes even that sunny afternoon when mounted park rangers, armed with ax handles, cleared the Yosemite Valley of hippies. But Gibbs? Who's he? Who cares?

They walked around the building to the front of number four bay, each wrapped in thought. Jack motioned Maxx into his cage and climbed into the truck.

"Jack?" Ev handed him the keys and pulled her seat belt down. "We can't talk to Durwin now. He left. He thinks he'll be back this afternoon. But we have to then." Her voice shook. "Someone's going to get hurt."

19

Amateurs

War. Jack's father had been in on that fracas in Yosemite meadow between rangers and hippies. It had rattled him for years afterward, and no one had died in that skirmish. This was different. You don't take on Hell's Angels without a few lives lost. Jack tried to put it out of his mind. He couldn't.

What would Jesus do in this situation? Something surprising, no doubt.

Ev sat beside him similarly wrapped in thought as they burned up the road toward Beatty—if fifty-five is burning up the road.

Ev broke the silence. "Jack? Why do you put the dog in his cage and then hook the cage door open? What if he jumps out?"

"That's the idea. If I put this truck over a cliff or something, I don't want him trapped in the wreck."

"Mm. Remember when you made that comment about bathrooms to Aubray White? When he was writing up the explosion?"

"No. Not really."

"I told him to look in my closet, and you said I do some of my best investigation in bathrooms. Referring to Leightons' bathrooms. It meant nothing to him, but it

184

meant something secret and special to me. Does everything you say mean something special to someone, and everything you do have a reason?"

"Not always. But I do try to function on a basis of reason."

"Cold and calculating. No place for emotion, right?"

"Don't I wish."

Marcia.

The silence returned, sullied only by the road roar always present inside a moving Dodge Ram.

They turned east and headed up the hill toward Beatty.

"Ever hear of Rhyolite?" he asked.

"What's Rhyolite?" she answered.

"We'll stop on the way back, and you can see firsthand." He imagined what her response would be to the derelict old ghost town with its colorful characters who fed off the tourists. It would be interesting to compare her actual reactions to what he anticipated. How well did he really know her? Not well. Not well at all. She constantly surprised him.

A lone biker was riding toward them. Jack hit the horn and the brakes simultaneously. "There's Hippo!"

He backed up. Behind them the hog with the monstrous man pulled to the berm on the westbound side of the road. Jack backed parallel to the big bike, turned off his motor and hopped out. Behind him Ev protested bitterly about the folly of being late.

Maxx barked, but his heart wasn't in it. Hippo was not a Superior Human Being like Rice and Gladys and Myrtle and Point Man were, but he wasn't a stranger either.

Jack dug into his cooler and waved a can. "Pepsi?"

Hippo climbed off his still-rumbling rig. "All you got?"

"Take it or leave it."

He took it. "Anybody sees me drinking this wimp water, I'm dead." He swilled. "Not bad, though."

Jack offered Ev a Pepsi. She declined, scowling.

"You going to the rally tonight?" Hippo drained his

185

can and tossed it aside. It clanked and rattled down off the berm.

"Wouldn't miss it for the world." Jack's heart thumped. "Say, Hip, you guys ever think of just chilling out some and—"

Hippo wasn't listening because he hadn't finished talking. "Y'know, when it comes to smarts, your flat hat dweebs are really down a quart. You got maybe a dozen rangers in the park. Less. I thought you people with military creases in your shirts would put out more manpower, y'know? Us nasty old bikers ain't—"

A bike came roaring from the east. It slowed as it passed, and took off. In the biker's right hand was a pistol!

"That's him!" Jack tossed his own can aside, still half full. "That's that guy!" Same full-face helmet, same bike, same rider, at least as size went. This was the creep that shot at him and broke his windshield. Maybe even hit him at Chloride.

He could leap into his truck, start it, wheel it around, and take off, or he could hop on the hog, already running and aimed in the right direction, and go. He grabbed Hippo's machine and took off howling.

Behind him Hippo howled even louder.

The bike very nearly jumped right out from under him. He must not underestimate its brute power, or he'd be grinding up blacktop with his face.

The rider ahead ducked off onto a dirt road. Jack knew the road. It wound through the hills a couple of miles and down into Titus Canyon. It offered lots of places for a bike to whip aside and hide. Twice in half a mile the rider left the road, bounced a hundred yards across the rough ground and returned, not that the road was all that much smoother. Both times, Jack gained a little by staying on the track.

If something didn't happen soon they'd be down in the canyon. The rider made a stab at turning aside into the ghost town of Leadview, gave that up, and leaned into the wind.

186

In the midst of the chase, Jack caught himself admiring the perfectly honed machine beneath him. The thrill tickled him. Chasing homicidal nuts aside, riding a Harley was really living!

He needed this joker up ahead too. If it was one of Hippo's friends, and Jack could convince enough people that this was the guy involved in the drive-by shooting, they might be able to use the incident. Maybe they could even start mopping up bikers on the scanty premise that they were engaging in gang activities or—remote chance but worth a shot. Anything to avoid war.

They crested out on the range and started down a wide notch in the hills. Jack wasn't gaining much, but he wasn't losing ground. That would change soon. As the road became snakier, he'd fall behind. He had the power, but that other bike had the maneuverability. That other rider no doubt knew his bike well; Jack was a stranger to this road monster. If he didn't smash it into a wall he'd lay it down in a cactus. In the narrow, torturous canyon, this guy had the advantage. Out on the open road, Jack would have run him down in five minutes.

It dawned on Jack that this bike was too much for him. Had he bad-mouthed that amateur arsonist? He was a much less artful amateur, trying to ride this thing.

If Hippo were on this machine, he'd have that dude by now. Jack should have sent Hippo out instead of taking off like this. Yell, "Fetch!" and Hippo would have grabbed the guy by the scruff of the neck, shook him around a little, and brought him back. In many important regards, Hippo was very much like Maxx.

They were down in Titus Canyon now, for better or worse. The motorcycle roar echoed and bounced off the confining canyon walls. Vertical cliffs of solid stone rose a few hundred feet straight up on either side. Occasionally a shrub clung with fingery roots to some insignificant crack in the flat stone wall. Very occasionally. The sandy floor, once broad and open, narrowed down further and further the farther they went. Jack could see dried clumps of grass and weeds—flood debris—lodged in crevices and bushes twenty feet off the ground. When flash floods filled this canyon, they filled it.

At least, within the first twenty minutes of this insane chase, Jack remembered prayer. Only twenty minutes? He appealed for help, for safety, for clarity of thought.

And the thought that came most clearly was: *If some tourist is doodling along in this narrow canyon, we're all dead.* The tourist's car would have nowhere to go. Jack wouldn't hear the other rider collide up ahead. Neither biker would know anything was wrong until he came upon it, for the canyon twisted too tightly for anyone to see more than two hundred feet at most—too short a distance to brake or avoid disaster.

And the second thought that came: *God is in control.*

So far, so good. Jack brushed the wall on a tight turn and took off the right side-view mirror. But he was still up. The howling, echoing noise deafened him. Then dead ahead he saw what he feared most—a tourist. No, it wasn't! Four bikes had stopped in this narrow neck. They must have heard Jack and the other guy coming, because they were scrambling, shoving their bikes off to the side, their eyes bulging wide. Jack missed them. Barely.

Another half mile, God, and we're out of here! Help us! The canyon had narrowed to a twenty-foot-wide vertical slit in the world, over a hundred feet high. The motorcycles' roar, deafening under the best of circumstances, reverberated back and forth and up and down. Sparse weeds dotted the ninety degree angle between vertical wall and flat, sandy wash. An occasional scrub mesquite reached its brittle twigs out in a transparent attempt to claw Jack off his bike.

A quarter mile more, and they'd be out in the open. Once the mouth of this narrow canyon opened out onto the smooth, limitless slope of the bahada, Jack would have that buzzard. This machine would outrace anything on a relatively straight way.

The sky was opening up ahead. They were almost there.

God, no! Not now! Not at the very end, when we had it nailed! Dead ahead, a big white camper shell waddled in slow, casual motion, right smack in the canyon mouth.

The smaller bike whipped *Zip! Zip!* around the camper, skidded and kicked dust, and evened out onto the open road. The camper emerged from the encasing walls. No way Jack could maneuver like that. He leaned it aside, swept past inches from the camper's back left bumper, and bucketed out across the open bahada. Brush and gullies threatened to unhorse him. He'd lost the race; that guy would be long gone.

He concentrated on saving himself from an in-depth study of dirt. He vaguely heard horns blowing over by the road. He dared not look back. Finally he got the machine slowed. The hind wheel skidded around, turning him a hundred eighty degrees, he put one happy foot down on terra firma, and he was in control again.

Over on the road a quarter mile away, the camper had stopped, and just ahead of it was Jack's truck. Above the dull rumble of this bike he heard Maxx barking purposefully. Hippo had pursued with the truck, obviously. How many of those parked bikers festooned the far side-view mirror? Did his truck actually collide with the camper or simply scuff it in passing? What was happening over there? He saw nothing of the other biker. He kicked the machine into motion and almost dumped himself again.

He roared over to his truck, but not too swiftly. This stupid headlong race had left him with a new and healthy respect for the sheer number of horses propelling this hog. He killed the motor when he arrived at his front bumper, lest Hippo hop on his bike and run over Jack in anger.

Anger? Hippo sat by the side of the road with a grin as wide as the camper. Under him, his seat as it were, was the biker in the full-face helmet. Where was the bike? Jack had to look around awhile to spot it, a mangled tangle of spokes and metal fifty feet back down the road.

Ev stood beside the truck, looking very white and very frightened. One hand pressed against the fender and the other against her breastbone. She was taking such deep breaths she'd hyperventilate if she didn't watch out.

Hippo gestured toward his own machine. "You don't do too bad on that thing, y'know? Not too good, but not too bad."

"Took off your sideview mirror and scuffed your wax job a little." Jack dug the borrowed nylon porta-cuffs out of his back pocket.

"Same with your truck. Didn't need all them mirrors anyway."

"Only once in a while. I notice you failed to mention you took out my right headlight." Jack looped the slim nylon strap around the guy's wrists and snugged it with a yank.

"Taking this dude down. Had to nudge the bike a little."

"You have the right to remain silent . . ." The biker beneath Hippo knew the litany as well as Jack did, and it gave him a perverse pleasure to recite it now, line on line. Jack frisked him, a fast pat down. "Where's the gun he carries at the small of his back?"

Hippo gaped. "At the small of my back. You know this dude?"

"Yeah. The chief ranger." Jack stood erect, suddenly very weary. "Has to be. A lot of people knew where I was some of the time, but only Rice knew all of the time. Where I'd be and what roads I'd be traveling."

"Chief ranger, huh? Don't that go to show ya. No wonder your flathats are such poops when it comes to law enforcement." Casually, Hippo leaned over and pulled the helmet off.

Myrtle Leighton, even whiter than Ev and her eyebrows bright blue, moaned. "Get him off me!"

190

20

Jackstraws

It was quite a mob. There sat Emery Leighton looking confused, Myrtle Leighton looking both angry and terrified, Ev looking bewildered, Bob Hodges the law enforcement specialist looking grim, Hippo looking bemused, Maxx looking half asleep, Myrtle's lawyer looking like he was ready to hang somebody, an assistant lawyer of some sort looking superfluous, and Jack who was just looking. The room was stuffed.

Jack sat at the head of the table, so to speak, for this conference was pretty much his show. A mixed blessing, being the arresting officer. He'd never been in quite this position before. He'd have to proceed carefully, thoughtfully. On the table lay the helmet and Myrtle's .38 automatic, all neatly packaged in sealed evidence bags.

The lawyer, named Regent, was explaining California's rules of evidence. Jack was operating under the code of federal regulations, so he didn't listen. It made the lawyer think he was doing something constructive, and it gave Jack more time to think this through. Finding Myrtle under that helmet had thrown his theories for a loop. Or maybe it didn't after all. He had to rethink this, to work out the puzzle backwards from solution (Myrtle Leighton) to question (Did she kill George Gibbs?).

"So you see," Regent concluded, "not only was your action toward Mrs. Leighton without reasonable cause, you just set yourself up for a nice, hefty lawsuit."

"Tort claim," Jack emended.

"Civil. We're going for the gold. Lawsuit."

"Neither, actually. I assume you were talking to Mrs. Leighton on your car phone the whole two hours it took you to drive down here from Lone Pine."

"So?"

Jack leaned back, grateful that this soft, padded arm chair didn't bother his laceration too much, and made an A out of his fingers, tips together. "Mr. Regent, I believe I have some insight—" He paused and started over. "I have a good friend in Albuquerque, a criminal defense lawyer. Handles homicides almost exclusively. When he first told me he doesn't care when he takes a case whether his client is innocent or guilty, it surprised me. Then when I thought about it, it's logical. His job is to get the client the best deal—off the hook completely if possible. All he wants to know is what the charges are. That's what he's working with. The charges. His real job, he says, is to keep the prosecution honest by making them work for their conviction. If they have a good case, he can't do much. If they get sloppy, he can walk all over them. The hooker, you see, is that sloppy prosecution could get an innocent man convicted. So he keeps the judicial process well tuned, you might say."

Hodges blurted, "What a crock!"

Jack spread his hands and brought his fingertips back together. "He's slimy as a slug in mayonnaise, but he has an excellent point. If the prosecution puts together a solid case with sufficient evidence, everyone wins. If the evidence isn't there, the prosecution has no business asking for an indictment in the first place, because the guy just might be innocent."

Regent scowled. "What does that have to do with this?"

192

"It gave me a deeper appreciation for putting together a solid case. I just explained why I'm careful."

"Then you know you can't hold her. She did nothing wrong."

"Why did she run?"

"She didn't recognize you."

"She knows my truck and me, and she got a good look at both. She knew. And she had her gun—that gun—in hand." He pointed.

"You're grasping at straws, Prester. It's your word against hers. Miss Brant didn't notice a gun."

"I saw it," Hippo growled.

"You!" Regent leaned around to look at him. "Your word wouldn't convince a jury of diddly squat."

Hippo bristled instantly. "You saying I ain't—"

"Hippo!" Jack barked at him. "Where's your pride, man? You're trying to get a guy in a white shirt and a necktie to be nice to you. The image, Hip! That Pepsi was bad enough, but—"

Hippo's funk disappeared as quickly as it had come. He cackled and sat back.

Jack pulled the other evidence bag, the small one, out of the breast pocket of his borrowed shirt. He tossed it onto the table beside the gun. "I really hate patching my upholstery with duct tape, but the vinyl repair wasn't open in Ridgecrest."

Regent scowled. "What's that?"

"The slug we dug out of the seat back in my truck, the one a passing biker put into it. Hodges did the incident report. If ballistics demonstrates that it—"

Regent glared at the law enforcement specialist. "If you wrote the incident report, why does he have the bullet?"

"I never saw it!" Hodges looked a whole lot grimmer.

At the same time Hippo was blurting, "A biker?" Then he nodded. "Oh, yeah. Tootsie here."

193

Jack explained, "A sheriff's deputy and I retrieved it in Ridgecrest while they were replacing my windshield. Fully documented. If ballistics demonstrates that it came from Mrs. Leighton's weapon, as I believe it will, proving her utter innocence is going to be quite a challenge for you. I'm sure you're up to it, but . . ." He let his voice trail off.

Aubray White knocked and entered without being invited. He carried an army surplus folding shovel, one of those little jobbies with a blade that folds backward against a short handle that you use to trench around your campsite on stormy nights.

"That's it!" Ev practically hopped up and stood on her chair. She pointed. "Jack, that's the tool!"

"What tool? What's going on here?" Regent was starting to look confused too.

Tall, lanky Aubray in his Smokey the Bear hat looked more like Smokey the Tack. He laid the shovel on the table.

Jack explained, "In the incident report, Evelyn stated that the person who knocked me off Chloride Cliff used a green tool she had never seen before. But then, she's never been camping."

"There's a million of those shovels in the world!" Hodges sat back scowling.

"True. I have one myself, behind the seat in my rig. Only I painted mine international orange, so I can see it better in near darkness. I got to thinking about a green tool. Garden tools are almost never green. The wooden ones are wood, and the plastic ones are bright colors so you don't easily lose them in all the greenery. Mechanics' tools are never green. Only old army surplus stuff is green. I talked to Aubray here awhile after we returned this morning with Mrs. Leighton, pursuing several topics. And I gave him some instructions. Among them, I asked him to search around the Leightons' for a folding shovel."

Regent's worried frown turned to a smug grin. "Search warrant?"

"Faxed from the courthouse in Independence. Yes. Specifically seeking tools."

The grin died beneath his returning scowl.

Jack hastened on. "I knew the person who attacked me at Chloride was known not just to me but to Maxx. You see, I sent Maxx out searching. He encountered the biker waiting behind the abandoned building. But that person had to be a friend in his eyes, because he did not report the find to me. He would assume a friend could legitimately be there. He continued his search. My first thought was Rice or a young lady who fed him bacon. That always earns his devout friendship instantly. He bribes like a corrupt ward heeler. But it could be any of the others in this room now except you, Mr. Regent. He would have reported you, a stranger, immediately. And possibly Aubray, though I doubt it."

"More straws. You're grasping at more straws."

"Aubray?" Jack gave the young ranger a wave of the hand.

White picked it up. "Following Dr. Prester's directions and remaining within the scope of the search warrant, Mel and I searched the Leighton garage. We found this shovel. We documented it and dusted it for prints. The most recent prints match those on file with Mrs. Leighton's concealed weapons permit. We also treated it with a product called Illumi-Chem."

Regent's eyes narrowed.

Bathed in the muted brilliance of the sunlit windows, the rusting shovel blade glowed faintly.

"What's that?" Myrtle's voice croaked.

"It's a product, Mrs. Leighton, that reveals the presence of blood," Jack replied. "Even if that blood is ostensibly washed off, enough remains to fluoresce. And to be tested. If the Vegas lab confirms that the blood thereon is mine, that's another nail in your coffin. I speak figuratively, of course." Jack shifted his attention suddenly to Emery. "You're dying of cancer, aren't you." He said it like a fact, not a question.

Myrtle gasped. "How did you know? Nobody knows! How—"

Regent yelled, "Shut up!"

Jack pressed on. "In March you and Myrtle flew to Mexico, ostensibly on vacation. She went off on the Copper Canyon tour alone, and you remained in Mexico City— I am presuming for experimental treatment for your cancer."

"You have absolutely no evidence of that!" Regent roared.

"I already have a researcher in the Washington office checking specific flights with Air Mexico. Find out just who flew where. You've been trying experimental medications not authorized or available in the United States. No insurance company covers experimental treatment. So to pay for them you embezzled funds here and there from the monument budget."

"This is preposterous!" Regent was fuming.

Jack shifted his gaze to Hodges. "Someone stumbled onto the embezzlement and was afraid Emery was botching the cover-ups—the spurious entries. So that someone moved some of them around a little, to what he thought were better hiding places. He or she."

"Of course!" Ev jumped in. "One of the entries, at least, was moved while the Leightons were in Mexico. That doesn't necessarily mean the person who moved the entry was the one who falsified it."

"Right. But when that person moved them, he made it worse, not better. They stuck out. If he—he or she—had left them where they were, in the resource management budget, for one example, Ev probably wouldn't have found them." He looked at Ev. "You have them documented?"

She nodded. "The drugs, what they are used for, and what they're not used for—tell Mr. Rice you can't catch burros with them, please, Mr. Hodges—with the dates they appeared, and their subsequent history."

"Anyone could have made false entries," Hodges protested.

196

Jack nodded. "True. That's the nature of these computer beasts. Anyone with any computer savvy at all can break into the records and alter the figures. We have Mrs. Leighton cold on the attempt on my life—the assault on the road and the attempted assault east of Titus Canyon. But that's a sideshow. The main event is the George Gibbs problem. You do defend homicide suspects, don't you, Mr. Regent?"

Regent never fluttered. "Now that, Prester, you don't have a bit of evidence for."

"Mrs. Leighton learned Emery had been embezzling. When George Gibbs discovered the chicanery, she silenced him. When Evelyn got close, Mrs. Leighton tried to scare her off with the explosion in the trailer and the incident at Chloride."

"That was your trailer, not hers. She's in the apartment," Hodges protested.

"At the time, you knew that, but Rice didn't. You forgot to tell him. He thought she was there. Therefore the trap was meant for her. And as a scare tactic, it's a dandy. Rice confides everything about this case to Mrs. Leighton, and surely to his boss, the superintendent, as well. Rice's misinformation was also hers—that is, the actual occupant of the trailer. Mrs. Leighton, you knew your husband was a suspect in the murders."

"But not a serious suspect."

"He's my favorite to wear the crown. You're a suspect also. You were not home Thursday when Gibbs was killed. I've confirmed that through your Avon lady. No alibi. You had three important things we look for, Mrs. Leighton: motive, means, and opportunity. Of course" —he shifted his gaze to Hodges— "so does the chief ranger. Did you get the medicines, Aubray?"

White looked a bit grim himself. "As instructed, yes sir." He set the sealed bag of medicine phials down beside the gun. "These are from the Leightons' bathroom and kitchen cabinets."

Jack pulled Ev's list out of his pocket. "This is a list Evelyn prepared independently. We compared the drugs on her list against the few drug names discovered among the spurious items in the park budget. We got enough matches to implicate you directly, Mr. Leighton."

Regent waved a finger. "You have a warrant for that?"

"Absolutely. I began this session by explaining my appreciation for an airtight case."

Ev turned to Myrtle. "Mrs. Leighton, I can see wanting to scare me off. I was the danger. I was the one who could find those entries. But why did you try to kill Jack?"

Myrtle Leighton's iron-hard eyes bore into Regent. "Barry, don't you dare say, 'Shut up,' to me again, do you hear?" The eyes shifted to Jack. "Tuesday morning I mistakenly thought she was with you when I threw those shots at you."

Regent exploded.

She skewered him with an icy stare. "You yell at me once more, and you're fired, do you understand? I know what I'm doing." The iron eyes returned to Jack. "But it didn't matter too much, as I thought about it later. I wanted you to back off too. This morning Durwin said you and Brant were going into Beatty so I rode out ahead, turned around at Rhyolite, and planned to pass you on the road again."

"And shoot again."

"To scare you."

"Why Chloride?"

"To frighten Brant. To get you both to back away." She sighed. "In hindsight, I see it was stupid. But I was desperate. Emery doesn't need this added stress. Not now."

"And the trailer?"

"I set the gas trap in the trailer Thursday too."

Jack had her on a roll. Could he trade up to some more information? "You removed the smoke alarm battery."

198

"I had to. I was afraid the butane would set it off."

White nodded slightly and tightened his lips down to a thin line. He wasn't enjoying this any more than Jack was.

Jack shifted to accommodate his back. "Why frighten us? Why not take Evelyn out permanently, like George Gibbs?"

"That's why I'm spilling this now. I'm telling you what I did. But I'm also telling you what I didn't do. I was prepared to give Gibbs a bad time if necessary. But I didn't have anything to do with his death."

Regent roared. "Great Caesar, Myrtle, quit trying to work your own plea bargain! You're botching it!"

She turned on him, and they screamed at each other like toms in a cat fight. Jack looked at Ev. She was nodding slowly.

"Stop it!" Emery's voice, usually very soft, pierced the hubbub like a flamethrower cuts through plastic wrap.

They stopped it.

"What do you plan to do, Prester?" he asked. "You wouldn't accuse her of the Gibbs murder if you didn't have clear evidence for it."

"She's demonstrated willingness to kill. Shooting at me on the road last Tuesday probably can't be prosecuted as attempted murder, but my death was certainly an expected consequence. She put all three of them within eighteen inches of me. What I plan to do, Mr. Leighton, is haul your wife into Independence on the assault charges. I'm assuming she can bail out immediately, but we have to go through the proper motions. In fact, Regent" —Jack turned to the lawyer— "you have to drive home to Lone Pine anyway. I'll release her to your custody, if you want to take her along and clear the legal hurdles. We'll send White here to get her when she can return."

"That's highly irregular."

"But not illegal. You're trustworthy. Mr. and Mrs. Leighton would never retain an attorney who would muddy up their case worse than it is. I'll send a deposition with you. When he goes in to fetch Mrs. Leighton home, White can bring along any other papers you and the judge think of."

They bandied that around a few minutes. If Regent actually took her in to Lone Pine, thence to Independence, she'd get her ears blistered for two hours about her gift of blab. Jack almost hated to send her with him.

But only almost. He did not want to spend the many hours it would take to haul her in himself. Besides, these borrowed pants were tight. They were cutting off circulation in his legs when he sat. And he had very nearly lost infinitely more than his clothes. No, not infinitely more. He was safe in eternity. But his temporal life. Finitely more. He was considerably down on the loquacious Mrs. Leighton.

Eventually White and Hodges left to do the paperwork. Emery and Myrtle went off to get some things together to take in to Independence. Regent tagged along, fulminating like a lawyer. His strange, superfluous assistant followed, mute.

Ev rubbed her face, both elbows on the table.

Hippo chuckled. "What a show! Wouldn'a missed it for all the fork oil in Texas, y'know? So that fake biker mama did Gibbs. Did she do Bo too?"

Jack shook his head. "We don't know she did Gibbs. I haven't been able to find a connection between her and Bo. She—"

Hippo tossed out a couple of stray expletives. "Bright boy like you should see that right away. She's tooling around on that silly little Yamaha of hers, y'know? Happens to bump into Bo, he propositions her, and she decides to try out a real man once, 'stead of that feeble wimp, y'know? From the looks of him, her tie-down's prob'ly dead meat. He couldn't even get a head of steam up when you accused his wife of murder, y'know?"

"A possibility."

"A certainty. Bo never forced himself on a lady, but no lady ever went without for want of being asked, y'know?"

"She insists she didn't kill Gibbs." Ev frowned at Jack.

"That means either of two things. One, she actually did not do it, and she's being forthright in her confession and denial. Two, she wants us to think she didn't, so she confesses to part, the less serious part, and protests her innocence of murder and attempted murder, feeling that we'll be more inclined to believe her since she came clean on the shootings."

"Do you think she did it?"

"I don't know. She is extremely protective of Emery. Emery could easily have done the first shooting and the gas trap. Maybe even Chloride. Perhaps she learned of his attempts and wanted to take the heat instead of him. So she copied his tactics this morning. If we didn't catch her this time, we'd catch her sooner or later and assume she had done all."

"I see." Ev sat up straight. "No, I don't. It's confusing."

"How'd you know she'd spill?" Hippo lurched to his feet.

"I didn't. But people love to talk about the crimes they commit. A matter of pride, I guess. I was firing ideas out into the clear blue, hoping she'd open up." Jack shifted again.

"They do, huh? So wouldn't she confess to the murders, then, if she really did them?"

"There's a limit to pride when your neck's on the line."

"Yeah, guess so. Want any more bikes wrecked?"

"Nah, I might want to drive after dark. Thanks, anyway."

Hippo chuckled. "Yeah, well, lemme know." He leered at Ev. "Want a ride home, little lady?"

"Uh, no—no, thank you."

"You sure? Hit'll be the ride of your life."

201

"Really. No."

Jack waved a warning finger at the burly biker. "Graze in my pasture, and it's to the abattoir you go. Got me?" It was a totally hollow threat. At full strength Jack was no match for this dude, and Jack's flag wasn't even flying at half mast.

With a few more choice epithets, Hippo cast aspersions on Jack's ancestry. "You just wrecked my record!"

"The pity of it. What record?"

Hippo cackled. "In eighth grade I hadda learn to spell *abattoir,* y'know? I bet the teacher I'd never use it or hear it again, so why? She didn't have no reason, y'know? But I was right. I didn't never hear it—till just now."

"How much'll it cost you?"

Hippo pondered the brown indoor-outdoor carpet a moment. "Probably be about thirty bucks now, allowing for inflation. See ya tonight." He turned to leave.

"Hey, Hip? You have lots of muscle with your dudes in leather. You can keep things cool, you know, if you set the tone. Hear what I'm saying?"

Hippo studied him a moment, as if at a loss for words. Jack knew better. Amid all that beard, the mouth spread into a knowing smirk. "Cool it? Think about it, Pine Pig. This reunion for old times' sake is only happening once. No reason to be polite. We don't intend to get invited back anyway, y'know?"

"And most of your guys haven't really had a first class party in years, right?"

"Right. By the time we're done reuniting, the L.A. riots are gonna look like tea time at the country club." And out he went, his bathtub-sized boots stomping, not the least cowed by Jack's show of bravado.

After the pandemonium, silence.

Aubray White came in and gathered up the evidence bags. "I'll be back from Vegas before they need me, right?"

"About two days before they need you, probably. This is Saturday. I doubt Mrs. Leighton can get released today yet, and the court doesn't do much on Sunday. But hustle anyway. Regent might be able to pull enough strings to spring her immediately. It's a small town."

White nodded.

"Tell me. I meant to ask you earlier and forgot. How does Son of Slim get around? Certainly not that miserable burro."

White smiled. "Naw. He drives a three-quarter-ton stakeside pickup less'n a year old. Four-by, spare wheel cover, KCs, the whole bit. Sticks the burro in back, goes wherever he thinks he'll make some money, stashes the truck, and saddles up."

"Then appears out of the sere and wrinkled hills as if by magic, a voice and a form from the past."

"Quaint, ain't?"

"Where does he keep the rig when he's home?"

"Parked by the back door of his cabin."

So the cabin Jack visited was not the cabin Son lived in. No pickup, no vehicle tracks. *Aha.* Had he stepped inside, Jack would have found a still, no doubt.

Aubray stared at the bagged gun in his hand, and the shovel. "Mr. Leighton's a great guy. Really great guy. This is hard."

"Yeah."

White left.

Ev propped her tousled head in a hand. "The lawyer's right, you know. You're grasping at straws."

"Sorta. Trying to shake something loose in this case."

"There's a poignancy here, in a way."

"Getting shot at is poignant?"

"The way everyone is so protective of everyone else. You could be right about Mrs. Leighton taking over her husband's tactics, so to speak. And Durwin is very protective of both of them. You can see it in the way he treats Mrs. Leighton, especially." She blushed a little. "I don't mean—I'm not suggesting there's something between them.

You know what I mean. Do you truly think she did it?"

Ev looked like she'd just finished an hour's scrimmage with the Denver Broncos. Riding full tilt down through Titus Canyon with Hippo at the wheel must knock ten years off one's life. It certainly takes a heavy toll of one's truck.

"I don't know. Not a glimmer. And unless you can bail me out with a few brilliant insights, I'm no closer to knowing the murderer now than I was five days ago."

21

It Isn't Easy Being on a Green

My college graduation class was four hundred and thirty-seven. Hey, I was impressed. In my whole high school, nine through twelve, there were only three hundred and fifty kids." Jack refilled Ev's glass from the two-liter bottle and sat back.

They perched on the rim of the patio fish pond, picnicking, so to speak, in the afternoon warmth.

Absently, Ev opened her package of Twinkies. "I don't know what's getting into me. I never eat this junk food."

"All food is provided by God, ultimately. Therefore no food is junk. Look on it as dessert."

"We haven't had lunch yet."

"Be honest. When you were a kid, didn't you always dream of getting dessert first, before the carrots? It's a dream come true."

She grimaced. "Wonderful, if you're six years old."

She might feel guilty about eating the stuff, but Maxx was just plain eager. He sat as close to her knee as he could get, his tail wagging.

Jack snapped his fingers and motioned Maxx away. It took two snaps to get the dog to move, such is the magnetic attraction of a Twinkie.

Jack continued. "Anyway, the college president wanted this big panoramic shot of the whole class, caps and gowns—the works. So he hired a guy with a pan camera. You line everyone up in a big semicircle, a ground row and three tiers as if you were a choir, and everyone stands still. The camera goes click at one side of the semicircle, and pans slowly across to the other side. The finished photo is one of those ten-inches-high-by-three-feet-long things."

Ev nodded. "They photographed my freshman class with one."

"Just the freshmen?"

"Twelve hundred in my high school senior class. We filled up the eight-thousand-seat colosseum when we graduated."

Jack wagged his head. "Charlie Begay and I were the first people in rows one and two on the east side. The camera started there, so we were the first photographed. Soon as it clicked and started to pan away, we ran around back and took positions at the far west end. Here came the camera, panned past us and quit."

Those humongous eyes were staring at him. "You didn't!"

"There we are forever, at both ends of the bleachers, like bookends. Charlie and I are not only recorded for posterity in the foyer of Old Main at Bethmont College, so are our evil twins. Charlie and I each had one. Photographic proof of them."

"You couldn't have been too popular with the president."

"Livid. He tried to block our degrees and couldn't. The committee were all laughing too hard."

She stared at him a few moments. "I'll bet your evil twin is still active, right?"

Jack smiled. "So is Charlie's, I imagine."

She shook her dark, shaggy, beautiful head. "I don't know how Hal teamed me up with you. Or why."

206

"Didn't your evil twin ever cut loose even once?"

"There's enough evil in the world without decent people adding to it."

"Couldn't agree more." He watched a couple minutes as she finished her Twinkie and licked the crumbs off her fingers.

Maxx got up and tried again to perch by her knee.

Jack ordered him away. "Why are you angry with me?"

The huge eyes flitted up to him. "I'm not. Not with you."

"With whom?"

"I'm angry and disappointed that Durwin isn't in the area. I can't understand why he would be gone now. What if he has car trouble? What if he doesn't get back in time for—for tonight?"

Then the war will commence as scheduled, and Rice can honestly say, "I would have stopped it if I could, but I was stranded beyond radio range." Rice could probably avoid official responsibility for whatever went wrong, if he were out of the area. But Jack didn't voice his thoughts.

Instead he said, "Not much we can do until he returns. I had a stack of papers high enough to shade a giraffe, but they burned. I should go make more copies. Investigating officers' reports, lab findings. Catch up on my reading. I'm way behind."

"I could do a little more snooping around in the special projects budget, I guess." Hunched over, she stepped out from under the mesquite. She stood erect and stretched.

Jack rolled to his hands and knees, crawled out from under the low branches, and stood up. It was easier than twisting his aching body all around. He let her in the back of the admin building, from sun brilliance into corridor dimness. She hit the fluorescent lights above her center-aisle table of printouts.

Jack flicked on the nearby dot matrix printer and plopped down at a terminal on the budget analyst's desk. Maxx, still grumpy at having been denied any Twinkie crumbs, splayed disconsolately beside Jack's chair and snarfed.

Jack typed in his code and broke into the reports. He hated reading from a monitor. He set the printer to putting the whole report and supplemental batch file on paper.

Durwin Rice. What was his game? Jack sat back while the printer did its thing, trying to piece together his puzzle and the enigma of Durwin Rice. He got nowhere on either front.

"They're gone!" Ev's voice practically croaked. "Jack, they're not here. He deleted them!"

Jack bobbed up—his body had been so stiff for so long, he was practically getting used to it—and crossed to her. He leaned on the back of her chair and bent over her shoulder, ear to ear with her. He watched her monitor as she scrolled down a file.

"Look, Jack. He took out all the most damaging entries. Except this one in July. He must have missed it. As if getting rid of them would cure the problem."

"Destroying evidence."

"I have it all backed up. He did it for nothing." She twisted around to Jack. Her breath moved warm against his cheek. "It isn't the superintendent. He left. It's not Durwin."

"Or Mrs. Leighton, though I doubt she'd have either the access or the expertise. No, wait. This could have happened yesterday. Everyone in the world had access to it yesterday."

Ev threw one of her Magic Markers across the room. "I hate this! They're all nice people, Jack. There isn't a bad person here. I don't want to crucify someone."

"'Nice' and 'bad' are subjective. There is a solid standard of judgment, and we're all measured by it." Here was his entree into a discussion of sin and redemption.

But she skated off onto other ice. "Let's take a walk. Let's go get wet in the pool. Let's do something. I'm so discouraged."

"Good idea. The golf course?" He leaned past her shoulder, backed her out of her program, and turned the machine off.

Two hundred and fourteen feet below sea level, awash in blazing sun, the world's lowest golf course spreads its 5,700-plus yards of greens through the Furnace Creek Golf Club. The greens are actually green, too, watered and manicured to perfection all year round.

Jack stood near the fifth hole, looking out across this tangle of roughs and fairways, the dozer-built hillocks, the artificially shaped terrain, and marveled at the incongruity.

"One of the few golf courses in the world" —he led Ev out past the third green— "where not even the sand traps are a natural element."

Under a whispering cottonwood she sat down in the grass and ran her fingers through the green blades. "I wouldn't dream of finding a golf course here. It's—well, it's unexpected. Hal plays golf. Do you?"

Maxx trotted up and shoved his big head against her arm.

"No." He smiled at the sudden memory. "But I'm familiar with this course. When I was seasonal here, about ten years ago, a stray sandhill crane showed up. Remarkably tame. Stood around on the fairway while the golfers played through. The greens keeper wanted to shoot it. It was tearing up the greens, he said. So some of us decided to catch it and transport it to safety."

"Is this another wrestling-with-moose story?" She almost smiled. "Go on."

"If you're sure you want to hear it. Ernie was one of us. Ernie's that good-looking guy in the warehouse yesterday who asked if you're available. Half a dozen of us took some rope and burlap bags and blankets and started

209

prowling the golf course here. Moonless night. The crane's gonna be sound asleep, right?"

"I assume from your tone of voice it wasn't."

Jack shrugged. "Ernie whispers, 'There it is!' We were right over there, behind those trees. We come sneaking across the fairway, up that way." He pointed with arm extended. "Then I spot it. I can see it in the darkness, sticking up. Piece of cake! We all leap up, slam forward, and throw a blanket over—" he pointed "—the ball washer. Broke it off at the base."

She smiled. For Ev, that was a paroxysm of emotion. "Did you ever catch it?"

"Nope. Got within ten feet once. The wingspan on those suckers—you know, when you're right under a sand-hill crane as it takes off, it's like a B-1 bomber. Turns out the greens damage was done by flickers digging for bugs, not the crane. It spent a couple weeks getting in the golfers' way and then flew off south, I guess. Anyway, it left."

Maxx flopped down on his belly by Jack's knee, content to watch the earth spin on its axis. He snarfed and began licking random parts of his anatomy.

Ev sat in silence awhile. Jack cast an occasional glance at her face, hoping for some clue to her thoughts, and saw none.

Finally, he asked, "What are you thinking?"

She dipped her head slightly in that way of hers. "I can't help it. It's the same old thing. I feel so left out. If that was ten years ago, you were what? Twenty-four? Having all these adventures. Park adventures. At twenty I was in college, busting my suspenders to get all A's. No play. Not even a steady boyfriend. And certainly no adventures. It seemed so important, then, to succeed brilliantly in college. It seems so sterile now."

"I got my share of classroom sitting."

"Earned doctorate. I know. But you have so much more as well. Anyway, I feel left out. Left behind. Disadvantaged."

210

"You're catching up now—at least the adventure part."

She shuddered. "Not fun adventures, like you talk about. I've never *seen* a crane. In fact, I'm not sure what a flicker looks like. This murder mess isn't fun. Or the embezzling."

"Amen and amen."

"I forget. Why did we come out here?" Ev rose to her feet.

Jack hauled himself up stiffly. He still hurt in too many places to count. "I don't know. Yes, I do too. It's green here. Green is the symbolic color of life and hope. I desperately need some green in my life just now. I suspect, so do you. Besides, it's a nice place for a walk."

She nodded. He expected her to head back toward the admin building. Instead she struck out across the fairway. He wished he had brought his binoculars out here, but it hadn't occurred to him. As they strolled the back nine he pointed out pipits and sparrows and even a flicker. Now she knew what one looked like. But none of the birds was close enough to really be seen well. The first of the robins were back. Early, this year. In Death Valley, robins are harbingers of autumn, not spring, as they migrate down from the north.

They walked clear out to the ragged little mesquites at the far side. Some people sneered at the mesquites. True, they weren't impressive when you compared them to the stately cottonwoods, the skyscraper date palms. But these were native trees accustomed to salt, to desert dryness, to privation of every sort. They grew, even flourished, along a scattered, broken line from the golf course clear out to the sewer lagoon. The birds, both natives and migrants, loved them. And that was reason in itself not to sneer.

"I have an idea," she said presently. "You know that entry the person who did the deleting missed?"

"The one in July."

211

"I think, if we set a careful trap, we can find who it is."

"That's your area of expertise, not mine. I'm lucky I can find the word processing program. Whatever I can do to help."

"Actually, you can help. I'll think about it some more."

Jack and Ev were not the only people out enjoying a walk. A lot of the greens were festooned with golf foursomes in ridiculous, gaudy shorts and vivid shirts. Maxx took a stab at chasing balls, but Jack managed to call him back before the mutt thwarted anyone's hole-in-one. Time to put the leash on. Jack called the dog and reached for his collar.

With a happy bark, Maxx wheeled suddenly and went thundering off. On the south periphery of the course, there lurched Gladys, staggering along in grim determination. She wore tight jeans that emphasized the strange double crook of her crippled legs.

Jack yelled at Maxx, but the mutt ignored him.

Maxx was off to visit his pal, his buddy. The lab bounded over to Gladys and very nearly flattened her. Had she not seen him in time and braced, she would have found herself sky-gazing.

She watched Jack as he came running. She did not look particularly pleased. "Good morning, Jack. Nice to see you." You wouldn't guess it was nice from the gloomy look on her face, or her flat voice.

Jack pointed to her red and blue nylon fanny pack. "No big bag today. That belt pouch must be a lot more comfortable."

She studied him curiously. "That's very observant of you. But then, that's a job specification, I would guess —being observant." She reached back and slapped the fanny pack. "It's old. I dug it out today because you're right; my handbag isn't comfortable. It flops against my hip too much."

212

"My mom uses one of those belt pouches all the time. I'm not sure she even has a purse anymore." Jack snapped the leash in place. Once under tow, Maxx settled down somewhat.

Gladys eyed Ev as if she were a slog of slime on the beach. "Miss Brant." Ice.

"Mrs. Gibbs." Just as icy.

Jack noticed a lot of bikers were swarming here and there but not in any organized groups. They acted more like tourists than makers of mayhem.

Gladys pointed herself toward civilization and started off at her unique gait. "Do you watch television much?" She lurched wildly as she crossed a small rut.

Ev murmured something negative, not at all with the program.

Jack shook his head. "Hardly ever. I have a suspicion that when I'm not home Maxx turns on the soaps, mostly for the dog food commercials, but I rarely have time."

Gladys laughed long and lightly, and her laughter was surprisingly musical. "I like those reality cop shows. It's amazing, some of the ways they have to trap criminals. I'll bet they don't tell you everything they can do, either."

"You mean keep some secrets of the trade to themselves?"

"Why show criminals all the ways you can catch them?"

"To deter them from being criminals, perhaps. So you've learned a little something about forensics."

"Fascinating. The things they do with ballistics, comparing bullets and things. Fingerprints. What is that test to see if a man is really a rapist?" Her eyes sparkled. Interesting eyes.

"DNA matching. They sort out repeated sequences in the DNA of a specimen—body fluids of some sort—and calculate the odds that it could have come from a particular person."

213

"How do you know you have a body fluid with DNA in it?"

"Nearly all fluids do, except urine. Even that sometimes. DNA is present in every cell of the body except red blood cells. Theoretically, every single cell has the complete body program coded inside it."

She shook her head. That simple departure from the centerline threw her for a loop. "I never had any science in college. In fact, I didn't finish my degree." She looked up at him, and it obviously took her quite a bit of coordination and effort to turn her head and walk at the same time. "May I lean on you? It goes better if I'm propped against someone."

"Certainly." Jack offered his arm.

Sure enough, once she could hang onto something, the lurching smoothed out quite a bit. She still staggered, but she managed to keep her limbs moving in more of a straight line.

"At home I have a three-wheeler. That's actually my easiest way to get around. You can pedal all over Alexandria once you know where the bike lanes and wide sidewalks are." She paused a moment, then added, "I don't have a driver's license—courtesy this epilepsy."

"Neither do I, at the moment—courtesy a trailer fire."

"Really! When was that?"

"Friday night. Your baby-sitter—what's her name? Meghan?—I assume she doubles as chauffeur."

"That's right. And if your license burned up, I assume Miss Brant here is yours."

Jack tugged Maxx back to attention. The mutt was distracted by every new aroma on the path. "I rarely let her drive. She treats transmissions as if they were replaceable."

"They're not?"

"Not on my salary."

He could feel the heat of Ev's glare. Silence.

What should he say? He opted for nothing at all.

Ev's voice dripped icicles. "I have work to do. If you two will excuse me, I'll go on to the admin building. You'll pick me up around five, Jack?" Without waiting for his answer she started off at a purposeful march.

Just then he got an idea. "Hey, Ev, wait a minute."

She stopped and turned to face him.

"Can you do an errand for me?" He patted his pockets. This morning, when he bought a toothbrush, he also bought some cheap Bic pens and a little wirebound notebook. He found it in a hip pocket where his wallet ought to be.

"Make this call for me, will you? And collect my faxes?" He jotted the number and the request.

She scowled, looking like she wanted most of all to stick shish-kabob skewers under his fingernails. She glanced at the note, paused to read it, and softened. "All right. Sure." She turned without good-byeing Gladys and marched off.

The silence tiptoed back and walked beside them.

Gladys spoke, and the silence fled. "What was that crack you made about Bo or something? Who's Bo?"

"Nice try at faking innocence, Gladys, but I know."

"No, you don't. There's nothing to know. I resent you mentioning George's name along with a total stranger. He wasn't perfect, but he was my husband. I owe him respect, at least."

Jack walked in silence, a real party-pooper. He thought about the deletions and who could have made them. He thought about any connections they would have to George Gibbs. He thought about Myrtle Leighton's fascination with police methods, and now Mrs. Gibbs's. He thought about the greasy pink stain in the seam of Gladys's fanny pack. Other thoughts, too, churned in his mind— and new solutions. Possibly correct solutions. And he knew how to double-check at least some of them.

They left the golf course and struck out along the roadside. As they walked, he worked and reworked the

215

scenario, discarding those possibilities that little details negated, until only one picture emerged. And the more he put little pieces together, the clearer the picture came. He was fairly certain. He knew who killed George Gibbs.

22

War and Peace

It was near dark. The ancient hills on the east side lost their golden glow as the sun slipped behind the Panamints. The valley was filling with the roar of motorcycles. In pairs and bunches and in high aloneness they came and went, restlessly.

"Getting a little tired of them motorcycles," the gas station attendant grumbled.

"Noisy." Jack would not have used the word *tired*. *Terrified* came to mind. He paid and walked out into the warm evening air.

Ev's trap was laid. They had called everyone they could find. With Mel and Aubray and Hodges, Ev had left a message for the absent Durwin Rice. "Tell him," she said, "that someone's been deleting material from the records but they missed one entry in July. It's the only one we have left to build a case with."

It was also a lie.

But then, the best traps are lies by their very nature. Deep tiger pits, covered with branches, pass themselves off as solid ground. Bait on hooks promises fish a good meal. Undercover gigs and elaborate stings exist as falsehood. Jesus called Satan the father of lies. Some aspects of police work bothered Jack a lot more than others.

217

Ev came out of the gas station rest room and crossed to the truck. Bikers roared past. She cringed. "I'm scared."

"So am I." He looked in vain for Point Man, for Hippo, for Cat, for any known face. None. Unwashed, unshaven faces aplenty, but none that Jack could call "acquaintance," let alone "friend."

The visitor center had closed early today. Jack had seen the blonde seasonal named Karen locking the front doors around four. There was a tension building, a foreboding. Something was going to blow, and it would take everyone in this valley with it.

He opened the passenger door for Ev.

She slid inside. "Does Maxx have an evil twin also?"

Jack closed her door and climbed in his side. "Twin nothing. A whole litter." He drove back to the admin building.

Jack let them in with his M-1. Ev hustled down the hall to her monitor and flicked it on. It glowed amber in the dim light. Jack hit the switch panel. The overheads popped on one by one, reluctantly. The room blazed bright.

She flopped into a chair, her face tilted upward.

All Jack could hear was motorcycles out on the road.

She asked, "Do you think something will start before dark?"

"Hard to say."

She looked at her monitor for the four hundredth time. "What if the deletions were made yesterday? If it's Durwin or the Leightons or someone like that, the trap won't work."

"Might not anyway, if our deleter is really savvy."

"It would help if we knew it happened this morning."

By tipping his aching body aside, he could just reach the in-house phone list on the sideboard. He ran his finger down the entries. Karen—Karen—Karen Husolt was

218

her name. There she was. She lived in one of the trailers. He dialed. She answered.

"Jack Prester, Miss Husolt. Who was in back in the admin building here this morning, please?"

"No administrative personnel. Just the rangers and José."

"José who?"

"Diego. Maintenance."

"What rangers, do you know?"

"I called back a couple times with visitors' questions. I got—let's see—I got Aubray two or three times and Mel once."

"Think they were the only two here?"

"No. People wander in and out all the time. And Aubray's wife. Diane. Aubray is here, and Diane works up at Grapevine."

"Mm. Did you notice anything at all unusual about today?"

"Closed the VC early. Mr. Rice's expecting trouble."

"Did he say anything about it?"

"Not really, but everyone knows. Oh, and Mr. Rice was back there. I heard him in the background a couple times."

"He's supposed to be out of the area."

Silence at the other end.

"Miss Husolt? Miss Husolt?"

Her voice came back moments later. "Mr. Prester. I don't know if this means anything, but a grocery company truck is pulling out of the maintenance yard. Here it comes past the trailers. One of those big eighteen-wheelers. I've never seen something like that back there."

"Are you authorized to carry firearms, Miss Husolt?"

"No." Her voice was soft, hesitant.

"Then stay at Cow Creek. You'd be wise to leave the lights off in your trailer. Pretend you're not home."

"What is—it's starting, isn't it? The trouble."

"Possibly so. Thank you, Miss Husolt. Good night."

Ev was looking at him. "Firearms?"

How much should he tell her? It would take the truck maybe eight minutes to reach Furnace Creek, and . . .

The monitor flicked. Jack pointed to it.

Ev inhaled audibly. Their trap had just sprung.

Sufficient unto the day is the evil thereof.

Ev slipped out of her hard-heeled flats and hurried into the hall stocking-footed. Jack followed her to the ranger office.

"Find the one we mean?" Jack leaned in the doorway. "The one over the Fourth of July holiday."

Aubray White jumped a foot and sucked in enough air to fill a tractor tire. He relaxed by degrees. Casually he punched an F key on his keyboard. "Howdy, Prester. Miss Brant. Which one? Oh, hey. I talked to that little Meghan girl like you asked."

"Gregory's baby sitter."

"She says she drove Mrs. Gibbs down to the convenience store late this morning in their rental car. That's all. She has no idea whether Mrs. Gibbs went out Friday night because they stay in separate rooms. Mrs. Gibbs comes and goes as she wishes, without Meghan knowing."

"Mm."

"The girl noticed one thing, though," Aubrey added hastily. "She insists she always leaves the car in park and sets the emergency as well. The emergency brake wasn't on this morning."

"Write it up?"

"Sure."

"Thanks."

Aubray looked from face to face. His own long, lanky Good-Ole-Boy face hardened, tensed.

Jack scooped up a chair and plunked it down beside Aubray's. "Ev had this great idea, so she did some reprogramming on this thing. She's a whiz at computers and any occupation with the word 'budget' in the job description. Here. I'll show you." He backed out of the spread sheet

Aubray had been in and punched in a command. The monitor flipped to blank for a count of ten.

In glowing amber letters it told the world the date and the time of day. Below that it announced:

CODE: AUBRAY WHITE
ACTIVITY: DOC 1 PG 83 COL 3

and proceeded to reproduce what had been erased and changed.

Jack sat back. "Ev's idea. Record whoever entered the system and what they did." He held Aubray's eye. "I thought for a while it was Rice. But you had means and opportunity as well. You've been jockeying falsified entries around. What was the motive?"

Aubray looked from face to face. "Emery Leighton is a good man, Prester. A great man. Great to work for. I overheard Rice confront him about the—ah— entries. Rice is a dumbbell when it comes to computers. Neat guy, but practically computer illiterate. I'd do all his zero-base budgeting for him. I figured if Rice could find the entries, anyone could, so I tried to hide them better. When Miss Brant found them too, I deleted them."

"Why?" Ev looked stricken, as stricken as Jack felt.

Aubray grimaced. "If you'd ever worked for Leighton at all, or Rice either for that matter, you wouldn't have to ask."

"Did you get any piece of the action yourself?"

"Piece?"

"Profit in any way from the embezzlements."

"Oh. No. I did it to protect them."

Ev popped a floppy into the A drive and copied the incriminating screenful.

Jack pondered all this a while. "Write a statement— a confession, if you will. You made yourself an accessory after the fact by hiding it instead of reporting it. As far as I can tell, that's your only crime, such as it is. I for one certainly don't have time to prosecute it, not with the Gibbs case. Your loyalty is misplaced, but the romanticist in me admires it all the same. Make sure you explain the motive."

Ev's huge eyes were studying Jack, reading something in his face, though he couldn't tell what. "I've already processed the evidence Hal wants," she told Aubray. "Recorded on disk separate from the system and on its way to Hal. You deleted them too late. But I'm new at this sort of thing. It's going to take all my time writing the reports and preparing the embezzlement case. I don't have time to prepare a case condemning you."

Aubray lurched to his feet. "I think I hear you two right—that you're going to be easy on me. Remember, I did what I had to. Leighton deserves some easy too, Prester. He's a nice guy."

"He's also an embezzler."

"Now you know there's embezzlers crooked as a hound's hind leg, and there's decent guys caught in a bear trap."

"Nobody forced him into it."

"Circumstances did."

"We all get circumstances."

Aubray watched Ev pull the floppy.

She punched keys. The monitor went blank, with only the C prompt glowing.

"Don't we, though." He disappeared out the door.

Jack heard his heels click up the hall toward the front entrance.

"I feel terrible." Ev moseyed out the door and back down to her bailiwick.

"I don't feel like sing-along at the Boston Pops, myself."

She sat down at her terminal and backed out gracefully, handling the keyboard as smoothly as she handled weird little forks at formal luncheons.

He sat across from her and listened to the motorcy-

222

cles. White. Jack felt as helpless as a garter snake on waxed linoleum. Why did it have to be good old Aubray?

Ev jumped up suddenly, walked to a window, and raised the venetian blinds to look out. Even from his chair Jack could see a thick pall of dust hung between earth and sky. They were ramming around all over this area, off the established roads.

She dropped the blinds back into place. She turned to him, her arms crossed tightly. "What are you thinking about?"

"I'm thinking of the safest place for you. If a riot starts you shouldn't be here. Or the inn." He consulted the phone sheet again. "Karen Husolt, the girl who works the desk, is in trailer C102. Why don't you go there? Take my truck."

"And where are you going?"

"Nowhere. The rangers are on the way. I can't leave this."

She crossed to him and parked nose to nose with him, except he was still seated, which made it nose to belt buckle. "That Tayes person is right. It's not your investigation. He said to stay out of it, and I think that's a splendid idea. I want to go home now. Drive me up to Cow Creek, please."

"Ev—" He hauled himself to his feet. "Ev—"

She moved in close and pressed her hands on his arms. Those quart-sized brown eyes begged him, puppy-dog style, their pleas stronger than words.

What could he say? How could he explain his grave concern for her—for every woman in Furnace Creek just now? She stood so close his breastbone tingled.

She gasped at a muffled *Poop! Poop! Poo-poop!* from outside.

Jack dashed across the room, killed the lights. He carried a borrowed .38 service revolver he had never fired, and there was no way he could crack the gun safe. He was worth zip if it came to protecting her. He looked out into

223

the gathering darkness, his night vision nonexistent.

Maxx, on his feet beside Jack, barked, instantly antsy.

"Fireworks!" Jack announced. "They're setting off fireworks." In the sky beyond the admin building, a cloud of red embers drifted down and winked out. Never in all of his Fourth-of-Julys had he ever been so happy to see fireworks.

Instead of bullets.

She pressed in beside him. Jack called Maxx to heel and escorted Ev outside. Obviously they weren't waiting for total darkness to begin festivities. Just when you least expected it, another spray of embers would rain down and evaporate. A white rocket howled up toward the stars.

"Maxx. On guard." He led Ev by the hand, around the building to his truck.

Ev hung back, paused. "Look!"

In the very midst of that chaotic mass of bikers, a huge bonfire crackled to life. What were they burning? Stacked among the wood were other combustibles—clothing, papers.

"Do you know what a real bonfire is?" she asked.

"The size? This one's a doozy. Twenty feet high, at least."

"The meaning. It's a signal fire, and a warning. And you burn symbolic things you want to destroy."

"Like girls in the sixties burning their bras."

She nodded, awestruck as flames burst up through the tower of wood and who-knows-what, leaping joyously into the night sky. "I wouldn't be surprised if there were some bras on that one."

"And neckties and a briefcase full of security analyses."

Twenty feet from the bonfire, a speakers' platform loomed four or five feet high. On it two guys arranged sound equipment. Amps, huge speaker boxes, mike stands. Their multitude of nickel brads caught the dancing firelight a million different ways.

Maxx was barking, not at anything in particular but just because the tension and excitement had tipped him past his silence threshold. It snapped Jack back to reality.

The grocery chain semi pulled to the road berm at the east perimeter of the rally. The bikers were too preoccupied with raising the noise level to notice it.

And then, suddenly, the crowd hushed. Like the wave in a football stadium, the silence began here and spread through and across to the far end.

Lined up facing the crowd, elbow to elbow, a solid row of rangers had assembled themselves. Jack assumed there were some women among them, but you couldn't tell. Orange fire glow danced on the riot helmet every man wore. Every man held a riot gun. Every man's belt carried the full complement of service weapon, jiffy load, cuffs, mace—they were geared for war.

Somehow, the state of the nation's economy, or even finding the murderer of George Gibbs, didn't seem real important now. Death Valley was about to explode.

Thanks to the thick quiet, you could hear choppers from far off. The ominous *plupluplupluplup* began in the distant south. The sound grew. Every head except the rangers' turned to the south, and a disquieting murmur started to build.

Jack happened to glance beyond the grocery truck to the low hills across the road. They were lined with tourists. Gawkers stood around or sat in lawn chairs in the gathering darkness, watching the panorama before them like opera patrons anticipating the "Ride of the Valkyries." Some, vultures, used binoculars. Didn't they realize that the moment this thousand bikers erupted, they would take the brunt? They were defenseless. *People are going to die here, folks. It's not a circus.*

Jack pictured in his mind's eye a crowd of bikers five hundred strong descending unannounced on Beatty, literally tearing the town apart. Beatty? Vegas! A thousand bikers could sweep through Vegas, destroy, kill, torch the place, and be gone before any effective resistance mobilized. For no reason? Sure. All those Nam vets, all those ancient Hippos, wouldn't need a reason. To raise one last never-to-be-forgotten death strike would forever write Hells' Angels into the Book of Infamy. Nero, Hitler, Stalin, the Gang of Four, Hippo and his ilk.

From the south, dark trucks came howling up the road. Four trucks. Five. They parked near the semi and disgorged dozens and dozens of fully armed young men in camouflage fatigues. Army.

Jack could see the choppers now, their white belly lights flashing. There had to be a dozen of them. They came up the valley low, below sea level, and their muted *plupluplup* grew into a thunderous roar that hammered the mountains on either side.

Of course! Less than a week ago, Jack had been talking to the CO at Edwards. Edwards and Ft. Irwin were on joint maneuvers, right? Why not a little actual battle practice, right here in good old Death Valley National Monument?

More fireworks went off. Maxx barked wildly. Fireworks always upset him and hurt his ears. So did guns, for that matter.

Jack grabbed Ev's arm and stuffed his truck keys into her hand. "You know where I'm parked. Get in the truck and get out of here. Take it clear to Beatty, understand? No! Past Beatty. Vegas. Go!" He gave her arm a pat. "Maxx! Go with Ev!" He pointed. "Guard Ev, Maxx." He turned toward the mass of bikers.

The choppers dropped lower, lower. One by one they parked out on the salt flat in the near darkness beyond the sea of bikers—big Chinooks, not dinky little glass-bubbles. From each leaped scores of soldiers in camouflage. They lined out around the far shore of the agitated sea of bikers. From behind them, the choppers trained glaring white searchlights onto the mob.

A war? A dress rehearsal for Armageddon.

226

What Jack needed most in all the world now was a horse. On horseback he could push through the crowd. From a horse he could see faces, get above the heads, find Hippo.

Lord God, I want to find Hippo. Lead me to Hippo. Where is he? How can I stave off this bloodbath, dear Lord?

Jack knew the answer to that even before he expressed the prayer. He couldn't. Not even the mighty Hippo could come near helping stem the tide. In His psalms, God warned His people about relying on man's arm instead of the Lord's strength. Only God could avert disaster now. It was infinitely past Jack's power to do anything.

The soldiers were here, the lines drawn. Let the war begin.

23
Jumping Jack

One of the most impressive pictures in Jack's high school history books was that of General Robert E. Lee returning to his troops from Appomattox. You knew he had lost, but he didn't look it. Astride the magnificent, gray Traveler, he rode with dignity and respect before lines of weeping soldiers.

The line of rangers, not weeping, guns in hand, stood at parade rest. From behind them emerged a huge sorrel horse in full NPS tack—saddle, breast collar, tie-down, white leg wraps, the works. Astride, in the splendor of his winter class A's, Durwin Rice rode out into the swarm of bikers. He looked a lot like that picture in the history books, and he lacked not a bit of the dignity of General Lee himself.

Jack gaped, and he realized everyone else was gaping too.

Rice urged his horse at a quiet walk straight through the mob to the speaker's platform. The sound men on the platform stopped what they were doing to stare. Jack expected Rice to borrow their sound system, but no such thing. His horse carried portable speakers where saddlebags normally would hang. He unwrapped the mike from his saddle horn and raised it.

"Ladies and gentlemen, your attention, please." His amplified voice rang through the chaotic night.

And he had their attention.

Of course, the choppers, rangers, and army troops certainly didn't hurt. But had he come alone, he would have struck just as impressive a presence.

"In 1964, my first year of seasonal Park Service work, I stood within a hundred yards of here watching the awards presentation at one of the last official motorcycle rallies in this Monument. I understand the history of this occasion today."

The summer uniform is a short-sleeve shirt open at the collar. The winter class A includes tie and jacket or coat. Rice wore the winter uniform, and with the tie and jacket gained an aura of respect the short-sleeve summer shirt would never have sustained. But there was much, much more to the authority figure he struck now than just a jacket. His voice was imposing, his seat on that big Point Reyes Morgan horse commanding. The gold badge on his coat told the world, "When I speak, the government of the United States is speaking."

Another rocket went screaming toward the stars. Rice's horse raised its head, but it stood firm. Jack could have told the rocketeer that park horses are well trained for crowd control.

Rice spoke again, but a voice from the crowd partially covered his. He kept going. "I realize some of you are lawyers, just waiting for me to step on your rights. Be aware I know the law too. You're in violation of at least seven articles of the code of federal regulations right now. I shall use those seven infractions to insist that you disperse."

Voices rose.

His rose above them. "The potential for disaster here tonight is too great. Let's defuse the situation before it starts. You've had your fireworks and your bonfire. You've had your rally. Now disperse voluntarily, or be dispersed."

Hundreds of voices bellowed against him. Jack realized how vulnerable Rice had made himself, hanging out in the open like that, head and shoulders above everyone else, trapped in the midst of the enemy. The leader, the spokesman, the perfect target. Were there deaths tonight, Rice's would be the first. Jack stood in dumbstruck awe of the man's sheer guts.

The moment hung suspended. Jack knew a little something about mob instinct, about what tipped off riots and what allayed them. Everything depended now upon the thousand surly bikers. If no one stepped forward to lead a revolt, if no one disrupted the general rumble of discontent and crystalized it, Rice might just pull this off.

The bikers milled and mumbled, uncertain. The lines of uniformed troops stood rock solid, absolutely certain. Any little incident now—an unruly biker, an antsy soldier, even a display of firearms in the biker ranks—would trigger a lethal melee 1,500-people big.

And then the crowd by the ranger line erupted. Somebody from within the mob was shoving his way over to the steady row of gray and green. He was screaming unseemly epithets at them, shouting, thrashing—and Jack recognized some of the words. He recognized the voice too, and the bulk.

"Hippo!" Jack broke into a run, headed for the mountainous man. "Hippo!" Jack couldn't make any headway. He squeezed and shoved and shouldered his way through the smelly mob. Didn't anyone bathe? He had to reach Hippo. He had to put that one small fire out before it torched off this whole valley.

A general hubbub was building. Jack lost sight of Rice. There he was, still astride, still by the platform. More choppers arrived, more reinforcements. The din around him was picking up.

Just before Jack reached him, Hippo turned away from the gray and greens and started plowing through the crowd, headed toward Rice. Jack changed directions, prodded and elbowed and shoved. He was sorely, sorely tempted to draw his borrowed .38. He resisted. *Don't be the first to show a weapon, you jerk! That's all this tinderbox needs.*

But he felt so vulnerable, a single struggling straight guy in a sea of alien subculture. He could be shot or stabbed or pounded or trampled in two seconds flat. He shouldered his way toward Rice.

Hippo reached Rice about five seconds before Jack could. The burly biker grabbed Rice by a pants pocket and his utility belt. Rice swung a baton high, ready to repel boarders.

"No!" Jack dived, covering Hippo's head with his arms. "Hip, back off!" He seized two great handfuls of random leather parts and dragged the man backwards a step.

"Come on, Hip buddy!" Cat was beside him now too, balanced precariously on his one good leg, clawing at the immovable rock.

Someone grabbed Jack's shoulder, but the hand fell away.

Rice was glaring at Jack. "Which side are you on, Prester?"

Until that moment, Jack couldn't have said. He knew, now. Above the ruction he yelled, "Tayes told me to stay out of this. So I am. Hip, get out of here! Come on. Come with us."

Hippo released another barrage of language that would make a streetwalker blush. He was babbling now, rambling, raving. His eyes were wide with terror, but it wasn't drugs. The pupils were normal for this light.

"I'm gonna lose more of 'em!" Hippo shrieked at Cat. "I'm gonna lose you! I don' wanna lose any more! I can't lose any more! Get these freaking—" his frantic tirade was drowned in another explosion of fireworks, red embers sprayed out across the heavens "—outta here!"

Cat had wormed his way between Hippo and the horse. Now he started shoving, using the same body English a piano mover would apply to a thousand-pound upright.

Jack started pulling. Hippo stumbled and moved a yard farther away from the horse. Another two feet. It was working.

Jack heard a few stray bike starters kick in, and the rumbling roar of Harleys. *Thank God!* A lot of shouting went on, and a lot of confusion, but no gunfire so far. No one was stepping forward as a leader and organizer to call these bikers to arms.

Jack was bumped and jostled, nearly suffocated in the crush, and then he wasn't. The crowd was loosening up. Hundreds of bikes with inadequate mufflers roared to life. The Point Reyes Morgan horse held his ground, but his eyes rolled so wildly the whites showed. The glaring white lights from the choppers cast black/white shadows across the ocean of leather and denim.

Lights. Action. Chaos.

And then a miraculous transformation took place in the mountainous Hippo. He was letting them drag him off. Jack had no delusions that Cat and he together could handle this raging maniac. Definitely a full-fledged miracle. The faceless bikers in this crowd let them by, as awestruck as Jack by the change in the furious, weak, angry, howling, muscular, ineffectual Hippo.

Jack kept a tight grip on Hippo's right wrist and wrapped his arm around Hippo's waist. Cat stumped along, pressed close to Hippo's left. They talked and coddled and yelled, and Jack had no idea what either of them said. It didn't matter. Hippo, still roaring obscenities, was letting them haul him away from the crowd to safety and sanity.

And the bikers were letting their rally end without mayhem. That, too, was an incredible miracle. Hell's Angels backing down? Not really. Perhaps, were Bo alive here, he would have prodded them into a full-scale riot. Perhaps he would have salted them down, calmed the mob. They churned, uncertain, apparently not quite ready to bull through the ranger line to reach those soft, vulnerable, retired spectators on the hill across the road, not keyed up enough to cut loose and set southern Nevada afire.

Bikes came and went, spreading thunder all over. Tension melted as the sheer decibels rose. A heavy dust cloud hung low, a blanket between the bikers and the night, glowing in the choppers' white floodlamps.

Jack and Cat, with Hippo stuffed between them, left most of the crush behind. A truck horn tooted. Ev pulled Jack's pick-up alongside, the window cranked down. Maxx barked in the back.

"Get in!" she yelled.

Jack looked around. He needed a place. Where—? "Ev, stay behind and keep the headlights on us. We're going over there." He flung a gesturing arm toward the empty parking lot.

Hippo was offering less resistance now. He spouted a constant stream of expletives, probably because he had no polite words to express the intensity of the feelings that had surfaced and exploded inside him.

Jack raised an arm, the wagonmaster's signal to circle the wagons. Ev pulled to a halt beside him, on the edge of the parking lot.

Jack stopped, and Hippo walked on six feet before he realized he was leaving someone behind. He paused and half turned, his face tight with inexpressible emotion.

Jack grabbed his glow-in-the-dark Frisbee out of the back of his truck and sailed it nearly straight up, high into the dark sky. "So talk to me."

"Nothing to talk about. What the—" Hippo's voice faded as he turned to run for the Frisbee. He grabbed it and spun around, remarkably light on his feet for such a hulking mountain "—kind of arrest is this?"

"Who said arrest? I said talk. I know what you're feeling, but I want to hear it from you." Ev had his single remaining headlight on bright. Jack stepped aside, well away from its cyclopian glare, so that Hippo could see him.

Hippo fell back very nearly to the far end of the lot, under the sickly yellow flood lights. He wheeled and put every pound of muscle behind his toss. "You don't know a bleeping bit of how I feel," and he punctuated it with a choice expletive. The Frisbee came burning, whistling.

Jack dived for it and missed. With a joyous bark Maxx dealt himself into the game. He leaped out of the truck and hit the ground running flat out for the disk. He caught it on a flying leap and came trotting back.

Jack took it from Maxx's mouth. He flung the Frisbee as he talked. "You lost Barbara. You lost Bo. When you saw all those rangers and soldiers you were sure the whole place was going to blow up and you'd lose more. You panicked—really panicked—and now you're mad and embarrassed because you fell apart."

"Bull!" Hippo's voice sounded distant. Here came the Frisbee, brighter and brighter in the headlight.

With a mighty jump, Jack deprived Maxx of the joy of catching it. "That's not all you're mad at. You're so full of anger at Barbara you can't stand it. And you feel so guilty you can't stand it, because she's dead and you don't think you ought to be mad at her." He tossed it high this time. And he hated himself because he could feel the tidal wave of anger rising inside him again, for the millionth time.

The Frisbee arched toward the stars, a ghostly gray-green blob in the headlight. It sailed to earth untouched. Hippo was standing there staring at Jack through the darkness. He expressed himself in a few more expletives. Belatedly he turned away and retrieved the Frisbee from the dirt.

It came soaring, right toward Jack.

"What makes you think all that?" Hippo called.

With only a bit of a jump Jack grabbed it. He put all his back and his aching ribs into it, throwing it viciously.

His eyes were burning. "Because I still feel exactly like that about my wife, and she's been dead three years."

"How'd she die?" Hippo had to fall way back to grab it.

"Car wreck."

"Drunk driver?"

"Nope. Her fault. She wasn't paying attention, and she tailgated a guy making a left-hand turn. When she realized she was going to back-end him, she swerved."

Here came the Frisbee. "Into the ditch or over a cliff."

"No. She was Australian. Learned to drive on the left side of the road. By habit and instinct she swerved left, smack into a dump truck in the oncoming lane. Seat belts don't help when a dump truck tears you apart." Tears were running down his cheeks now. He hated that. He really hated it. He grabbed the Frisbee backhanded and jogged a couple steps to bring himself around again. He flung it wildly, not caring.

Maxx knew a wild toss when he saw one. He took off after it.

Hippo didn't try. He let the dog go catch it. "Any kids?"

"Boy, five and a half. That's another thing." Jack's voice caught in his throat and choked him up, so he waited while Maxx retrieved the disk for Hippo. The white ghost came sailing.

Jack caught it with only a couple of steps and a jump. "She had him along that day. She took him away with her. I try to forgive her, and I can't." He slung it skyward in a violent attempt to dislodge a star. "She left forever, and she took my son too." The tears were rolling freely, his nose blocked up. He slurped.

"Cute kid, I bet."

"He could read already."

Across the darkness the Frisbee bobbed and headed this way. "Barb didn't have to die. If she wasn't feeling so good she woulda just got outta the way, y'know? Like Cat

235

and I did. She coulda made it." The anguish in Hippo's voice jacked its pitch. "If she hadn't been snorting snow like one o' Santa's reindeer, she woulda been sharp enough to get outta the way, y'know?"

"And it was you who gave her the coke."

Hippo unleashed a string of expletives with a "y' know?" in the middle. His choices told Jack he had fingered it exactly.

They tossed it back and forth in silence a couple rounds. Hippo was moving in closer; Jack had to lower his trajectory and shorten the arc. He needed the pause and the time, so he could clamp a lid on his own harried memories. He was ashamed of his tears and welcomed the darkness that hid them.

It didn't help a bit that Jack heard open weeping. A woman. Over in the truck behind the headlight.

Behind them and all around them, motorcycles were roaring up and down the road, the rally dispersing. God—through Rice—had just worked an authoritarian-type miracle. The helicopters still added their decibels to the noise. Jack could barely hear Hippo.

But Hippo closed the distance to half. "So what'd you do?"

"What works for me might not work for you. You committed to Jesus Christ?" Jack tossed the disk lightly. It curved casually, gracefully, practically right to Hippo's hand.

Expletives, including some new ones, laced his negative.

"That first. You're not going to get far till you do that, whether you're angry or not. That's what kept me going. I'm mad at God too, but God's nice enough to shine it through. He takes care of me whether I deserve it or not, and I appreciate that, because a lot of the time I don't deserve it. Like when I hate my dead wife.

"The Park Service sat me down with a shrink to help me sort out my feelings. I quit theirs and found a Christian

236

counselor, who could help me at the spiritual level too."

Another expletive. "A shrink, huh?"

"Or adviser. Friend. Someone you can trust. It'll take some time yet, but I'll make it. Now that I know what's going on inside, I can work on it. I couldn't before."

"Barb was a good woman." Here it came, gently, on the cooling air.

Jack caught it easily, without stretching his aching ribs. "I believe you. And I can see for looking that your relationship was the real thing." He tossed.

Hippo abandoned the Frisbee, to Maxx's delight. It skidded into the dust. Maxx raked the edge with a practiced paw, bobbling the disk enough that he could grab its rim. He came trotting to Hippo, and then to Jack. His tail sagged as it dawned on him by degrees that the game was over.

His face still twisted in anguish, Hippo took the Frisbee out of Maxx's mouth and handed it to Jack. "Talk to me some more."

24

Jack of All Tirades

Good old Ev looked a wee bit confused. There she was in the administrative office, putting in some donated time early on a quiet Sunday morning, playing with her computer toys, streaking lots of colored lines across printouts with her beloved Magic Markers, building her embezzlement case. Then along came Jack to whisk her away on a romantic walk out to the sewer lagoon.

"Sewer lagoon?" She wrinkled her delicate nose.

Romantic?

Hardly. For one thing, any walk in which Maxx was involved could not be considered romantic. The mutt barged around gleefully to the full extent of his leash, tugging here, nosing there, hanging back whenever he got a whiff of something particularly interesting in some clump of brush. Jack's right arm had grown an inch from being jerked around. As soon as they had walked beyond the usual haunts of tourists, he turned Maxx loose. The tugging was really playing hob with his lacerated back.

Also, this was business.

"Yes, but the sewer lagoon?" Idly she fingered the binoculars hanging around her neck.

"All sorts of great stuff visit the Death Valley sewer lagoon. Wait'll you see."

238

"I'm not sure I'll be able to see. Daddy has some huge binoculars you use aboard ship, but I never could use them well. Things bob around when I try to look through them."

"I pawed through all the binoculars in the ranger cache. I think you'll like these. The seesaw focus is easier than the old gnurled wheel, and eight by fifty is a good field to find things with. Get used to these, and we'll promote you to ten fifties."

She paused. "It's so quiet. Just birds chirping somewhere. And to think it could have been a war."

War. Yes. It could so easily have escalated to an all-out fire fight extending hundreds of miles, were the rioters so inclined. Both sides were ready. Both were mobile enough. Jack thought again about the image of Rice on the horse, riding into the very midst of the enemy. Bold move. Gutsy move.

Rice knew about the embezzling. He could possibly have been party to it as well. Whether or not Ev found Rice culpable in that matter, Jack would always admire the man for his wisdom and his deep, quiet bravery. Jack had just watched a legend happen. Just what Rice wanted.

They meandered out across the bright, open, sunwashed flats. What a glorious day!

Ev stopped dead and scowled. "That's Gladys Gibbs coming."

"I told you when we left the office this is business."

"But you didn't say her." She pouted, instantly grumpy.

Maxx thundered off to greet his buddy. Gladys braced. Maxx veered. Another catastrophe averted.

Gladys didn't even bother to say hello to Ev as they approached. She nodded to Jack and smiled, sort of. "Out early."

"Perfect morning. Clear skies, and what? Seventy?"

"About. Maybe seventy-five."

"Maxx, get outta here. Go on." Jack waved an arm. Maxx trotted off and resumed his exploration of aromas.

Gladys nodded at Jack's binoculars and ignored Ev's. "Out bird watching?"

"Yeah. I was a naturalist in my seasonal days. It's sort of like malaria. You relapse every now and then."

Gladys smiled suddenly. "I'm headed for the barn. Jack, will you join me for a drink? I'm ready for one."

"I'd like that. Sounds good."

Ev's voice put an inch of ice on the sewer lagoon, and it was 'way over there. "I'll go back to work if you two don't mind. I have a lot to do."

Jack nodded. "Sure, if you wish." Ev had done her part, simply by giving him a convincing excuse to be out here and encounter Gladys. He probably should have warned her—he'd been watching Gladys for nearly an hour, timing the meeting. "I'll be along soon."

"Not very soon, I'll bet." She turned and walked away.

"So you work on Sundays." Gladys resumed her hike.

Jack ambled alongside, not at all accustomed to keeping his speed down to two miles an hour. "When we're on a special project, yeah, sometimes."

"Somehow you seem like a person who goes to church. The language you use—something."

"Church starts next week, when the student minnies arrive."

"Minnies?"

"Christian Ministry in the National Parks. Student ministers work for the concessioner during the week and hold church services on Sundays in the campgrounds."

He extended his arm. She latched onto it, and her gait smoothed out. She had to shift her fanny pack a little; it kept bumping Jack's hip.

"So what does a Christian drink on Sunday?"

"Orange juice. It's not just for breakfast anymore."

Way out there, Ev paused to watch a brace of shovelers come whistling in. As ducks go, shovelers are just plain gaudy with their bright green and white, and long,

240

long bills. Jack was glad they caught her eye. She even turned and tried out her binoculars to look at their landing spot, the distant lagoon.

Gladys was studying him. "Married?" she purred.

"Not at the moment."

"Since you apparently don't have a place to stay, come on over to my room then and freshen up." She looked right at him. "Perhaps one of us will think of something else."

"You indicated the first time we talked that you have —shall we say—scruples. Remember, 'Does it make any difference?'"

She smiled, but not cheerfully. "And it does. Marriage makes a difference, I mean. But I'm not married now. You're not married. There's no difference to make." She paused, and added, "You interest me. And you said I interest you. It's safe. Gregory and Meghan have one room, and I have another."

"So I hear. And George didn't sleep in either of them. He had a room down the hall. Mrs. Gibbs. Gladys." Jack dug into his shirt pocket with his free hand. "This is a search warrant to inspect your premises and your person. Ev requested it yesterday at my behest. We're seeking lipstick and cigarettes, specifically, and any weapons."

"I'm not carrying a weapon, and you already checked my lipstick and cigarettes. You took samples and everything."

"True. But that was your black purse. I'd like to take a look in your belt pouch here. You've changed cigarette brands in the last week. I'm wondering if you changed lipsticks as well."

"A ranger was talking to Meghan yesterday. Is that what he was asking Meghan?"

"No. Other investigators asked her that days ago, and she says she doesn't know what brand you smoke. You don't smoke in her presence, at her request. Thursday morning when I came for Gregory, you stopped in the inn shop to buy cigarettes. The girl started to give you Dorals. You became angry and directed her instead to the Virginia Slims."

"That was her error."

"I doubt it. She remembered Dorals as being your brand. A cigarette butt was found with Bo's body. It showed traces of lipstick. The Vegas lab identified it as a Doral, with Maybelline's Peach Blush."

"I'm not wearing Peach Blush."

"And the lipstick from your leather bag was Cover Girl's Candy Apple. So now I'd like to see your belt pouch."

"What are you trying to do—implicate me in George's death? Is that what you're trying to do? Better cops than you have been questioning me, and they didn't find anything wrong. You have to pin it on somebody, so you've chosen me. Is that it?" Gladys's brain was obviously racing down the track a mile a minute. She snapped the search warrant open and read it. "I'm not saying anything without a lawyer."

"Good for you."

"And there's no reason to go through my stuff again."

"The oily pink stain in the seam of your fanny pack there. Looks like a lipstick melted down in there, probably some time ago. I'm willing to bet it's Peach Blush."

They were coming up on the hedge of mesquites that extended from the back of the golf course just about to the sewer pond. Jack tried to justify this light and airy day, this dazzling morning, against the dark things happening. The contrast jarred.

"I'm not saying anything." Gladys looked like the hangman was leaning on her shoulder, and Jack hadn't made any actual accusations yet.

"You don't have to. I've formed this scenario in my mind. See what you think of it. You and big, rough-tough Bo were an item. I'd guess sneaking around made it more fun, so to speak. You went with him to Wildrose. You went with him up to Chloride."

"If they're not in walking distance, I've never been there." Gladys was looking around, peering into the distance, apparently checking out activity a mile away. Was she looking for a way out?

Jack had lost sight of Ev, but then, the low, dense mesquites now masked Furnace Creek. "George suspected something. When he would learn of a possible assignation, he'd try to follow you. I doubt he ever caught you though." Jack paused for effect. "Then he followed you and Bo out to Salt Creek."

She paused and turned to study the empty desert behind them.

"A witness claims three persons walked out onto the salt flat that night, and two of them appeared drunk. Bo's blood alcohol level was below normal intoxication parameters. He wasn't drunk. Neither was George. What the witness saw was you on Bo's arm. Your lurching, uncertain gait would appear as drunkenness, especially from a distance.

"Here was your chance to dispose of George. He was an albatross around your neck, worth nothing to you. Bo the biker was a seriously mixed-up guy. He would have no compunctions about doing the deed. When George followed you out into the middle of nowhere, and the moon not yet full, Bo beat him to death with a tire iron. But frankly, Bo was a liability also. What if he threatened you or coerced you? What if he were arrested and the truth revealed? You couldn't trust him.

"You certainly could not have bested him physically, so you pulled a gun and shot him in the back." Jack paused, watching her face.

She grimaced. "Ludicrous. Why would this Bo have a tire iron 'way out there?"

"Shake down these jolly rogers, and you'll be surprised the weapons of choice they carry around—screwdrivers, tire chains, switchblades. Tire irons. But I'm guessing you two knew George was onto you and following you all over the park. I think you and Bo expected him to find you out there, and Bo came prepared. Which spells premeditation, Gladys. Maximum penalty."

Her face was a gaunt, tight death mask.

Jack pressed on. "You don't know much about ballistics, but you're sure bullets can be traced. You didn't want Bo found with your bullets in him. You were certain that somehow, by some mystical magic of modern forensics, they would surely be backtracked to you. So you used the tire iron to dig a grave in the sandy creek bed and bury Bo, assuming that way out there he'd be gone forever.

"But you couldn't collect George's insurance until his body turned up and he was legally dead. So you left him out in the open to be found eventually. You wiped the tire iron clean of prints and buried it some distance away. After all, investigators have arcane things like metal detectors. Even if they found the tire iron, you didn't want them finding Bo."

"My lawyer will feel bad taking my money, it'll be so easy to destroy your so-called case. You can't prove any of this."

"You'll be unpleasantly surprised." Jack kept on, piling item upon item, loading her down, he hoped, to the breaking point. "I doubt you would have brought Bo into it, but you didn't want your bullets in George when he was found. Your only choices of murder weapon, besides Bo, would be knife, gun, or poison. You are terrified of forensics and don't know enough about the science to know what's traceable and what's not. You were certain they'd lay George's death at your door unless someone else actually did it."

"If so, where's my gun? And why didn't someone hear it?"

"Silencer. Possibly you buried it out in the valley somewhere. If so, we'll find it. Possibly you mailed it home. It and its silencer. We'll have someone at Hal's end go out to your home and check incoming packages. You have a .38 automatic, Gladys. Is that right?"

She glared, tight-lipped. "Done with your tirade, I hope?"

"This isn't a tirade. I'll show you a tirade if you want one. I told a lady with blue eyebrows—and I'm telling you —when you're not trained for an occupation, stay out of it. Crime, especially. Rank amateurs who don't know the ropes can only mess things up. A couple TV shows are no training in forensics."

"I'm sure even a biker has a few brains. No man would kill for a woman he only knew a few days. No."

"Bo didn't just meet you. Bo worked in Washington as a chef. George worked out of the Washington office. You probably met Bo somewhere in the Washington area. Another source says Bo wasn't the least bit shy about propositioning women. George took on a temporary job, much like this one, at Mount Rainier and then North Cascades. You went along with him, but you stayed in town while George was out at the parks. The nearest large towns are Tacoma and Seattle. Just by coincidence, Bo worked in Tacoma and Seattle in hotels. That angle will be easy to confirm too."

"You're saying some shiftless bum followed me around? And you expect to convince a jury? Me?" She arranged a get-outta-here look on her face.

"Bo was in on the organization of this rally, including the choice of time and location. We'll check with the other bikers, but I bet we'll find that Bo engineered it so that it would coincide with George's project here. Yeah. You. Bo was in love. He followed you around. His spotty employment record is a little spottier because of you."

Gladys, pale and shaken, looked ready for intensive care. But defiant to the end, she still managed a black scowl.

Jack shrugged. "I was hoping to lay the trailer fire on

you, too, but unless we turn up witnesses—and there don't seem to be any—we may never get to prosecute that one."

"And the trailer fire too. Dump it all on Gladys."

"No trouble at all for you to leave the inn in the dead of night and drive up to Cow Creek. Just because you don't hold a valid driver's license doesn't mean you don't know how to drive. That very day, Friday, I had frightened you when I first linked you with Bo. I was much closer than you could tolerate."

"Ridiculous."

What was she seeking as she gazed all around?

Jack kept it up. "Maxx didn't growl or defend his turf. Which means one of his buddies was at the door, and that narrows the list of suspects right there. He thinks you're the greatest thing since liver-flavored candy."

Speaking of the mutt, where was he? There, cruising along the edge of the mesquite thickets, sniffing and probing in plain sight. He couldn't be what Gladys was seeking.

"How did I know it was your trailer?"

"You're acquainted with the residence area at Cow Creek. You and George had luncheon with the supe, remember? Just cruise the area looking for my truck. I admit the trailer fire's iffy. If we never prove it, we never prove it. But we can nail you solid on Bo."

Jack looked at Gladys. "I'm sorry for you. But I'm a whole lot sorrier for Gregory. He didn't ask for any of this."

"It sounds like you're so thoroughly convinced, protesting my innocence won't do any good."

"Show me where I'm wrong, or provide a better scenario."

A bezillion insects buzzed in the twelve-foot-high mesquite trees beside them. Jack wondered, idly, what kind of bugs they were. It was the naturalist in him coming out again. He suppressed it. This was law enforcement time, not posy-sniffing.

She stopped to study the search warrant again. Apparently she couldn't read and walk at the same time.

Judge not lest you be judged hopped into Jack's mind. He wasn't judging—he was accusing. But was the line between accusation and judgment so fine it was non-existent? Someday, when Jack entered the gates of heaven, he would sit down with Jesus to discuss the unique problems Scripture poses for the law enforcement officer.

She unwrapped herself from Jack's arm so as to have use of both hands. Slowly, her face a mask, she folded the paper enough to fit in her fanny pack. As she lurched back into motion at her usual staggering gait, she pulled the pack around front and unzipped it. "I suppose you want to go through this now."

"Back at the VC would be better. I want witnesses."

"I'm sure you do. Make certain all the knots are tied up tightly in my noose. I suppose the offer of a drink is off now."

"By no means. My treat."

"You're chivalrous." She held the pack open and tucked the paper in. It wouldn't tuck. She jammed. Finally she managed to work it down in. It was quite a feat as she lurched along. She stopped and turned to him. Her hand came out and with it the maw of a .38 automatic, pointed at Jack's middle. The maw moved up to heart level.

He froze. His mind went blank.

"I have a dilemma," she announced.

"You think *you* have one."

"I don't dare mount the silencer, but I hate to make all that noise. I bet the shots will carry clear to the visitor center."

"Count on it." He watched her back up a couple steps. Her reverse was neither more nor less controlled than her forward gears. She was too far away for him to jump her before she could pull the trigger. He thought of the holes in Bo's back. She was going to put some just like them in his chest. He looked around briefly for Maxx. The dog was three hundred feet out, intently stuffing his nose into a clump of saltbush.

"Don't call him. I'll shoot him too." Her voice remained firm. Killing didn't seem to bother her much. "I've been looking around. There haven't been any people or any vehicles close enough to monitor a wire. Am I using the terminology right?"

"You mean a listening device recording what we say from a remote location?"

"Like the police use on television. Yes. For sting operations. I'm pretty sure no one has been listening."

"Besides, you've been very careful to avoid self-incrimination. I noticed that."

"That's true. Here's another dilemma. If I kill you I'll go to prison. If I don't, you'll send me to prison for Bo's death. You're determined to do that. I can't win."

"Then why get sent up for two?"

"Because I think I can beat this one." She smirked.

He remembered she was good at smirking.

"No one can see us because of those trees. What sort of trees are they? I read it once."

"Mesquites." He started to move in closer.

She raised the gun slightly, a simple but eloquent gesture.

He stopped.

"That's right. They're thick enough no one can see us. You thought I was an easy victim because of my handicap and accosted me. I refused your advances. We struggled. I defended myself. It's too bad. You feel sorry for Gregory—I feel sorry for you." When colder killers were invented it wasn't Jack the Ripper they'd have to beat. Gladys displayed all the passion of a rattlesnake striking mindlessly at a warm moving object.

Jack took a big, big chance. He rotated on one heel, a full hundred and eighty, presenting his back to her. "If I'm attacking you, how will you explain the bullets in my back?"

"Turn around! Look at me!"

"I don't have to look at you. These shadows on the

ground—with the sun pretty much behind us I can see everything you're doing, just by watching your shadow. You've raised your gun a little higher, and now you just wrapped your left hand around the grip to steady it better. I suppose you saw that two-handed grip on TV too. 'Miami Vice,' maybe."

She called him an impolite name she certainly never heard in church, or even on TV. Suddenly she gasped, sucking in air clear to her toenails. She too was watching the ground. A second shadow had entered the periphery of Jack's vision, a person moving in behind Gladys.

Ev's voice barked, "Freeze!" Ev must have watched cop TV also. Her shadow showed two hands gripping in a firearms stance just like Gladys's.

Jack twisted around enough to see over his shoulder. He ignored the pain of all those damaged body parts when he moved, especially his back.

Gladys glared at him, transfixed.

"Don't multiply your woes, Gladys. Drop it on the ground."

"He was such a donkey, Jack. They both were. I wanted happiness like normal women have, that's all. And I could never get it. Not from George. Not from Bo."

"No reason for you to destroy more of your own life than you already have. Or Gregory's. He needs you. You can't blow us both away before Ev takes you down. It's over."

Her lower lip trembled. Her face sagged. Then, thank God, her arms sagged. The .38 *plupped* in the warming desert hardpan.

Smoothly, quickly, Jack yanked out his own borrowed revolver. He leaned forward and scooped Gladys's gun out of the dirt, up and away. Crisis past. He broke into a cold sweat.

Here came Maxx, the worthless pooch, now that he wasn't needed. He bounded to Jack, to Gladys, to Ev, and bounded on past to sniff at trees some more.

Gladys studied Ev's shadow beside her for a moment. Then she wrenched her contorted body around and stared straight down the barrel of Ev's Magic Marker.

25

Jackpot

Activity in the airport hadn't slowed down one iota in the ten days or so since Jack last came here. The slot machines still clinked and churred, the lights burned as bright at midday as at midnight, the chrome and neon glowed as dazzlingly as ever. People still scurried frenetically, not laughing nearly as much as you would think they should in the Entertainment Paradise.

He and Ev stood around as her flight preboarded first class and families with small children. And what was this "preboarding" business, anyway? Either they boarded, or they didn't. Once passengers started boarding the plane, they were boarding. Period. Preboarding was when you checked in at the desk.

Ev stood so close their arms touched. "Know what impressed me most about Durwin's horse thing? He didn't leak it to the media so that the news reporters would be there. He could have been on network news with his grandstand play, and he didn't. He kept it—you know—not under wraps exactly . . ."

"Private. In-house."

"Right." She lapsed back into silence.

"You didn't say specifically in your statement. The sewer lagoon foray. Why didn't you just return to the VC

251

Sunday morning? Why did you come back to Gladys and me?"

She shrugged. She took a breath. "Well, to be honest—" another breath "—I was afraid you and Gladys might, uh—you know—way out there, no one could see you. I wanted to know if—besides, that search warrant I got. The one you asked me to call in for when you were walking with Gladys on Saturday. I knew you had it with you, and I thought you might spring it on her."

"Thought I might need help? Good instincts. I sure needed the backup. I didn't think Gladys was bold enough —or foolish enough—to be carrying that .38 with her. I was sure she dumped it somehow. Fatal error on my part, making that assumption."

More silence, if you don't regard clanging, talking, laughing, announcing, and the million other airport sounds.

Jack broke the noisy silence. "You were great, coming up behind Gladys like that. Good outdoorsman stuff. Am I reading you right, that you're getting used to the desert?"

"I guess." She added hastily, "But I'm glad you didn't say am I starting to like it. I'm not. It's dismal. Bare. Empty."

"Botanists list four hundred fifty different plants in the Monument."

"I don't believe that, even if there's only one of each of them. There aren't four hundred fifty of anything there, except stones."

"And birds."

"That second walk out to the sewer lagoon was amazing. The one the next day, Monday. All those birds. I'd never heard of most of them—like the phalaropes, for instance—and there they were. I like the avocets best, I think."

"Great place to see unusual birds, sewer lagoons. And the parks around Washington. Look around. You'll enjoy it."

252

"I will. Thanks again for giving me your bird book."

"You're welcome again."

Silence.

An airport person called the back ten rows. Travelers crowded at the gate doorway, briefcases and carry-ons in hand. If the families and first class preboarded, was this postboarding?

He cleared his throat. "You're going to be the envy of your officemates with that tan."

"And I didn't even try to get it." She licked her lips. "When are you coming back to Washington?"

"In a couple days, then home to Kansas."

"I saw your Kansas license plates."

"Yeah. I got an apartment in Hutchinson. It's a two-day drive or less from there to any park in the lower forty-eight."

"What will you do in Washington?"

"Appear before that evaluation committee that's going to decide whether to continue the program, talk to Hal, and wrap this up. Think I'll look up Gregory and take him somewhere to play in the sand." Jack waited for a count of five, watching her face melt into a sort of well-concealed pout, before he added, "I'll keep you abreast of what's happening out here, of course, and call you just before I come. I'll need a ride in from the airport—that is, if you don't mind. Dulles, probably."

"No. I don't mind a bit. You drove me all over Death Valley, and to the airport here. I'll be happy to drive you around there." More awkward silence. "Anywhere. Sure. I'd love to."

He extended his hand. "They're calling your row."

She took his hand, and her handshake seemed stronger. She no longer looked the least bit worried that there might be snakes up his sleeves. "Yes. I better go." She didn't move. "Jack? Do you think the committee will approve continuation of the program?"

"At least for the next fiscal. We hit three cherries,

253

clearing both the murder and the embezzlement—and demonstrating they were unrelated."

She looked confused, so he rephrased. "Jackpot. Three cherries is a slot machine jackpot. Exactly what the program was designed to do, and within two weeks of the crime. Unqualified success."

"I'm proud to be a part of it. When you kept including me in the murder investigation, I resented it at first." She smiled. "But not later. I think I could get hooked on adventure."

"All the same, let's hope the next one's more sedate."

"I guess. Well—uh—good-bye." She stood there.

He mumbled something. He felt the strongest urge to kiss her, and that was ridiculous. She was a co-worker. That's all. Besides, you don't mix romance with work—ever. He learned a long time ago the folly of doing that.

Just a co-worker.

His co-worker picked up her laptop and suitbag. Suddenly she tilted up to tiptoe and planted a soft, gentle one on his right cheek. She wheeled quickly and headed for the plane. Most of the passengers had postboarded; she had a clear shot down the jetway. She turned in the door and smiled brilliantly at him.

She disappeared.

He waited until her plane lifted off and vanished in the Vegas blue. He took his time wandering back to his rig. Maybe he wouldn't wash his right cheek tonight.

As always, Maxx saw him coming long before he could see Maxx. The barking echoed clear through the place.

Maxx had company. The two big Harleys behind Jack's rig seemed weirdly out of place in this yuppie-looking parking garage.

Jack grinned and high-fived the guests. "The Hip! H'lo, Cat."

Cat grinned. His cast was starting to get awfully dirty.

Hippo's rumbling growl pretty much matched the motor sounds of his bike. "Cat hadda get his leg looked at, so we came in. Hey, feel like some serious talk?"

"Always. Where? How about that Gearjammer north of town?"

"Sounds good. See ya there." Hippo gunned his bike and took off, from zero to thirty instantly.

Cat grinned at Jack and winked before he shoved off. He was wearing a Point Man T-shirt. He roared up behind Hippo. They turned aside and out of sight at the end of the parking aisle.

The howl of their Harleys faded away.